NEVER
WASTE
TEARS

GLORIA ZACHGO

Never Waste Tears

Cover Art: Gloria Zachgo

Other books by this author

The Rocking Horse

ACKNOWLEDGEMENTS

Thank you—Linda and Marion—for being there from the start of this journey into the 1860s. It was with your help I realized I needed to tell this story in five different voices.

Thank you—Carla, Jan, Melody, and Mike—for your invaluable feedback. Your critiques inspired me to keep going.

Thank you—Annette, Barbara, Becky, Jeff, Judy C, Judy J, Marion, and Mary—for your endless encouragement.

Thank you—Barbara—for sharing your adventures in the publishing end of your endeavors.

Thank you—Marion—for helping me edit.

Thank you—Connie, Irma, and Nona—for helping me find information into the past.

Thank you—family and friends—for believing in me.

Thank you—Ron—my husband—for I know living with someone who has different characters playing in her brain at odd hours, cannot always be easy. I couldn't be a self-published author without your help, encouragement, patience, and the little fact that you put together my book cover and helped me with formatting, and—yes, the list goes on and on.

DREAMS

✢✢✢✢✢

The Civil War took a heavy toll on people's bodies and souls, often leaving deep scars that affected generations. New loves and new dreams were possible for some, while others never recovered from their wounds.

✢✢✢✢✢

Rebecca Louise Martin
born on September 9, 1851

Nathaniel Jacob Carter
born on April 12, 1848

✢✢✢✢✢

Rebecca's Diary...

April 12, 1861—People were standing together and talking in the streets outside our house today. I asked Mother what was happening. She said, "It's nothing, dear." Later I heard her and Father talking in very quiet voices. I couldn't hear what they were saying, but they sounded worried. I shall ask Mother again tomorrow.

Nathan...

I turned thirteen years of age on April 12, 1861. I will never forget that day, for it changed my family forever.

My father owned Carter's General Store in Eaton, Ohio. My mother, my two older brothers, and I were expected to help run the store when Father wasn't there. I don't recall where he was that day, but he wasn't in the store.

Early in the afternoon Mother sent me outside with a broom to sweep off the steps on the storefront. As I was going out the door I overheard her tell William and Emil to mind things while she went upstairs. William answered her and walked outside where he could watch me sweep. He gave me a lopsided grin as he leaned up against the open doorway.

"Bet Mother's going upstairs to bake someone a gingerbread cake," he said. Then he winked at me, turned, and went back inside.

With my mouth watering at the thought of gingerbread for supper, I hurried to finish my chore. It was when I swept the last bit of dirt off the steps and onto the street, that I noticed something had people excited. A crowd had gathered in front of the telegraph office.

Voices were raised, but I couldn't make out what they were saying.

I heard my mother open the window above the store. She yelled down at me. "Nathan, see if you can find out what all that ruckus is about."

I leaned the broom against the side of the building and ran over to where everyone was standing. Sideling close to a group that had broken away from the main crowd, I listened intently. Most of the women were whispering. Their eyes wide with fear. Many of the men were raising their voices. I caught words I didn't understand, but they were said in a manner that gave me goose bumps.

I looked back down the street and saw Mother leaning part way out of the window, waiting for me to return and tell her what I heard. So I ran back to her, looked up, and repeated some of the words.

"They said there were shots fired…I…I…think they said Fort Sumter…or…something about Lincoln…a secession…and oh, yeah…troops."

The look on my mother's face made the goose bumps come back. I stopped talking because she shut the window and turned away. William and Emil were standing in the doorway listening to what I had said. They both took off lickety-split toward the crowd.

I stood there, wanting somebody to explain what had happened. Then I went inside to mind the store, but no one came in the rest of the day.

At the supper table there was no mention of my birthday, even when Mother brought out the gingerbread. I was one to always be hungry, but that night I got this big lump in my stomach. Even the gingerbread tasted off.

At first Father kept talking about how wrong the secession was and that President Lincoln had no choice but to declare war. But it was when he stopped talking and got all quiet that I felt a change happening. Finally Emil broke the silence.

"We have to fight for our country," he declared. He looked at William.

William nodded, and said, "We have to fight for what's right."

I wanted to fight too. I wanted to be right there alongside my brothers. I was about to say as much when Father spoke.

"It won't last long, Mother. The Confederacy is ill-equipped to fight for long." His voice was calm and determined. "We will all do our part, including me." He was looking at Mother, though his next words were directed at me. "Nathan, when your brothers leave, you will be the man of the house. I expect you to mind your mother and help her run the store." He waited while we all soaked up what he had said. Then he added, "I'll leave in the morning."

I tried to swallow. I tasted real fear for the first time in my life. "Are you going to fight too?" I couldn't keep the panic out of my voice.

He finally looked at me and said, "No, Son. I doubt that I'll be marching into battle. But I know how I can help. I'll be back soon enough."

My father was about to leave me. My brothers were going to leave too. I hardly slept at all that night. My father had told me I would be the man of the house.

Father left the next morning after showing William and Emil things they should do before they could leave. He never told any of us how he was going to help in the war, but he said he needed to go immediately.

My brothers were left with the task of trying to teach me the things they thought I should know. I helped them unload the wagon and carry supplies into the store. I wondered how I would ever manage those heavy sacks and kegs when they weren't there to help, but I said nothing to them.

I prayed every night for Father's quick return and I prayed the war would end before my brothers had to go. But all too soon, they left too. I did not cry when they left. Father had said I would be the man of the house. I didn't think a man should cry.

Rebecca's Diary...

June 2, 1861—Martha's brother left yesterday to fight for the Union. She told me she is proud of him, but also worries for him. Almost all my friends have someone in their family who has gone off to fight in the war. Mother and Father do not talk about it when I'm with them. But I overheard Mother say she was glad she had no sons to send off. When we went to the mercantile today, Mrs. Carter said her sons had left last week. I saw Nathan, but he paid me no heed. He was busy wrestling a big barrel by himself. He must really miss his brothers. I wonder if he'll be in school this year.

Nathan...

During the day I didn't have much time for the distraction of missing my father and brothers. When I had watched Emil and William do their chores together they were always teasing each other and laughing. But I found the work was not all that easy. At first Mother had to help me with the lifting of some of the heavy things. But, I was determined— that I was. As the days turned into weeks, I could feel myself getting stronger. I learned how to load and unload the wagon by myself. Oh, I had a few hard lessons along the way, but it only took one time of busting a seed sack open to teach me to put something under the sack before I drug it across the floor. And I learned how to move a keg or barrel, by dancing the edge of it around on its rim.

I didn't think about the running of the store being hard on Mother until I overheard her talking to herself one day.

"I don't understand this. How am I supposed to know how to do this?" she was saying.

She didn't see me standing around the corner of the room, so she kept right on talking, with her voice growing a little louder each time she said something. "I've never been good with numbers. I don't understand them at all."

"I do." I said, as I stepped out where she could see me.

She jumped. Then her face turned red. She looked pitiful. Mother was a strong woman, but I thought she might start crying that day.

"I always got high marks in arithmetic. Besides, I like working with numbers."

"You do?"

"Yeah," I said as I took a look at the records she'd been working on. It surely was clear that she didn't understand numbers. That was the day I started keeping the records for her and that night she surprised me with gingerbread for supper. It brought back memories of everything that had happened on my birthday.

"Nathan, I guess we all forgot to have a celebration that day."

"Yeah." I didn't like remembering it, so that's all I said. I thought it was a nice thing for Mother to do, but when we ate the gingerbread it didn't give me the satisfaction that it used to.

On Sundays I didn't have my normal chores to do in the store, but Sundays were the longest day of the week for me. I went to church with Mother in the morning. The middle of the day was time for being myself. Even when the weather wasn't so nice, I usually took off for the creek to go fishing. It had always been with Emil and William before, so I would pretend they were sitting there on the bank with me. When I wrote them letters I'd tell them about all the whoppers I'd caught. I don't suppose they believed it, but I thought maybe it would remind them of home and get their minds off their own situations a little.

We didn't get many letters from them. I know it was a continuous worry for Mother. At first Father's letters always told us that the war couldn't last long. But as the season changed it seemed to me the war had already lasted long enough. We heard a lot of rumors of battles and skirmishes, but none of the letters we received mentioned them. We didn't know what to believe.

Rebecca's Diary...

September 12, 1861—Martha and I worked on our embroidery stitches today. It is not so unpleasant to do when we do it together, because she thinks it is fun. How I dislike it. I would much rather practice on my music. Martha's family finally received a letter from James. He said he had seen no battles yet. Martha and her mother were very relieved. As soon as Martha left, I practiced scales on Mother's piano.

October 4, 1861—Martha's brother has died. Mother and I called on the Owens family. They received the letter yesterday that told them James died from camp fever in the month of September. His letter the month before had said he had seen no battle. Poor Martha, I don't know what to say to her.

November 12, 1861—Martha and I went to Carter's General Store today with her mother. I saw Nathan again. He saw Martha and me, but pretended he didn't. I wonder if he will ever come back to school.

Nathan...

Because of the war, Mother and I had trouble getting some provisions for the store. The war caused problems for everyone in one way or another. Father's letters came real regular at first, but then the letters didn't come so often, and he sent no more promises that the war would end soon. Still, we considered ourselves mighty fortunate when we heard the woes of some of the other families in Eaton.

Church bells tolled often that fall, announcing the loss of the town's family members. Mother and I would look at each other, sorrowful for the family, but relieved it wasn't one of our own. We knew most everyone in town, since everyone came into our store at one time or the other, and we grieved with those families. We prayed hard for the war to end soon. I could hear Mother saying those prayers at night in her room after I'd gone to bed. I knew she was a strong woman, but sometimes I heard her crying too. Those nights I had a hard time getting to sleep.

That fall I saw Rebecca Martin and Martha Owens in the store with Martha's mother. Mother was talking to Mrs. Owens in the way she always had of saying the right things to those who lost someone, but I didn't know what to say so I got busy and pretended that I didn't see them. It seemed like it had been a long time since I'd been in school, but I thought how it really wasn't that long ago when I saw those two girls playing Jacks at recess and having so much fun together. Martha looked so sad. It reminded me that Mother and I hadn't gotten a letter from William or Emil in a while. I wrote both of them a letter that night.

Rebecca's Diary…

April 12, 1862—Church bells were ringing early this morning when I awakened. At first I thought it was Sunday morning and I would be late for church. But Mother said it was to mark the anniversary of the war and a tribute to all who had lost someone the last year. It will make Martha sad again. Even the songs Mother wanted me to practice today seemed sad and melancholy. She said I play the piano as well as she does. I have been practicing on a song of my very own when she is not at home. I will surprise her one of these days. It's a happy song.

Nathan…

Sometimes it was hard to remember what our life was like when my father and brothers were still home. At first I was kept really busy with learning how to lift sacks and barrels on my own. But I learned ways of carrying and moving things without breaking my back. When the farmers came into town for supplies I liked to listen to them talk about their crops and livestock. Harvesting crops and milking cows sounded more pleasant to me than wrestling a keg of pickles around inside the store. They started visiting with me like they had visited with Father before he left. One of them, Benjamin Thomas, and I were talking one day when he surprised me.

"Nathan, you're doin' a mighty fine job while your Daddy and brothers are away," he told me. It was almost an embarrassment when he said it, but it sure made me feel proud that he thought it. His only son had enlisted about the same time Emil and William had.

"Thank you, Mr. Thomas."

"Nathan, do you think you might call me Benjamin?" He wasn't fooling with me. He was serious and smiling like he used to do with Father.

I nodded in a sort of casual way, but I was about to pop my buttons. I was only fourteen and it surely was a compliment for him to ask me that. I started looking forward to talking with him whenever he came in. He would tell me how hard it was to run the farm all by himself with only his girls to help.

"Sure wish you could help me out. I see how hard a worker you are. You'd make a mighty fine farmer too. Yeah, that you would." He would chuckle and wish me a good day. It was plain to me how much he loved farming. Maybe he planted some kind of seed in my head with telling me that I could make a good farmer. I started dreaming about working outside, beneath the sky all day.

Rebecca's Diary...

August 20, 1862—Mother and I were in the mercantile today when Mrs. Carter suddenly became quite ill. I found Nathan in the back of the store helping someone load a wagon. He rushed into the store and helped his mother to their living quarters. As there was no one else in the store, Mother found the items she wanted and we waited for Nathan for some time. When he came down the stairs he seemed quite distracted as he tallied Mother's purchases. However, his demeanor changed when he gave Mother and me a piece of horehound. He has grown to be most handsome. I have missed seeing him in school. It appears he will not return, but will have to continue helping his mother in the Carter store.

Nathan...

I'd been out back of the store helping Benjamin load some seed onto his wagon when Rebecca Martin found me and told me something was wrong with Mother. When I went inside I found Mrs. Martin standing beside Mother urging her to sit down. Mother's face held no color. Mrs. Martin said Mother might faint if she did not lie down.

Mother seemed embarrassed and insisted she was fine. She didn't look fine. She reached up with a shaky hand, rubbing the side of her head. I put an arm around her and walked with her upstairs to her room. She laid down on her bed without further complaint and told me to finish taking care of things in the store.

When I went back downstairs, Mrs. Martin had found most of the items she needed and all I had to do was tally them up. She seemed very concerned for Mother.

"Nathan, would you like Rebecca to fetch Doctor Palmer for your mother?"

"She said she just needed to rest," I replied. But it was hard to tally the amounts on a piece of paper when I was thinking of how my mother looked when I left her.

When I finished, I placed Mrs. Martin's things in her basket and held it out for her. Instead of taking the basket, she gave me an impish grin and asked if she could have the usual. I didn't have any notion as to what the usual was. I turned to Rebecca for a clue and I'm ashamed to admit all thoughts of my mother's plight were forgotten when I looked at her. No longer a little schoolgirl, I was so smitten with the look she gave me that I almost missed her nod toward the candy jar at the end of the counter.

"Oh... the usual," I said, remembering that Mrs. Martin had a sweet tooth for horehound candy. I had often heard Mother tell Father that Mrs. Martin never forgot to get a piece of horehound for herself whenever Mother offered a piece of candy to Rebecca.

I got two pieces out of the candy jar and handed one to Mrs. Martin, who then took her basket from me.

"Give your mother our best wishes," she said as she turned to leave.

I handed the other piece of candy to Rebecca. Her eyes never left mine. I wondered why I'd never noticed those pools of golden brown before, that didn't even blink.

Mrs. Martin turned and started to walk toward the door, calling over her shoulder, "Rebecca, your father will wonder whatever happened to us."

I was looking into those eyes when I saw the corners of Rebecca's lips turn up ever so slightly. She turned and walked away with her mother. I stood watching and wishing she'd never leave.

By the time I got the store all closed up that day and went upstairs to peek in on Mother, she was sleeping peacefully, so I didn't wake her. My belly growled as I slipped out of her room. I had done a lot of things since my father and brothers had left, but I'd never tried my hand at fixing my own supper. I was tired from running the store most of the day, I was worried about my mother, and I was hungry. I guess I felt some sorry for myself too. So I cut off a couple good sized hunks of bread for my supper and I went to my own bed for the night. I put my head down on my pillow and it seemed like no time before I woke up to the smell of bacon frying.

Mother was up and moving around like she did most days.

"Time to get up and eat breakfast. The store won't run itself," she said.

She tried to smile. She was not one to complain, but the dark circles under her eyes put a new worry on me.

Rebecca's Diary…

September 9, 1863—My twelfth birthday started out to be such a fine day. Then Mother told me something that was quite upsetting. She said this dreadful war had altered her plans for me to attend the finishing school she had attended when she was my age. She is considering sending me East to live with Aunt Emily instead. I was so surprised that I told her I didn't want to ever go to finishing school or to live with Aunt Emily. Mother became very unsettled and said I was being disrespectful and I definitely need finishing school if I can sass her like that. She said she would talk with Father tonight. I said no more, but the rest of my day was frightful. When I practiced my piano I couldn't concentrate, and mother criticized my playing. I don't understand why she wants to send me away.

Nathan…

I longed for the safe return of my brothers and my Father. I had lost all my boyish desire to ever go away and fight in the war. Mother's headaches afflicted her often and came on suddenly. She would put both hands to the side of her head and grimace with the pain. I would stop whatever I was doing and help her to her room. I hated seeing her in so much pain, so when she complained the light hurt her eyes I'd hang a blanket over the window and get her a cold cloth to put on her forehead. Doctor Palmer prescribed laudanum as a remedy. It helped her some, but she would be of little use to anyone after taking it. It usually took a day or two of rest and then she would come back down to the store to work, only to become ill and have to take to her bed again.

"I don't like this at all, Nathan," she said each time, "but I'm just no good today."

"Don't worry, Mother," I'd say, "I'll take care of things." And then I would help her back upstairs. It left the running of the store to me and I made some mistakes, but I did my best and learned from them. I'm proud to say I usually didn't make the same mistake twice.

During the week I kept busy with the running of the store and taking care of Mother. I missed her good cooking and had to learn to fend for myself when she was down. When she was feeling better she taught me how to make a pot of stew or fry up a skillet full of potatoes. It made for a lot better eating when she couldn't do the chore herself.

I still went fishing on Sundays whenever I could. It was a pleasure to be outside in the fresh air and not think about running the store. I still thought of my brothers sitting with me, but now I often included Rebecca Martin in my daydreams. She seemed to always come to the front of my mind whenever I thought of my future.

Rebecca's Diary...

April 12, 1865—Church bells rang again today. They kept ringing and ringing for news that was good. The war ended several days ago. Mother said my future could now move forward. I think she still wants me to go to school back East.

April 13, 1865—Yesterday everyone was rejoicing with good news. Today church bells tolled for the Carter family.

Nathan...

It seemed to me that my birthdays were marked for the deliverance of significant news. I turned seventeen the day we heard of the war's end.

I saw a joy in my mother's face that I'd not seen for many years. It was a sight to see and I had the expectation that she might no longer suffer with her headaches. When a letter arrived the next day we should have been in celebration, but it was instead a letter that no family wanted to receive. It held the painful news that Emil had died on a battlefield in Virginia while bravely serving his country.

Mother didn't say anything. She looked old and heartbroken when she handed me the letter. She went to her room and shut the door. Benjamin happened to be in the store at the time. He looked at me and shook his head. Grief was fresh for him too, for he had gotten news of his son's death back in March.

"I'll watch the store for you," he offered.

I nodded. I had no words to say. I walked out with the letter in my hand and headed out the door toward the church. The town's mood was still happy with the news of the war being over, but when I walked down the street and people saw the letter in my hand, they knew.

The reverend met me on the steps of the church. I handed him the letter.

"Emil was a good man," was all he said. He walked with me to where the bell's rope was hanging. Too many times he'd let a family member pull on that rope. He stood silently beside me as I let the town know that Emil wouldn't be coming home from the war. It had been a long four years since my brothers and father had left to fight for what they believed in. I had become a man since they left. How I longed to go back in time and just be a boy again.

~ 8 ~

Rebecca's Diary…

April 14, 1865—Last night I heard Mother tell Father that he needs to think about my future. I fear she still wants me to go away. I was going to talk with Father today when the church bells tolled on and on. This time they announced the assassination of President Lincoln. Both Mother and Father are highly distressed with the news. I cannot comprehend what will happen next.

Nathan…

Mother came out of her room when she heard the church bells the day after we'd gotten the news on Emil. They tolled on for a long time. She looked to me for an answer. Just then a young boy ran by the front of the store shouting out the news—President Lincoln had been shot. When I turned back to look at Mother she had closed her eyes. Her shoulders slumped. At first I thought she was about to faint from the shock of it all, but as I rushed to her side, I realized she was saying something.

"Why?" a moan escaped from her lips.

"Mother?"

"Why won't your father write and let us know that he is alive?" She opened her eyes and went on. "Nathan, I have to know. Is he even alive? What is he doing? Is William alive?" Her voice suddenly changed from pleading to a snarl.

"How much more God? Will you take my husband and other son too?" she spit the words out. Without warning her arm swept across the counter and everything on it went crashing to the floor. I grabbed ahold of her, afraid for her.

"Why?" she asked once more, before she collapsed in my arms.

Life went on and Mother came back to me, yet it was another month before we got any answers. Father returned after our supper one day, as though he had only been away for a stroll down the street. I hardly recognized him. He looked like a very old man. His eyes were sunken into a hollow face and his jaw was set into a hard line. When Mother ran to him he stood like a wooden statue. He did the same for me.

"What's the news of Emil and William?" were the first words he spoke to us.

Mother's shoulders sagged as she looked down. "We've not heard from William, and…" her voice cracked, "Emil won't be coming back to us."

The muscles in Father's jaw moved, but he said nothing. There was only the sound of the clock, "tick-tock, tick-tock". Finally Father looked at me.

"You've grown taller," he said. He turned and walked toward his bedroom, speaking into the air. "Anna, I'm tired. I'll go to bed now." He went into their bedroom and closed the door. Mother and I looked hopelessly at each other.

It was a week later that I saw Father's eyes light up just a bit when William walked into our home. But when Father's gaze moved to the place where William's left arm had once been, his eyes darkened again.

"The bastard's took your arm, Son," he said, as though William didn't know his own arm was gone.

William nodded to Father, "But they didn't get the rest of me."

Mother ran to William and hugged him proper. While he held her with his right arm, he looked my way.

"I go away for a bit and you grow up before I get home," he said.

Mother stepped back so that I could hug my brother. I had held back all my tears for four years. That day I held back no longer. I could feel the warm touch of his hand patting my back like he did when I was just a kid. My brother was home and I had no shame in my tears. But my Father stood there shaking his head with condemnation.

Rebecca's Diary...

September 12, 1865—Mother has resigned her ambitions of sending me away to school. She is trying desperately to teach me to be a cultured young lady so that I will be a benefit to society. She has told me my talents should never be wasted and has me practice the piano for two hours every day. Then we have tea together. I like tea time with her, especially when she invites Martha for tea too. Mother seems quite pleased that I am learning to be proper. She said she would help Martha become proper too, for she feels she is sometimes a bad influence on me.

Nathan...

The times I spent with my father when he was the kind hearted man I once knew him to be, were almost impossible to remember. He told us nothing of what part he played in the war and we were forbidden to discuss anything political in his house after he returned. Even though William wanted no special treatment of his misfortune, Father doted on him. While he could find no fault in anything William did, he could find no good in anything Mother or I did.

"You've set the price too low on all our goods. Our family must eat too," he criticized. "I'll certainly have a time getting things back in order again from the mess you both have made."

When he complained, Mother would send me a look. I knew it was best to grit my teeth and say nothing. How could he be so blind that he couldn't see how hard our life had been while he was gone? Mother and I talked about it one day.

"Nathan, your father's a good man, give him some time," she said.

But time seemed to make no difference in the way he felt about me. I could do nothing right in his eyes.

I'd been living the last couple of years as the man of the house and my Father's feelings for me were a hard thing to take. One day when I went to the train station and was loading provisions onto the buckboard for the store, I overheard a couple of farmers talking. When their discussion changed from the weather, to talk of owning more land, I envied them, for I had a love for working outside.

"I hear there's still plenty of land the governments givin' away with The Homestead Act."

"I heard as much as 160 acres."

"If I was younger, I'd give it a try. Course, Mattie wouldn't be none too happy to leave her family to go off to Nebraska or Kansas."

The men moved on, talking about free land and how hard it would be to start all over again. It was then I wished I knew a little more about farming.

~10 ~

Rebecca's Diary...

July 16, 1865—As we were going to church this morning, we saw Nathan and William Carter heading for the creek with their fishing poles. Mother shook her head and said it was contemptible that the Carter family no longer went to church on Sundays. Martha said she thinks it is remarkable that William can do so many things with only one arm. I think Nathan is remarkable.

Nathan...

It was a hot Sunday morning in the middle of July when William said he thought it was time he and I started fishing again. I thought that was more than fine. When Father saw us leaving together he looked at the fishing poles I was carrying and then he looked where William's left arm had been. He did that a lot. William saw the look too.

"Here, Nathan, I'll carry my own pole," he said.

When I gave him the pole Father looked away.

We didn't let Father spoil our fun that day and soon we were sitting under a tree on the creek bank. I put a worm on William's hook. He got a far away look on his face when I handed the pole back to him. When he tried to drop the line into the water, the pole slipped from his hand and fell into the creek. I started to go after it.

"Let it be!" His words were sharp.

I stopped. I tended to my own business, as he struggled to retrieve his pole. It didn't take him long before he was sitting back beside me again. He put the line back in the water, held the pole with his right hand and balanced the end between his knees.

It was a hard thing to watch sometimes when he tried something new. But I was proud him. He accomplished tasks I didn't think were possible with only one arm.

We sat quiet for awhile, enjoying the familiar "brak-brak" of frogs calling to each other. When William moved a bit, and the frogs quieted, he looked over at me with his cock-eyed grin.

"I'll learn to bait my own hook again too," he said.

I figured it wouldn't be long before he'd figure out how to do just that.

Neither one of us cared so much about the fishing that day as we did about the remembering. We talked like we had when I was a tadpole myself and he was teaching me how to bait a hook. I got up enough courage to ask him, "Can you tell me what the war was like?"

He looked away from me to something I'd never be able to see on the other side of the creek bank. It took a long time for him to answer.

"No." He shook his head a little. "I'll tell you this though," he paused. "I think I saw what hell must look like." He kept looking at that spot and finally turned to look at me. "I'm a cripple, but I'll not act like one. There were more than a few that were much worse off than me."

We both studied the water for a bit before I asked, "Do you know what happed to Father?"

"No." He turned his head and looked across the creek bank again. Then in a whisper, he said, "I think maybe he saw more hell than I did." We didn't talk anymore that afternoon. We just fished.

After William told me Father might have seen more hell than he had, I tried to understand that maybe our father wasn't all the way back from his war journey. Every time he started harping on me though, I'd find some excuse to be somewhere else. That's when I thought about leaving Eaton and heading out on my own.

Rebecca's Diary...

September 21, 1866—Mother and I went to the mercantile today to pick up the beautiful fabric she had ordered. She hopes to have it made into a dress by the time I am to play for Sunday services. Reverend Finch has asked Mother if I could be the church pianist while his wife is visiting her sister in Philadelphia next month. I saw Nathan in the store and I do wish he would be attending services. I think Mother might think better of him if she saw his family in church again.

Nathan...

I was moving a keg of nails in the store when I heard Rebecca's voice. Half hidden behind some shelves, I took advantage of looking without being seen. A beam of sunshine was pouring through the front window and touching the top of Rebecca's head. She wore no bonnet. Her hair shimmered like golden honey in the sunlight. I stood perfectly quiet, enjoying everything I was seeing, including the soft curves as she moved slightly. It was a sight that I imagined was the closest I would ever get to seeing an angel.

Mother's voice was somewhere in the distance calling me.

"Nathan, whatever's gotten into you? Didn't you hear me?"

"Coming Mother," I said as I stepped around the shelf, brushing my hands together and trying to look as though I didn't know three women were standing there looking at me.

"Nathan, I can't reach that bolt of fabric," Mother said.

I looked down at my mother's feet and saw the stool she used for the purpose of getting things off a high shelf and I saw the grin she was trying not to show the others. It was strange how my mother knew my feelings for Rebecca before I did.

I reached above her head, retrieved the material, and smiled at the ladies. Mrs. Martin's eyes were only on the cloth she was already running her hand over, but Rebecca's eyes were on me. That look made my belly do a little jig. My head went fuzzy. Then Mother's voice was directed at me again.

"That's all I need, Nathan."

I didn't look at Mother, but I nodded and tipped my imaginary hat at Rebecca to bid her farewell. I walked away knowing that Rebecca's eyes were still watching me, and I smiled at the thought of it all.

I went outside to the back of the store where a wagon full of supplies needed unloading. I was still wearing the smile I'd had minutes before, but it was soon wiped off my face with my Father's bitterness.

"Do you expect your crippled brother to unload this wagon by himself?" he bellowed.

William gave me an understanding look and a bit of his crooked grin. He nodded his head toward a crate sitting on the back of the wagon. I walked over and grabbed one side of the crate and William grabbed the other with his right arm. We carried it into the store where Father was waiting for us.

"William, I need you to help me with some records," Father said, walking toward his desk. "Your brother can earn his keep and finish this job."

I knew William hated doing sums, but he followed Father without complaint. I went back to the wagon to unload it by myself, puzzled as to how William seemed to accept Father's sour attitude.

When I started unloading the wagon, I crowded out thoughts of my Father and replaced them with the smile Rebecca had shown me earlier.

Rebecca's Diary…

September 22, 1866—Mother has started making my dress already. It will be striking. I certainly have not inherited her love for sewing or her skills as a seamstress. She told me I will look lovely, but I must practice the piano more, so that I am able to play the hymns better than Liota Finch. Then she told me that I must stay modest and humble at all times.

September 23, 1866—Martha told me after services today that she saw Mrs. Carter yesterday and told her I would be the pianist in church next month. She is sure Nathan heard them talking. Martha agreed with me that Mother would surely approve his calling on me if he would start coming to church again.

Nathan…

One minute I was happy. The very next, I was miserable. And even when Father yelled at me, I didn't take it as hard anymore. I'd never been taken with a girl before and I had no idea how to court one. The only time I'd been around girls was in school and that seemed like it had been a long time ago. It sometimes felt like I'd been busy helping Mother at the store for all of my life.

My hands got all sweaty every time I thought about how pretty Rebecca was. I doubted Carrie Martin would ever think I was good enough for her daughter. So I didn't know how to go about calling on her, but I knew I would find a way. Then I overheard Rebecca's friend, Martha, and Mother talking in the store.

"Reverend Finch has asked Rebecca to play church services on Sunday mornings when his wife goes back East to visit her sister next month," Martha said. "So her mother is making her a lovely dress out of that green silk she ordered."

"That's one of the finest pieces of fabric I've ever sold in our store." Mother added, "She will look lovely in that shade of green with her fair coloring."

Martha talked a little more about church. Mother tried to change the subject.

"Maybe you could come and hear Rebecca play..." Martha said.

Mother said nothing. It was then that Martha noticed me. She could tell I'd been listening. She smiled at me like we'd just shared some kind of secret. Then she turned and walked out of the store.

That Sunday I slipped into the very back row of the church right before the Reverend started the service. The pew where the Carter family used to sit was empty, like it was waiting for my family to come back.

The Martin family was sitting in the third row from the front. Rebecca surely did look nice in her Sunday finery. The Reverend looked where I was sitting once while he was preaching. I listened, but my eyes couldn't seem to keep from going back to the third row. I should've felt some guilt about it, but I didn't, and I slipped out of church just as the Reverend said the last Amen.

~ 13 ~

Rebecca's Diary...

October 7, 1866—I was anxious before I started playing this morning, but Mother's face had that look that always told me to love the music and pay no heed to the listeners. I forgot about the congregation and missed no notes. I also know I looked my best, because Mother's needlework was stunning. She surprised me with a fashionable bonnet made from the same fabric. Mother also told me that the Reverend thought the hymns had never sounded better. The morning was a fine day for me and was made even better when Martha said she saw Nathan Carter in the back row of the church. She said he left just as Reverend Finch was saying Amen. I hope it isn't boastful to think he knew I was going to be there and he wanted to see me.

Nathan...

I thought I wouldn't have to answer to anybody if I slipped in and out of those Sunday services. Then Reverend Finch came into the store one Monday morning with a smile and a mission. Father was walking toward the front of the store when he saw the Reverend. He didn't say a word. He turned around and walked right outside. I pretended to be very busy with getting an order ready for the widow Ferguson, who could no longer come into the store.

"Praise be to the Lord! It was good to see Nathan in church this Sunday," the Reverend said to Mother. Mother raised one eyebrow and looked my way. "It would be a mighty fine thing if his family could join him."

Mother started to say something, but the Reverend went on.

"I know it's been a while Mrs. Carter, but we've missed having your family with us," his voice was filled with kindness.

I hadn't seen Mother say a prayer of any kind since the letter of Emil had been delivered to us. She stood perfectly still, not saying a word for a long time. Then I saw her take a deep breath and look into the Reverend's eyes. His words had sounded heartfelt and inviting.

"Reverend, I've missed your services. But it's too soon for John," Mother said.

The Reverend nodded with understanding. "Your pew sits empty," he said as he turned his head and looked straight into my eyes. "Would John keep you and your sons away?" He smiled kindly. He left Mother to think on what he had said as he walked out of the store.

"Nathan, do you want to tell me what's been going on?" Mother asked me.

"Uh, I've got to get widow Ferguson's order delivered," I said.

William walked around the corner just then. He'd heard it all.

"Nathan's sweet on the Martin girl," William answered with that grin I usually liked to see.

"Oh, that's right. Martha said she was going to play the piano for the Sunday services now," Mother added. She looked at William. It was the first time I ever noticed how they shared the same cock-eyed grin.

A look passed between them as they both turned and looked at me. It was then I understood. They knew the feelings I'd been having, and both of them were having fun with my discomfort. I suppose I couldn't expect to keep my feelings secret any longer.

Rebecca's Diary...

October 14, 1866—Playing for church services is most delightful. Reverend Finch told Mother that several people said I have a gift. It is true that playing brings me the greatest joy. But the best part of the day was when Nathan smiled at me from the Carter pew. His mother and William were also there. Mother said it is about time the Carters come to their senses and come back to the church. Father said it was sad that John Carter would not come to church with his family.

Nathan...

Father wanted nothing to do with God after the war. But the visit from Reverend Finch made Mother soften her heart. She started reading her Bible again. Father started to forbid her, but she defied him on this one thing.

"I will go back to church," I heard her say to him. "I've been angry at God for too long. And the boys will join me."

Father raised his hand and slapped her across the face. It was a hard thing for William and me to see. But Mother never backed down, and Father walked away, grumbling to himself. I started to say something to her, and she held up her hand to warn me that she would not hear me.

"Your father is a good man," she said. Then she walked away, leaving me to wonder how a good man could hit our mother for wanting to have God back in her life.

I went to church with Mother and William on Sunday, and we sat in the Carter pew. Rebecca looked like an angel when she sat at the piano and played the hymns. I've never had an ear for music, but I could see she had a gift for it. I heard others whisper the same thought to Carrie Martin, and while I could see the pride she took from it, it seemed to bring a discomfit to Fred Martin. I wondered on that a bit. I came to the conclusion that Rebecca's father was a humble man. It made me think I might muster up enough courage to ask him if I could court his daughter. William had courted a few girls before he lost his arm to the war. I talked to him that very afternoon.

It was a fine autumn Sunday to get in one of the last times we would be fishing for a while. William was struggling to put a worm on his hook. I knew it was something he could learn to do himself, and sure enough he did a fair job of the task. I had learned not to help him unless he asked, and he didn't ask very often. Sometimes I forgot he only had one arm, he did such a good job at most things he made up his mind on.

"So, you're smitten with her, eh?" he asked.

I nodded.

"You sure can pick the pretty ones," he teased. "Don't let her get away, Brother. I've seen the way she looks at you, too."

"I don't have any experience at courting."

William got quiet, the way he sometimes did, then he said, "Do you remember how Father used to be with Mother?"

I thought back to a different time and smiled at the memory of the father I once knew. I then listened as William told me what he thought would be the proper way to court Rebecca.

"Course you're gonna have to get Mrs. Martin's approval too, you know," he said. His smile said it might be a bit of a challenge. That's when my stomach tied itself into a knot that I carried with me for a few days.

Rebecca's Diary...

October 18, 1866—Mathew Porter wants to court me. Mother thinks he is a splendid suitor and said he comes from a very well-to-do family. I have seen him look at me and do not like the way it makes me feel. He is also much older than I am. But Mother insists I be nice to him when he calls. I so wish Father was here so that he might talk with Mother, for I think he does not care for Mathew either.

October 20, 1866—Mathew Porter called on me today and Mother asked that I show him my talents on the piano. I did not play well. Mother was angry with me. She accused me of being most obstinate. I told her it is hard to become one with my music while someone leers at me. Mother was most upset with me and said I shall be destined to become an old maid.

Nathan...

Martha Owens was in the store today and came right up to me and told me that Mathew Porter was calling on Rebecca. She said Rebecca was miserable. She then gave me a look of utter disgust. She turned around. When she saw William had heard her, she looked at him and said, "Can't you talk him into doing the right thing?" She didn't wait for an answer, but marched out of there like I was supposed to know what to do for Rebecca's misery.

"I think she was trying to tell you something, Brother," William said. I saw something of admiration as he looked at Martha departing our company. I wondered if maybe he didn't have some feelings for Martha.

"I was waiting for her father to get back from his trip," I explained.

"Maybe you need to go right to the formidable Mrs. Martin," William's cock-eyed grin was setting in.

"Flowers will melt almost any woman's heart," my mother chimed in. She had heard Martha's comments too. "Of course, since the leaves have fallen, there aren't many flowers around right now. I would recommend going straight for the most vulnerable part of Carrie Martin."

I didn't get the implication right at first. Then I saw that Mother had already put a supply of horehound candies into a pretty little tin box and was tying a bow on it.

"But what do I say?"

"You'll think of the right thing when you need to find the words." Mother's smile gave me the little push I needed.

16

Rebecca's Diary...

October 22, 1866—Mother and I have been in disagreement ever since Mathew Porter called on me, so today when I was practicing my music I was surprised to hear her laughing. When I stopped playing, Nathan was standing beside Mother and smiling at me. Mother invited him to have tea with us. I can't imagine how he convinced her, but she gave her permission for him to call on me.

Nathan...

When I was standing before Mrs. Martin and tried to speak, my voice squeaked. My stomach was flipping around like a fish out of water, and my mouth felt like it was full of dry straw. I kept thinking of Martha's words and knew for a fact that any girl as pretty as Rebecca was going to have other fellows wanting her attention too. The thought gave me the courage I needed to find my voice.

"I'd like very much to call on Rebecca, Mrs. Martin," I finally got the words out.

And that was the first time I'd ever sat down with ladies and had an afternoon tea. It seemed to me like it was an important thing for Mrs. Martin. She even insisted we have some of that lovely horehound. I took a piece for the sake of being polite, but I've never really appreciated the taste of horehound.

Things were no better between my father and me. I wanted to strike out on my own, but knew I couldn't leave without Rebecca by my side. I had a dream for some of that free land in Kansas or Nebraska, but all I'd ever done in my life was work in the store, so I knew I surely had a lot to learn. When I told William about my yearning, he gave me some good advice.

"Why don't you talk to Benjamin Thomas? I've seen how you and him talk, and I know he respects you."

I set out that afternoon for Benjamin's farm. I suppose it was strange that I could talk with him about my future and all, when I couldn't talk with my own father. But somehow it felt right.

Benjamin got a far away look in his eyes when I asked him if he'd teach me how to farm. "Thought my own son would take over someday," he said. He gave his head a little shake, like he had to get rid of the thought. He smiled at me. "I'd be right proud to teach you what I know about the land. Mama and me…well…we just got the two girls left. The farm will go to them now. Are you looking for a wife too?"

I couldn't tell if he was serious in his question, so I explained my dilemma to him. I thought he looked a little disappointed, but then he told me he'd be glad to hire me on and pay me in a percentage of what the farm crops would earn. It sounded like a good deal for me, though I surely had no idea what my father would say about it.

17

Rebecca's Diary...

November 1l, 1866—Nathan has accepted a job working for Benjamin Thomas. Mother says Mr. Thomas is just a dirt farmer and he'll do nothing for Nathan's future. Nathan has told me he wants to own his own land some day. I've not told Mother that. At least she is happy Reverend Finch has asked me to continue playing for Sunday services. His poor wife, Liota, fell at her sister's house. She now is burdened with a broken arm and won't be able to play for some time. Of course I am sorry for her misfortune, but I do so enjoy playing for the church.

Nathan...

I was hungry to learn all I could about farming from Benjamin. I made a promise to work for him for a year. He told me I would learn about the land in the warm months, and in the winter months he'd show me how to repair harnesses, sharpen tools, work on the implements, and even make some furniture. Of course we had the livestock to take care of too.

I was surely surprised at how some of the simplest chores were the hardest to learn. I thought milking a cow was an uncomplicated thing, but learning how to squeeze and pull on those teats at the same time took a bit of getting used to. It took me near a whole week to be able to milk a cow as fast as Benjamin could.

The Thomas family treated me like I was one of their own, and I'll always be grateful for their kindness. They were a happy group and weren't filled with bitterness that the war had taken one of theirs. Instead, they talked about their Jonathan with the fondest of memories almost every morning when we sat down for breakfast. And almost every breakfast Mildred Thomas cooked up the lightest stack of pancakes I'd ever tasted. Of course I never mentioned that to my mother when I went home and sat at her table.

I made it home almost every Sunday. I would meet Mother and William at church and still get to see Rebecca as she played for the congregation. Then I would usually go home for Sunday dinners with Mother and William. Father's feelings for me had not changed, and he hardly ever spoke to me. He hadn't shown displeasure when I told him I was going to work for Benjamin. He had just turned and walked away.

After my Sunday dinners at home, I spent the rest of my free day at the Martin house. Fred Martin always seemed interested in hearing about my week, but I had the distinct feeling that Carrie Martin had severe displeasure when we talked on the subject of farming. She would usually try to direct our attention to parlor games, her favorite being charades. It was always Mr. Martin who would make some excuse that gave Rebecca and me a bit of time alone. I was most grateful to him for that.

18

Rebecca's Diary...

January 13, 1867—Nathan and I are engaged to be married. The ring he has given me fits me perfectly. He said it once belonged to his grandmother. I can hardly wait to talk with Martha tomorrow.

Nathan...

It was the ring—my mother's ring—that I gave to Rebecca. I wonder if Mother would have given it to me if she could have foreseen the wrath it brought forth from my father. The ring had been my maternal grandmother's. It was too small to fit mother properly, and she'd never worn it. She said she would be proud for her first daughter-in-law to wear it.

I had no doubt Rebecca would marry me, but when I asked her Father for her hand I was uncertain how he would react. I was even more nervous than when I had first asked if I might court her. I felt as though Fred Martin's eyes bore into my soul that day, and when he said yes, I thought I might pass out with relief, right there in the Martin parlor. Carrie Martin must have heard the whole thing. The next thing I knew she was standing beside her husband.

"You *will* have a proper engagement," she announced, as she looked first at me and then at her husband. She added, "I believe in *long* engagements, Nathan Carter."

While I was trying to get my voice, Mr. Martin looked at his wife and smiled. "Why, my dear Carrie," he said, "we were already married when you were fifteen."

Silenced, Mrs. Martin's face showed a blush.

I couldn't help but smile too, though I knew better than to say more.

I wasn't the least bit nervous that very afternoon as I asked Rebecca two things.

"Will you marry me?" was the first question. I was on one knee looking up at the prettiest thing I had ever seen and I was holding out Mother's ring. She looked at me with those golden brown pools that didn't blink. She nodded as she let me slip the ring on her finger. So while I was on that one knee I asked her something else I'd wanted to ask her for some time. "May I call you Becca?"

That's when tears started falling out of those lovely eyes.

"I'm sorry, Rebecca," I stammered. "I thought…I won't…" I raised myself off of my one knee and stood.

"I love the name," she whispered. "But my mother would never let anyone call me that. Not even my Father."

"I won't," I promised.

"Oh, but please do. Only not around Mother," she whispered in my ear as she gave me the softest kiss on the cheek. It was a special moment for us, and I thought the name meant as much to her as the ring. I wanted to take her in my arms and carry her away with me, but I heard footfalls coming down the hall. Carrie Martin walked in carrying a tray with tea and tiny little cakes.

"We'll celebrate the occasion," she announced.

I wanted to dance a jig to celebrate. Instead I had tea and cakes with my fiancé, and called her Rebecca whenever her mother was present.

19

Rebecca's diary…

January 20, 1867—When Nathan called on me today he told me he is no longer welcome at his home. He would not tell me why.

Nathan…

Before I headed back to the Thomas farm the day I gave Becca her ring, I was going to stop by and tell Mother how much Becca liked it. But when I stepped through the door I heard shouting coming from another room. I was going to leave when I heard a loud slap and then I heard my mother weeping. I went into the kitchen.

"How could you give Nathan that ring? It should have gone to Emil!" my Father's face was twisted and ugly.

"But Emil's gone, John," my mother said so softly I could barely hear the words.

"Then William should have it!" Father was spitting the words in my mother's face.

"William and I talked and he wanted me to give it to Nathan. The ring was *my* mother's ring. It was *mine* to give." Mother's face wore a red mark across it where Father had struck her. She looked confused and so tiny. When she dared to utter those defiant words I saw Father's fist double up as he raised his arm.

I caught his arm in the air. I could not watch as my father beat my mother. I was a man now and strong enough to hold him.

"Please, Father," I pleaded.

"You! You didn't go and fight. You don't know what it was like!" Father ranted.

"John," Mother's soft voice tried to reason with her husband, "He was only a boy then."

"He's not a boy now," Father said. He turned to me, spewing out his anger. "Do you know what it's like?" he caught his breath. "It's hell. You didn't see that. Your brothers did. You were here safe with your mother while Emil died in some God-forsaken battlefield. William gave part of his body for the bloody war and now he's a cripple. What did you do? You stayed here nice and safe."

"I was thirteen years old! I ran your damned store for you while you went away and never told us where you were." That's when I let go of Father's arm and that's when he hit me. I staggered backward and tasted blood.

"I'm your father and I will be respected in my house."

My own fist tightened just as William came into the room. I think I would have fought the stranger that had just hit me if William hadn't stepped between us. I knew I wasn't at fault for my brother's death and William's misfortune, but my Father blamed me anyway.

"Go! Go out into that world and figure it all out then." He threw the words at me through gritted teeth. I knew at that moment he would always blame me for something I had no control over. He couldn't bear to put any blame on himself.

"Get out of my house and don't bother coming back." I glanced at my mother and felt her helplessness. William closed his eyes and was shaking his head. I walked away, knowing I would never be welcome in my father's house again.

20

Rebecca's diary...

April 7, 1867—I wish it were possible to see Nathan more often than just Sundays. Mother wants me to ask him why he doesn't spend time with his own family anymore. He wants to go fishing with William as soon as the weather warms and asked if Martha and I would join them. I told him I had never been fishing. He assures me it is very enjoyable. When I told Mother, I thought she might faint.

May 5, 1867—I may never see what gives men enjoyment about fishing, but I must admit the time the four of us spent together was quite delightful. Martha even caught a fish today.

Nathan...

That spring and summer Benjamin surely kept me busy. We got up at dawn, ate supper after dark, and worked between the two. I was bone tired every night. My hands had blisters and calluses. But I could see why Benjamin thought it was the best life possible. He understood the land like it was a part of him. I was grateful that he wanted to share that with me. When he knew I was serious about owning my own land he took the time to help me plan a way to make my dream come true. I figured he would get tired of my questions of ignorance. Instead, he helped me make lists of the things I would need. Even though he said I earned my keep and then some, I will always feel obliged to him.

On the Sabbath we did no field work. I'd get up earlier than normal and have the cows milked by breakfast time. Then the Thomas family went to church together. I'd follow them to town on one of Benjamin's horses so that I didn't have to walk back to the farm. Since I was no longer welcome at home, church services were the only time I spent with Mother and William. Then I'd go spend the rest of the day with Becca.

William and Martha were getting kind of sweet on each other, and William came up with the idea that maybe the four of us could all go fishing together on Sundays. I wasn't so sure Becca was keen on the idea, but Martha seemed to really like to fish. Becca and I mostly just sat and talked about our upcoming wedding. We decided to wait until next spring, and then we would head West.

21

Rebecca's Diary ...

June 12, 1867—Mother is quite distraught that Nathan and I will be going West after we are married. She told me there are still savages in those parts of the country. I think she just wants to scare me so that I won't want to move so far away from her. She has told Father he needs to speak to Nathan.

June 13, 1867—Mother is now quite upset with Father too.

June 16, 1867—When Nathan came today, Father spoke with him. Mother now insists that I cannot marry Nathan.

Nathan...

When Becca told her mother I intended to take us West after our marriage, I didn't feel as welcome in the Martin house as I once had. It was that very summer when I called on Becca one Sunday that Fred Martin said he wanted to speak with me. I was sweating buckets by the time we finished with our talk. He was an easy going man, but even though his wife wasn't in the room with us, I got the feeling she was directing part of his conversation.

"I truly love Rebecca, Sir," I said. "I want what is best for her too."

I was sure his eyes were looking into my soul.

"It's only because of my daughter's great affection for you that I'm even considering your marriage to her," he explained. "If she is still willing, come next year, I will allow it. But you'd damned well better take good care of her," he concluded.

After my talk with her father, Becca finally came down the stairs. Her eyes were red and swollen, and I thought how beautiful they were. She was followed by her glaring mother, who said not one word to me.

We went out to the porch where Martha and William were waiting for us. As we walked to the creek, Becca and I let them get ahead of us to that we might talk privately. She assured me that she wouldn't change her mind about wanting to marry me.

We'd become engaged in January and promised we would wait a year before we wed. But if we didn't leave to go West until the spring, we would have nowhere to live but with the Martins. I didn't fancy that idea. So we set our wedding date for the first day in April.

22

Rebecca's diary…

March 31, 1868—Tomorrow I will become Mrs. Nathaniel Jacob Carter. Mother is most unhappy. She refuses to help me pack my trunk for my departure. She also told me that if I see even one savage, Nathan is to bring me back to Eaton immediately. Father and I have been trying to reason with her, but she is highly distraught. I played her song that I composed for her today, thinking it would make her happy and she wept the entire time I was playing it. She told me she doubted there would be any pianos anywhere in my uncivilized future.

April 1, 1868—It is my wedding day. Father has told me I look as lovely as Mother did on their wedding day. Of course that made Mother weep again.

Nathan…

I felt much obliged to Benjamin for the lessons of farming he'd given me. He had a plentiful harvest that year I worked for him, and he paid me fairly for my help in the venture. He told me if I could get land for free, I'd be showing a profit on my own farm in a couple of years. It was sweet music to my ears that he had that much faith in me. By the time our wedding day came, I felt I could make a fine future for Becca and me.

It was the parting with our families that was the hard part. I knew the Martin's were none to pleased with us leaving Ohio, but Fred Martin told me, if I was determined to go, he'd help us out. The day we wed he gave me a considerable amount of money—a thousand dollars. It was a generous gift, but he made sure I understood that it was for Rebecca's future.

"You will take good care of my daughter, Nathan." His eyes were boring into me.

"Yes, sir," I answered with as much conviction as I could muster.

"And I think it best that this gift be between you and me."

I knew what he was meaning, though he didn't say the words. Carrie Martin would not be a quick one to forgive her husband for making anything in my life any easier. She had wanted a glorious celebration for her daughter. Instead we got married in the Martin parlor. Only the Reverend, the Martins, Martha, William, and Mother were there. My own father would not come to my wedding. I could see the sadness on Mother's face. But William was the one who surprised me the most. He took me aside before we went to the train depot.

"Mother and I talked it over and we want you to have this as a wedding present," he said as he pressed some money in my hand. "You more than earned it when you helped run the store, little brother."

"I can't," I started to say when he held up his hand and gave me that grin I loved.

It surely was a hard thing to leave our families.

23

Rebecca's diary...

April 2 1868—We are finally in St. Louis, waiting for our steamboat to take us to Independence. The city is bustling with all sorts of activities. I would be very content to stay here and explore it for a while, but Nathan is anxious for us to be on our way.

Nathan...

I would've been the happiest fellow in the country if Becca wouldn't have taken the leaving of her family so hard. I knew she was trying not to cry, but I saw a few tears slip out. Her mother had no kind looks to throw my way. I suppose I could understand those feelings.

"I know I will never see you again," her mother said, and then she hugged Becca as the conductor yelled for all to board. We stepped onto our train, found our seats, and looked back at the platform where our families stood. Becca and I said no words to each other as the train pulled out of the depot. We watched the people we loved get smaller and smaller until we couldn't see them anymore. One part of me didn't like that at all, but another part of me knew we were going to have a good life together. We were both excited and a little more than anxious as to what awaited us at our new destination.

When we reached St. Louis we took in the thrill of it all. As soon as I purchased our steamboat tickets we took advantage of the waiting time to see as many of the sights of the city as we could. We had a ferrotype taken of the two of us, and Becca managed to write to her mother. She wrote that we were having a wonderful time.

"I hope it will make her feel a bit better that there is civilization in this part of the country," I said to her as we posted the letter. Then we had to hurry to embark on the next leg of our journey .

24

Rebecca's diary...

April 5, 1868—Our steamboat ride is quite soothing and enjoyable. I much prefer this travel than the sooty train ride. However, last night we came very close to running up on a sandbar. Nathan said we have the most adept Captain on the Missouri River. He maneuvered us skillfully out of danger's way. Today we spent leisurely time on deck with a most delightful couple who are on their way to California. They too will be joining a wagon train when we reach Independence.

Nathan...

Our travels on the Missouri River were pleasant enough until I met a man named Charles Rudd. He and his wife had plans to join a wagon train in Independence too, but they were going to travel all the way to California where his brother needed help to run a new business he had started. His brother had surely made California sound like a grand place to be. I started talking to him about my plans for getting a homestead somewhere in Nebraska. It was then I was glad our wives were talking some distance away and couldn't hear us. Charles lowered his voice and told me something I didn't want to hear.

"My brother told me of some Indian troubles he heard about in Nuckolls County in Nebraska last year." He went on, "He said the quicker we could get through that part of Indian territory, the better."

"Is there unrest there now?" I asked him.

"I'm only going by what my brother told me. He said there's still plenty of land available if people want to risk their scalp to get it."

I know he meant well by giving me the warning, but it surely did put a damper on my disposition for awhile. It was something I was glad Becca didn't hear right then. It started a doubt in my thinking, but I didn't see any benefit in worrying my lovely young wife.

25

Rebecca's diary…

April 7, 1868—We are now in Independence. I stayed in our hotel today when Nathan went to find a wagon train to travel with. He came back and said we would be leaving day after tomorrow. It gives us little time to purchase all that we will need, but Nathan is confident that we can accomplish the feat. He said he looked at a team on the way back to the hotel today.

Nathan…

When we got to Independence we found a hotel right away. Becca stayed in our room to freshen up, while I walked down by the river, where wagons were being ferried across. When I inquired as to the possibility of joining their caravan, several of the gents told me I would have to talk to Skinner, the scout and wagon master. When I caught up with him he was busy overseeing the crossing.

"I'm looking to join up with a wagon train, Mr. Skinner," I said to him. "A couple of fellows told me I needed to talk to you about that."

"Ain't no Mr. Skinner here," he said to me while not looking in my direction. "It's just plain Skinner." He turned toward me, but was immediately summoned to help a man with a skittish horse, so I waited and watched.

I liked the man right off, but I couldn't tell the reason. I suppose it was because he stood a head taller than myself and he looked like a man who was in control of the situation. When he finally realized I was standing there waiting, he came back to where I was. While overseeing the activities of the crossing he spoke to me.

"You got your wagon with you?" he asked.

"No sir," I started to say and saw immediately that he didn't like being called sir either. "I need to buy it yet. We just got off the steamboat ourselves," I explained. "My name is Nathan Carter and my wife is Be...Rebecca."

He gave his approval with a nod. He added, "It'll take us the rest of today to get all the wagons across. Then we'll rest a day and give ever'one a chance to pick up supplies. If you kin be ready to go, we'll be leavin' the day after that—at sunrise."

I took it that he meant if we could not be ready, we would have to find other accommodations.

"We'll be ready, Skinner." I held out my hand to shake on the deal. He didn't take my hand but gave me a good stare.

"Your word's good with me. But we won't wait," he warned.

Turning, he helped another man whose wagon was coming off the ferry. I couldn't believe my luck at finding a train to join so quickly.

NEW BEGINNINGS

✧✧✧✧✧

A New Frontier welcomed those who were willing to leave their families and everything they knew. For some it was the promise of adventure and great fortune. For many it was the promise of free land. Had they foreseen the hardships they were about to face, it is doubtful some of them would have been so eager to go, for the demands of the prairie were many and only the hardiest survived.

✧✧✧✧✧

Carl William Taylor
born on May 12, 1839

Hannah Jane (Lucas) Taylor
born on February 16, 1846

✧✧✧✧✧

26

Nathan…

I surely would've liked to have had more time to get our supplies, because I thought I could have bargained some. The price of goods was much higher here than back home, but I was told they were even higher the farther west we might travel. I thought the list I'd been working on for the last year would cover everything, but the storekeeper added a few more things. Then his wife talked Becca into some things she would need once she was away from the city. We gave the merchant our list of our needed supplies, and went to the livery where we got a good deal on a sturdy covered wagon.

It was the horses Becca pleasured in buying. After much consideration on a team of two or a team of four, we settled on a team of two. They were huge gentle animals that Becca didn't seem to fear in the least. By the time I finished bargaining for them, their harnesses, and their oats, she was talking to them like they were her pets.

"I didn't know horses could be this big," she said as she reached up to stroke the tallest one's muzzle. "The brown one with the blond mane is Jake and the one that's all black is Polly," she said as I put the bill of sale in my pocket.

"It's fine with me, but maybe you want to switch the names around?" I teased her.

Her face crinkled up and her brow furrowed. When she saw her mistake she rolled her pretty eyes, and patted the neck of the mare, "I'm sorry Polly, I won't get your names mixed up again."

"Well, Polly and Jake it is. Let's get you two hitched up to our new home," I said.

"It's funny to hear you call a wagon our home," Becca looked over to our wagon and giggled. And then her voice changed, her smile disappeared, and she sighed and said real quiet like, "Mother certainly would not approve."

When we got back to the general store and saw the provisions that were stacked up for us out front, I wondered if I'd be able to get everything loaded before the day was up. I went in and settled up our bill and got straight to work on the task of packing our wagon.

I was wrestling with the plow in an attempt to tie it onto the side of our wagon, when I heard Becca cry out. I dropped the end of the plow that wasn't tied up yet and went around the wagon to see what happened. What a surprise I received when I found my wife in the arms of a stranger.

"Are you sure you're all right, Miss?" he asked.

Becca gave a slight nod as the man gently placed her safely on her own two feet. "Oh, thank you," she whispered. Her face held a pretty red blush when she turned and looked at me.

The man looked my way too, as Becca tried to explain the situation. "Nathan, this gentleman just caught me when I tripped as I was coming down the steps."

She looked down at the parcels scattered in the street. "Maybe I shouldn't have tried to carry so many things at once," she said.

"I guess I'm obliged to you," I said, as I shook the man's hand and properly introduced myself. "I'm Nathan Carter, and this is my wife, Rebecca."

"Carl Taylor. Pleased to meet you both."

When I told Carl Taylor we were joining the train that had just ferried across the Missouri, he offered to help me load the rest of my things.

"Me and my wife, Hannah, are on that train too," he said.

As he helped me finish strapping down the plow, I found him to be a man of few words. He reminded me of Benjamin, and I felt I could learn from him. With his help we had our wagon loaded and ready in short time.

"I'd be grateful if I could ride back to camp with you," he said.

I was embarrassed that I'd not offered it before he asked. Once again I felt obliged to the man. "We could use the guidance," I said.

We waited while Carl posted a letter and did a little trading in the store. Then with Carl's direction we headed out for the campground, where we met our traveling neighbors and companions.

27

Rebecca's diary...
April 8, 1868—We are with the wagon train.

Carl...

As soon as our wagon was ferried across the Missouri River and I got our animals tended to, I headed back into town to post our letters. They was for our kin in Millersburg, Illinois. Near a month had gone by since we'd left both our families.

When the war was over, it took me some time afore I come back to my family. I seen so much killin' that I wasn't the same as I was afore. My Hannah seen that.

I talked to her, of a place I'd found in Kansas when I was on my trek home. It was a place where I felt at peace with myself. I couldn't get that feelin' anywhere else — not even when I got back home. I asked Hannah if she'd go there with me.

"You want to move away from our families?" she asked.

I couldn't explain to her the why. I didn't know the why myself. When I nodded and told her it would be a new start for us and it was something' I yearned for, she said the words I needed to hear.

"We'll go then. I don't ever want us to be apart again."

It took a lot from her. She'd growed to love my family as much as her own. She lived with them and helped my daddy keep the farm goin' whilst his boys was all gone off to war. Then I come back home and asked her to leave both our families. I knowed how much she loved me when she said she would.

The day I took the letters to be posted, Hannah stayed at the campsite and caught up with some things she wasn't able to do when the wagon train was movin' ever' day. And when I come back to camp I brung back some coffee, tobacco, and a newlywed couple who was to join our train.

Hannah...

It was near suppertime when my Carl come back to our campground. He went straight off to talk to Skinner, 'bout a new couple he brung with him. When he come back he helped the newcomers pull their wagon into our circle—right afore our own wagon.

It was one of Skinner's rules that any newcomer be the last wagon on the train, but since this was a tenderfoot with a new team, Skinner told Carl to put them in front of us for a few days. Skinner trusted Carl to help them if they had troubles.

As soon as they got their wagon to where they wanted it, Carl helped the woman down whilst her husband unhitched their team. She was such a tiny thing, I thought she was a child at first. It sent a wave of homesickness over me for Carl's younger sisters. We introduced ourselves to each other. Then Carl showed Nathan where to stake his horses. Rebecca stood waitin' for her husband to get back to her. Her eyes was wide with questions, as she looked around. She reminded me of a frightened little rabbit.

Luther Rangel's wagon was the last on the train, right behind ours. When his family seen there was somebody new joinin' the train, they all come over to our wagon. And when Carl and Nathan come back and Rebecca and

Nathan introduced themselves to the Rangel's, Luther started grumblin' under his breath.

"I thought the rule was that newcomers move to the back of the train."

When no one paid him any heed, he said the words a little louder. My Carl gave him a warnin' look.

"Guess we get to eat dust from one more wagon," he mumbled again.

The Rangel's had joined us a few days afore we got to Independence. When our wagon train come on them, they was all alone on the trail. Luther said he had an axel break, and the train they was with had gone on without them whilst he fixed it. Skinner took on the extra wagon and asked Carl if he'd keep an eye on them. I don't think he trusted Luther, and I knowed my Carl didn't trust the man.

I didn't like Luther either, and when I seen the way he was lookin' at Rebecca Carter, I knowed I should warn her 'bout him. She didn't seem to notice his look, as she was already in conversation with his girls, Clara Beth and Minnie.

"I've supper ready and you're welcome to eat with us for your first night here," I offered.

Rebecca's face showed relief and Nathan kept sayin' how grateful he was for all our help.

Whilst we ate, we got acquainted better. Carl answered lots of questions from Nathan. Then after supper the men joined the other men-folk who was havin' their smoke of the day. I thought back to my own discomfort the first days of travel with the wagon train, so I told Rebecca what the train's routine was.

"Hannah, I've so much to learn," she said. "Mother taught me how to make a lovely cup of tea, but I've never learned how to cook a meal."

"That will come in the mornin'," I said. "Let's get started by me showin' you how to make a comfortable bed under your wagon."

"Outside?" she looked around. "But I thought we'd be sleeping inside the wagon."

I smiled with the way she said it, 'cause it reminded me of my Carl's youngest sister, Elizabeth. "Unless you've got a tent, it's more comfortable to sleep under the wagon," I explained. "It's might chilly when the mornin' gets here, so you'll need some warm blankets. And, we get up afore dawn to make breakfast, so we best get our beds made up."

Nathan...

By the time Carl and I checked on the animals again and got back to the wagon, Becca had a nice little nest made for us.

"Hannah said it's the most comfortable place to sleep when the weather is nice," she explained. Then she got out her diary. I saw her write one line and close it. "I'm too tired to even write," she said. She yawned. "Let's go to bed."

"I'd been worried that she'd have a hard time sleeping in the wagon, but here she was, already willing to sleep on the ground. It surely was a wonder. It seemed like she no more laid her head down than she was snoring softly. I was tired too, but it took me a while to fall asleep, and when I did, I dreamed about the adventures ahead of us.

28

Hannah…

I'm not one to interfere in other's business, but I figured with Rebecca's genteel upbringin' she'd need considerable help for a few days. Even though she was more proper than Cora, it was the likeness that made me feel so kindly to her. When Carl and his brothers left to fight in the war shortly after we was wed, I lived on the Taylor farm and worked with his daddy and little brother. But it took his sisters help too, when his daddy got laid up with a busted leg. Cora and Elizabeth both did as much as they could to help but Cora needed lots of guidance to know what to do. Carl's daddy always said I was a good teacher, so I figured maybe I could help Rebecca too.

I woke up afore most of the others that mornin'. I seen to the campfire, milked our cow, Bossy, and then went to the Carter wagon and woke Rebecca.

"I'll show you how to cook up some bacon and cornbread if you're wantin' to learn," I said. She looked a little lost when she first woke up, but she nodded, and as soon as she come back from doin' her business in the bushes, we got started. By that time others was stirrin' and ever'one in camp was awake. As we was bent over the campfire the Rangel girls joined us.

"Pa wants my biscuits for breakfast," Clara Beth, the oldest, bragged. "He says I make the best biscuits in the whole wide world."

While Clara Beth prattled on 'bout how much her pa liked her cookin', Minnie's eyes didn't leave Rebecca. It was like she'd never seen a real lady afore. Rebecca didn't pay no heed to the stares of Minnie. She was in the process of learnin' and she did real good at it. Her bacon was a little burnt, but her cornbread was cookin' up mighty purty.

"We've made enough for our noon meal," I explained. "We won't have a campfire then."

"You should also have some biscuits like I make in case it rains and we can't have a campfire," Clara Beth was sayin'. "I kin teach you how?" she said as a question.

Rebecca only smiled.

"Them's purty shoes you have too, but how you gonna walk all day in 'em?" Clara Beth went on. I looked down at Rebecca's shoes.

"I bought others from the merchant in Independence. She said I'd need them."

"You will," I said as we started back to our wagon.

Clara Beth was still yammerin' while Minnie was still starin'.

Nathan...

When Hannah woke Becca, I went with Carl to tend the horses. Skinner showed up and said he wanted to talk to us. He said since I was the greenhorn in the bunch, he wanted to make sure I understood the procedure if there was any trouble.

"We'll stay on the Oregon Trail for a bit and later we'll connect up with the Smoky Hill Trail. But I hear there's some troubles with a couple of tribes in some of the area we'll be crossin'. I expect no troubles, but I want you to know if I give the signal to circle, I want no delays. Move'm as fast as you can and have your rifle ready at all times."

I nodded.

"Your missus know how to handle a rifle?"

I shook my head.

"Teach her. And don't let her wander away from the wagons at any time."

I nodded again.

He looked at Carl. Carl nodded once, like he'd been through it all before. It brought an apprehension on me, that I'd not felt since I'd heard people talking about Indians on the river boat. I didn't know how I'd go about telling Becca.

Skinner mounted his saddle horse and rode into the early dawn as Carl and I took our teams to the wagons and hitched them up. Carl explained the way one wagon would go one way and the other would go another when we were ready to make camp.

"It makes a nice tight circle that way. We're to the end, so the circlin's mostly for the others."

"What about the Indian scare?" I asked.

"Skinner just wants us to be prepared at all times. He said we had quite a few more miles to travel afore there's much worry."

I nodded. I had lots of questions going through my mind but I couldn't think of one to ask just then.

29

Nathan...

Becca and Hannah had breakfast ready by the time I got Jake and Polly hitched to the wagon. No one said much of anything while we ate. Becca kept glancing my way, every time I took a bite of my cornbread. There was a question on her face, but she didn't ask it. When I complimented our breakfast, I figured I'd guessed what was on her mind.

"This is a fine meal," I said between hungry bites.

Her smile made it plain to see she was pleasured with the remark, "We have Hannah to thank for that."

Hannah only shrugged.

Since Carl was saying nothing about the warning Skinner had just given us, I said nothing.

When someone banged on their plate a couple of wagons away, Hannah and Carl stopped eating, and got to their feet.

"Time to pack up," Hannah said as she looked in Becca's direction. "We'll be movin' soon."

I reached for another piece of cornbread, but Becca grabbed the skillet and started wrapping the leftovers in a towel.

"You'll thank me when we stop for our noon meal," she said, as though she had the wisdom of a seasoned traveler.

I didn't want to take my eyes off my lovely bride, but I heard everyone in the camp moving together for the common purpose of preparing for the day's journey. In no time at all we were on our way.

We'd gotten the train in a line formation before Becca and I said much. That's when I related Skinner's warning to her. Becca's brow creased into a slight frown, though she said nothing. I went on.

"Carl doesn't think there's anything to worry about. He said we've a ways to travel before we even see any Indians." I tried to make myself sound convincing. Then I added, "But, Becca…"

"Yes, what is it?"

"Don't wander away from the train at any time." I said, "And…Skinner wants me to teach you how to use a rifle."

Her eyes held fear when I said that. The wagon hit a rut just then and she nearly bounced off the seat. She straightened herself and held on tight to the underside of the bench. We hit another rut. She leaned to the side of the wagon and looked back.

"I'm going to walk," she informed me. "Hannah, Clara Beth, and Minnie are walking."

"I shouldn't stop the team right now."

"I'm going to walk," she said again.

With those words uttered, she immediately threw her legs over the side of the wagon bench and jumped. I tried to make a grab for her and nearly fell off the seat myself. My concern was needless, for when I looked back to see if the wheels were going to crush her, I got an improbable surprise. She'd landed perfectly on her feet. She looked like she'd been jumping off moving wagons all her life.

I looked back again. She had already joined Hannah and the Rangel girls. I wondered what she was thinking, as I craned my neck to get another glimpse of them. The two women and two girls were talking and laughing like they were on a stroll to attend a Sunday picnic. I seemed to be the only one that was worried about Skinner's warnings.

Hannah

When Rebecca jumped down off the wagon and joined us, I think Clara Beth talked even faster than usual. Rebecca asked Minnie where the cow she was leadin' come from, but Minnie got no chance to answer afore Clara Beth told her all she would ever want to know about Bossy.

"Oh, it's Hannah's cow. When our wagon broke down, our cow stepped in a hole and broke her fool leg, and when we joined up with Skinner's train Hannah said she'd share some of Bossy's milk with us, and then Pa found out and said I had to earn the milk, and so I milk Bossy after we travel all day and Minnie likes to lead Bossy when we walk cause she doesn't like to see her tied to the wagon."

"Oh," was all Rebecca said when Clara Beth finally stopped long enough to take a breath. But Clara Beth started off again as soon as she got a good lungful of air.

"Do you know how to milk a cow? Cause I kin teach you how to do it. It's not hard, but it's not as easy as it looks either and Bossy really likes me so it's a fun thing to do, and she gives almost a half pail of milk, even after she's walked all day."

"Speakin' of walkin' all day, when you gonna pick up your share of the kindlin'," come the deep voice of Clara Beth's daddy. He come up behind us whilst he was ridin' high on his saddle horse.

Clara Beth said nothin' back to her daddy. She just moved away from the rest of us right quick to look for kindlin'. Luther watched her for just a bit afore he tipped his hat to me and Rebecca. His eyes lingered on Rebecca afore he tipped his hat again.

He gave his horse a small kick, and rode off to help Skinner scout. Unless it was rainin', Lucas liked to ride his horse up at the front of the train, sayin' that he was helpin' Skinner *scout* the trail. It left poor Eunice, his wife, to drive their team by herself most days. As the last wagon in line, it left her to eat the dust from the other wagons.

30

Carl…

The air smelled sweeter to me after we'd crossed over the Missouri River into Kansas. I felt like I was goin' to the place I should be. On the trails, where wagon ruts, hooves, and feet had tramped the grasses down, I seen nothin' familiar. It was the high places, far-off in the distance, that I seen the tall grasses I'd trekked through when I come back from the war. I knowed some of those grasses reached higher than my Hannah stood. But we had some travelin' to do yet afore we'd reach the part of Kansas that I wanted for our homestead—the place where I'd found peace inside myself.

When my Hannah walked, I had all day to let the team do the work of pullin' the wagon, whilst I kept my dream in front of me. It'd been a full three years since the war ended and I still had nightmares at night. My Hannah would wake me sometimes if they got too bad. I don't know where my thinkin' would've taken me if she hadn't understood my need to leave our home in Illinois.

When the war finally ended I didn't go home right away. Instead I fulfilled a promise to the boy from Kansas who saved my life and gave up his own. He stepped in front of a bullet that was meant for me. I killed the man who shot him. And then I held that boy in my arms whilst he took a while to die. He asked me to tell his mama that he loved her and was goin' to see Jesus. And so when I was discharged I went to see his mama. She cried. She hugged me, fed me, and offered for me to stay awhile. But I lied and said I needed to go home.

I didn't go home. I couldn't. I wandered instead. I started walkin' in the opposite direction of home. One day I come upon this little creek in the middle of nowhere. When I got myself a drink, the water was cool and fresh, and I figured there was a spring feedin' that creek. I looked 'round. For the first time in a long time I didn't have to go anywhere else. The rattlin' in my head stopped and I no longer smelled the stench of death in ever' thing. I heard a meadowlark's sweet melody. I took a deep breath and smelled the sweet grasses. Some kind of miracle happened to me in that place. I stayed a couple of days and then I went back to my Hannah.

Home wasn't the same. My Hannah was there, but four of my brothers had been taken by the war. Two had died, fightin' for the Union. Two had joined the Confederacy. No one knowed if they was still alive. My thinkin' was we'd never see them again. Levi, my youngest brother, had done a fine job helpin' my daddy, my Hannah, and the girls keep the farm runnin'. And I was grateful that Evert, my oldest brother, made it back from war to his family. He had a passel of children that would grow to help him. I tried to make it work, but then the nightmares started. That's when I asked my wonderful wife to come with me to this place unknown to her.

31

Nathan…

The first night we camped after our travels all day, I had the pleasure of talking with Carl Taylor again. We'd had our supper and were standing away from the others after we'd enjoyed our smokes. Stretching out the tired muscles we had from bouncing around on a wagon seat all day, I was enjoying his company. He didn't tell me the why of his story, but he told me he was headed for a place he'd already seen in Kansas.

"Good farm ground?" I asked.

"With hard work I think it will be. When I first seen it, there was still some buffalo roamin' the area."

"You're joshing me?"

"It was near empty of people back then," he said, as he chewed on a piece of dried grass he'd picked up earlier. He took it out of his mouth and studied it, like maybe it held some secret. It was something I'd seen William do sometimes after he came home from the war. Then he said real quiet like, "I kinda needed to be alone."

I figured then that he'd seen his share like William had and I knew better than to ask. So I said, "Sounds like there's a lot of land to pick from."

"There was, then. But it's been some time."

We both held on to our own thoughts for a while before Carl spoke again.

"Since your destination is Nebraska, we'll be partin' ways tomorrow. I wish you the best of luck."

Confused, but not wanting to show my ignorance, I stayed quiet. My face must have worn a question on it though.

"Skinner's train is takin' the Smoky Hill Trail." Carl explained, "Half the train will head north, to Nebraska. Me and my Hannah will be goin' on with Skinner's train."

I mulled over what Carl had just said and was wondering if I was the fool my father thought I was. I had us on a wagon train not knowing it wasn't headed to our desired destination. I felt like a damned greenhorn. I'd been thinking Nebraska all this time, but what would the difference be if we went to Kansas instead? The things I'd heard from Charles Rudd when we'd traveled the Missouri River came back to me. He'd talked about an Indian massacre in Nebraska only a year ago.

"I'm considering Kansas myself," the words came out before I even thought about what I was saying.

I knew I could learn a lot from Carl Taylor. I trusted him that he knew what he was doing. He never said anything more, but pulled another piece of dried grass out of his shirt pocket, stuck it in his mouth, gave the slightest nod, and started walking toward his wagon. I walked beside him, pondering what my decision would be tomorrow when the trail divided.

32

Hannah…

Ever' mornin' afore the wagons started rollin' I checked the saplin's my daddy gave me afore we left Illinois. My Carl had carefully packed them in two big crocks and they was doin' a fine job of travelin'. As I tended to them I thought on that first time I seen my Carl.

It was in my daddy's orchard. Me and my twin sister, Sarah, was five years of age when our daddy started takin' us along to check on his fruit trees. That particular day we walked around the corner of the barn and seen the backside of a young feller. He was bent over puttin' our apples in a basket and didn't hear us. My daddy reached out to me and my sister and stopped us from goin' any closer He put his forefinger to his lips to shush us. Then we all tiptoed and was careful how we trod, so as to move closer to catch the thief that was stealin' our apples. When our daddy stopped again, we did too.

"Are you enjoyin' *my* apples?" our daddy's voice boomed.

I jumped when he said it. The boy jumped too. He dropped a half-eaten apple out of one hand and another apple out of the other.

"Uh… no sir. I…uh… mean yes sir."

"Well, which is it? Do you think *my* apples are good enough to steal?"

The boy stood there like he wanted to run, but instead he explained his situation. "I didn't mean any harm sir. I was only takin' the ones on the ground."

Our daddy gave him a look that me and my Sarah clearly knowed. It meant he wanted more of an answer. The young man knowed what the look meant too.

"They're the best apples I've ever had, sir."

Our daddy looked the culprit over and finally gave him a smile. "I'm gonna need help to do the pickin' this year. Think you might be interested? I could pay you in apples, if you'd like?"

"My mama would like that sir. We've eleven to feed in our family and we all like apples."

"Very well then, but I need to know who I'm offerin' employment to."

Wipin' his hands on his pants, the boy held his right hand out as an introduction to hiself.

"I'm Carl Taylor, sir. My family just moved onto the farm next to your apple trees."

Our daddy nodded his approval of the situation and shook his hand. Then he reached up and picked three apples from the tree, handin' one to me and one to my sister. He took a big bite from the one he had left. He smiled with the satisfaction of the taste. "I think you're correct in your assumption. These *are* good apples." Without lookin' at us girls he started pullin' more apples off the tree. Me and Sarah held out our aprons as he filled them with what he thought we could carry. He winked and added, "We'll take enough for your mama to bake us a pie."

Our daddy told the boy he could pick his basket full for his folks too. It was the beginnin' of Carl Taylor and his younger brother Jacob helpin' harvest in my daddy's orchard. Even though me and Sarah was only five that summer, it was the beginnin' of us likin' the Taylor brothers. I liked Carl, and my sister was sweet on Jacob.

If things had only turned out in a different way, I figured Sarah and her Jacob would've been right alongside me and my Carl on our journey. Instead, Sarah moved back with my daddy and my mama since her Jacob is gone forever. Carl's brothers, Jacob and Robert, was both lost at the Battle of Shiloh.

Ever' time I tended the saplin's I got that bittersweet recollection. I tried to remember the sweet more than the bitter, but the memories got mixed together now and then. I gave the seedlin's a bit of water and joined my Carl. He had the team all hitched and ready to go. We talked 'bout the day that was facin' us.

"Skinner said we'll only have nineteen wagons that'll be travelin' the Smoky Hill Trail," he explained. "We'll camp early whilst Skinner guides the other's north."

"He'll be leadin' us again, won't he?"

"He'll be goin' our direction," Carl said as he climbed aboard the wagon.

I liked Skinner. I thought it to be true that some of the tales he told was purty tall, but I trusted he was a good guide, and I was glad we didn't have to join up with a new train. I'd said my good-byes to most of those headin' for Nebraska the night afore in camp. As Clara Beth and Minnie walked over to our wagon, I was glad I didn't have to bid them farewell just yet.

33

Nathan...

I figured I needed to have my mind made up before we came to the fork in the trail that day. I'd wanted to talk it over with Becca, but the night before, she was so tuckered out she fell asleep before I had the chance. I listened to her gentle breathing and felt blessed to have her by my side. Then doubts crept upon me. That night I had plenty of them. They always seemed to come to me after the sun went down and I had more time to think. They weren't about my dream of owning my own land. They were about my providing what was best for Becca. Some of her mother's words had stuck with me.

I rolled out of bed and sat by the side of our prairie schooner where I could see the stars and the heavens. The air had a chill. The night was clear. I felt like I could've reached up and plucked some of those stars right out of the sky. My mother had taught me that I needed to get on my knees and fold my hands to pray. I didn't do that. Instead, I felt like I was talking to God with my thoughts. I asked Him to help me with the decision I had to make. Then I laid back down beside Becca and slept peacefully. The next morning when I woke up, I still hadn't figured out what to do.

Carl...

Midafternoon Skinner took off in a northern direction. Some of the wagons followed him, whilst others circled for a camp. I seen where the trail split. I knowed my Hannah had made friendships with some of those that we'd never see again, but I was lookin forward to not havin so many wagons to follow. One by one there was a lot of wagons headed in the same direction Skinner had gone. There wasn't near so many that was goin' our way. I wondered which way the Carter wagon would go. I smiled to myself when it joined those that was goin' our way. The Carters would be our neighbors for a while longer.

Hannah...

It was a hard thing to be distressed around Clara Beth. She wore a smile most times I seen her, and she seemed to know ever'body's business. She prattled on that mornin' and let us know which wagon was gonna turn north and which would turn south. She was so proud to have the knowledge of where each family was headed.

"Clara Beth, where do you find all your particulars?" I asked her.

"I listen."

"When?" Rebecca asked with a giggle.

"Clara Beth, how do you listen when you're always talkin'?" I asked.

Clara Beth immediately looked contrite.

Minnie piped up, "Ma says Clara Beth talks to you way too much."

Clara Beth looked at her little sister as though the child had betrayed a confidence. Her gaiety disappeared. Her tone of voice changed as she said, "I'm sorry Hannah."

"I don't care, you know," I said. "I like to listen too."

"It's just...well...you're so easy to talk to. I cain't talk to the others the same way."

She fell silent for a short time. I realized I'd not seen the girls play with the other children when we camped.

And when they was doin' their chores 'round others, I never seen them talkin' with anyone else.

We walked on for a ways with Clara Beth keepin' silent. I heard the labor of the horses and the creaks and groans of wagon wheels as they bounced in and out of the ruts on the trail. The walkin' wasn't near as pleasant.

"Clara Beth, I'm glad you talk to me," I said.

The child's face brightened. "Fer sure?"

Rebecca and I both laughed out loud. Clara Beth looked back and forth betwixt us. Taking a deep lungful of air, she started chatterin' about each family's destination again. Her voice was like music after a short time of not hearin' it.

34

Rebecca's diary...

April 10, 1868—We've been with the wagon train for two days. I finally find time to journal our travels while we are camped in midday, waiting for our wagon master to return. He is joining part of the wagon train to another train on the Oregon Trail. Since Nathan has changed the direction of our travels we will not go north to Nebraska, but will stay with a small group going across Kansas along the Smoky Hill River. Nathan made the decision after talking with Carl Taylor. I know it is his decision to make, but I am not pleased that he didn't think it necessary that I know. Our wagon master and scout is a man named Skinner. I find him to be the most interesting of characters. I don't doubt the sincerity of the man's nature, but he has told Nathan I must learn how to shoot a rifle. The road is so rough at times that I prefer walking with Hannah Taylor and the two Rangel girls. It does tire me though, and when we camp I can hardly wait to lay my head down at night. The weather has been mild so we make our bed under our wagon. I am learning how to cook over an open campfire. Clara Beth Rangel is only a child, but she has promised to teach me how to make biscuits and also how to milk Hannah's cow. I have so much to learn. If not for Hannah Taylor and the Rangel girls, I fear we would have nothing to eat.

Nathan...

I don't know why I didn't tell Becca that I wanted to go to Kansas instead of going to Nebraska. Maybe it was because I didn't know myself until I turned Jake and Polly onto the southern trail. Then when I told her she needed to learn how to shoot the rifle while we were camped, her demeanor changed.

"When can you show me? May I learn right now? Clara Beth has promised to teach me how to milk Bossy later today."

I looked into Becca's beautiful eyes. She tried so hard in everything she was learning. I wanted to take my bride in my arms and tell her how much I loved her, but there were others around.

"How about right now?" I got the rifle from under the seat of the wagon. I was anxious to shoot it myself, since I'd not used it yet. I had purchased the Winchester Model 1866 repeater rifle in Independence. The merchant had assured me it was what I needed if I was going to homestead. I'd never shot one like it and I didn't want Becca to know I was learning the same time she was.

We walked a ways from the camp along the creek where we could practice shooting into the creek bank. I wondered if some other fellow that'd traveled this trail before us had needed to show his wife how to use a rifle too.

"When am I going to shoot?" Becca asked me. My feeling was that it was not because she was eager for the learning, but I knew she wanted to get the lesson done as soon as possible. As I looked over the rifle with admiration at its craftsmanship, she asked, "Wait, you've never shot this gun either, have you?" I ignored both questions.

"Soon as I get a target set up, I'll show you how to load the rifle," I said. I picked up a piece of bark and set it on the ground a good ways away and in the opposite direction of the camp. I explained how it was safer to point the gun down until we were ready to use it.

"And never point it at anything you don't intend to shoot." I added, "Especially your loving husband." Becca's shoulders relaxed just a bit. Then her lips curled with a sneer, but her eyes were flirtatious. Since there was no one around us right then, I stole a kiss. I thought how few kisses I'd had from my new bride since we'd left Eaton. There was little privacy on a wagon train.

"We'd better get on with this lesson," she said, pulling away and turning prim and proper.

While I loaded the gun, she watched over my shoulder. Then I showed her how to hold the gun, cock it, and how to take aim. I pulled the trigger, felt Becca jump beside me, and smiled when I saw a hole in my target. It was a good feeling to know that I had purchased a gun with a good sight on it. I cocked the gun for another shot and held the rifle out toward Becca.

"My turn," she said. Her voice was confident, but her hands were shaking when she took it. I watched her closely. She did exactly as I had done, and I thought she looked like she'd surely done this before. But just as her finger pulled the trigger she closed her eyes. Again, she jumped at the crack of the rifle. A puff of dirt flew up in the bank on the other side of the creek.

"Did I hit it?"

"No, but you get to try again."

"Do I have to? I really want to learn how to milk Bossy today." She tried to hand the gun back to me.

I didn't take it. I said, "Becca, this is important. You need to know how to do this."

She glared at me. Then she put the rifle back on her shoulder, lined up the sight and pulled on the trigger. Nothing happened. Looking bewildered, she looked to me for an answer. I said nothing in the hope that she would remember how I had pulled on the cocking lever to reload.

And she did remember. But in her concentration, just as she pulled the cocking handle forward, she pointed the barrel of the rifle in my direction. I grabbed the barrel with my hand and pointed it down.

"Remember, how I said you should never point it at your loving husband?" I tried to say as gently as I could. That's when my beautiful bride stopped her charade of bravado and started weeping like I didn't know she could.

"I could have killed you!" she said between sobs.

"But you didn't, that's why I'm teaching you."

She begged me to not make her try anymore. I myself wanted to let her learn how to milk a cow instead of shoot a rifle, but I knew how important this lesson might be. Finally, resolved that I wouldn't let her quit until she hit the target, it took her only four more tries. When she saw that she'd accomplished the feat, she handed the gun back to me. Without a word, she turned away and started to leave. I tried to assure her that she had done a really good job but she paid me no heed.

As we walked up to our wagon Clara Beth met us with a pail half full of milk. Becca's eyes were filled with disappointment and I knew I'd not steal another kiss that day.

35

Rebecca's Diary...

April 12, 1868—This morning everyone gathered around the campfire for the Sabbath. We sang "Rock of Ages", while Skinner played his harmonica. I could hardly join in with the singing as I was overcome with a longing for my piano. A man named Samuel prayed for our safe journey. He no more than said "Amen" before we dispersed and went forth with our travels. That was all there was for this day of worship. Nathan has reached the age of twenty years today. We traveled eight miles.

Nathan...

It surely was a surprise at how well Skinner played the harmonica on Sunday morning. I thought the music would've made Becca happy. Instead, I think she suffered greatly with homesickness. I could see pain in her beautiful eyes. It brought on my doubts about taking her away from her family. I asked myself if we should turn the wagon around and follow the trail back from where we just came. Then I hitched up Polly and Jake and I breathed the sweet smell of the grasses. I thought how much I hated moving barrels and kegs around inside the store all those years. I remembered the satisfaction of planting and harvesting when I worked with Benjamin on his farm.

Once we started moving the wagons again, Becca appeared to be happy as she walked with the Rangel girls. Doubts for our future faded away. I had confidence I could make a good life for us on a farm if we found good land. I believed Carl when he told me about the land he found. I was looking forward to seeing the buffalo and the deer that he saw. I promised myself that when I got my first good crop, I'd buy Becca a piano of her very own that she could play every day until her heart was content.

Carl...

I didn't mind that our wagons was fewer in number now. I figured it meant we was gettin' closer to the place I'd found. My only worry about that was that it'd been three years and I didn't know that someone else might have found the place as promisin' as I had. If someone else had already filed a claim on it, I didn't have another plan.

Hannah...

With each day of travel, I could see a new hope in my Carl's eyes. There was a difference comin' over him the further west we went. That day we first left our families back in Illinois, I wanted to tell him to turn the wagon back. I thought my heart would tear in little pieces when I seen my Sarah standin' in the distance and watchin' us go. As twins, we'd been a part of each other all of our lives. We even married brothers on the same day. Her Jacob was lost to the war. My Carl come back. But he was a changed man and when he needed to seek this place where he'd found peace, I needed to be with him.

My mama's words had given me the strength to follow him.

"You've married a good man, who treats you well," she said. "Now go with him. You have your daddy and your mama's blessin's."

"And mine," my sister added.

It was a true fact that I missed them more ever' day the further west we went.

36

Rebecca's Diary...

April 13, 1868—The weather was cold all day with a sharp wind that carried even Clara Beth's voice away, and the air was wet and damp. After we made camp it rained enough that we had no satisfactory campfire to even warm us. But Clara Beth finally showed me how to milk Bossy. The task is much more difficult than I had thought it would be. Bossy kept turning around and looking at me while I balanced on Clara Beth's little milking stool and Clara Beth showed me how to pull and squeeze at the same time to produce a little stream of milk. It took me a long time but I was able to contribute a small amount to the pail before Clara Beth finished the chore. I'm grateful to Hannah for sharing the milk with us and the Rangel family. It wasn't much, but it was the only warm part of our supper. It is getting dark early and my hands are shaking so that I can't even write anymore. We are going to sleep in the wagon tonight as it is too damp to sleep on the ground. I am going to ask Nathan why we are going to Kansas instead of Nebraska.

April 14, 1868—The morning started out gloomy again and the walking was cold, but by noon the sun came out. Luther Rangel rode inside the wagon until the day warmed and then he rode past us on his saddle horse as Eunice drove the wagon. The girls walked with Hannah and me. It is strange that Clara Beth says little when her father is around. He always tips his hat to me and smiles, but I cannot bring myself to think good thoughts of him.

Nathan...

The traveling seemed easier when there were not as many wagons to follow, and Skinner said we were making good miles every day. When Becca finally got her chance to milk Bossy she took great pride in her accomplishment. I didn't particularly like the chore, but Becca didn't seem to mind.

"Well, Bossy wasn't so sure about it all, but it's a lot more fun than shooting a rifle," she told me.

We were sitting in the wagon trying to warm up from the cold day. The milk was rich coming straight from the pail. It helped to get our dry cornbread down. So I told her I intended to purchase a milk cow for us as soon as we reached the land we were going to homestead. She got real quiet then and I knew something had her unsettled. I waited to hear what was on her mind.

"Just where are we going to do that?" she asked. She turned her face away from me and looked out the back of the wagon. "I thought we were going to Nebraska, but you changed your mind without asking my thoughts on it."

I didn't understand why she was questioning me. I started to tell her it was my decision to make, but I caught my tongue before it spit out the words. She didn't look at me, as she waited for my explanation. I remembered my mother doing that to my father a lot after he came home from the war. And I remember my father never explaining any of his actions to mother or me. We were just to accept that he was right in whatever he said or did.

"I did what I thought was the right thing," I told her. "When I heard Carl telling about the land in Kansas, it sounded right for us. I also didn't tell you about the Indian massacre in Nebraska last year."

Becca turned to look at me then with her eyes wide. "What?"

"When we were on the steamboat, I heard about it. I thought we'd be safer going this way so I made the decision." I'd never seen Becca look at me that way before, and I only guessed as to what she was thinking. I tried to explain, "I didn't know myself until I turned the wagon south."

We bedded down in the wagon. Becca snuggled into my arms for warmth, though I knew she was still angry at me. When her breathing told me she was finally asleep, I lay beside her, questioning why I'd not included her in my decision. I remembered those days when my father wasn't there and mother had to make decisions on her own. I'd longed for my father to be there. I'd wanted to be like him—a strong man. Then I thought how he was after the war. I did not want to be like the man my father became.

37

Carl...

I knowed my Hannah was fond of the Rangel girls, but I seen some things in the girl's daddy that I was afraid might cause some problems. My Hannah told me.

"I seen Luther watchin' Rebecca when she brushes her hair at night," she said. "It ain't right—the way I seen him lookin' at her."

I nodded that I understood, but I didn't think Luther's just lookin', was enough for me to get riled up 'bout it.

Hannah...

I told my Carl 'bout Luther watchin' Rebecca one mornin' and that very night I looked back and seen that Eunice was watchin' Luther, while Luther was watchin' Rebecca. She didn't say anything to him, but later that night I heard them arguin' in loud whispers. The voices started to turn louder than whispers, until there was a loud slap. Then there was only hushed sobbin'. My heart could feel no kindness for Luther, and I pitied his wife.

The very next mornin' I seen Luther follow Rebecca when she went to do her business in the bushes. So I followed him and let him know it. He looked at me like I was interferin' with his day. Then he walked away.

By the time I come back to get ever'thing ready for our travels, Luther had brought his team 'round to his wagon. As soon as he seen me, he left the animals for Eunice to hitch up by herself whilst he went off to get his saddle horse. That's when I noticed an ugly mark against the side of her face. She didn't look my way and I figured it wasn't the first time she' been hit by her no good skunk of a husband.

My daddy had never hit my mama. I knowed I'd take a fryin' pan to my Carl if he tried to hit me. Maybe it was Luther's right to handle his family the way he seen fit, but it didn't give him no right to take advantage of Rebecca. I gave her warnin' to pay heed to who was followin' her when she was alone. Her eyes got big as saucers when I told her what I seen.

"He what?" she whispered.

Just then Minnie walked up leadin' Bossy and hummin' a tune. Rebecca didn't say anymore when the girls was 'round, though her face kept askin' me why.

I hadn't meant to put fear into her, but I thought she needed to know. As things turned out later in the day, I suppose I wouldn't have had to tell her anything.

Nathan...

We'd been making good miles since we'd left Independence. But on day nine there was trouble when the Rangel wagon got caught up in the middle of a creek bed. Since they were still the last wagon in the line and it was getting late in the day, Skinner had the rest of the wagons circle on the other side of the creek to make camp.

No one seemed to know where Luther had been during the crossing, but he suddenly came racing back on his saddle horse. He headed straight to his wagon. Carl and I were on the other side of the creek. We were getting ready to go back to where the Rangel wagon was stuck, when Luther started cussing and yelling up a storm.

"Fool woman, what in hell did you go and do that fer?" he screamed at Eunice. "Cain't you do nothin' right?"

Poor Eunice was sitting on the wagon seat trying her best. One of the wheels on the wagon had slipped into a hole. The horses were pulling with all their might, their eyes starting to show panic. The wagon wouldn't budge. Instead of getting off his mount, Luther kept yelling to the sky how stupid his woman was.

Carl shook his head as he watched.

"I'll try to calm the horses, if you want to help Eunice," he said.

I nodded. But before we could get near the horses or the stranded wagon, Eunice tied the reins to the bench and climbed down. She was in water knee high, but she managed to stay on her feet and walk to the other side of that creek.

By that time Skinner had ridden up. He got down off his horse and helped Eunice up the creek bank. She walked off to where Hannah was and sat down on the Taylor's wagon hitch. She sat staring straight ahead like a statue.

Luther was furious! He was sitting in his saddle, cussing and beating his hat against his pant leg, working his saddle horse and the team into a frenzy.

Looking the situation over, Skinner stood quiet for a minute before he yelled, "Luther! If you want help, I'd suggest you stop actin' like a jackass in heat."

Luther immediately stopped ranting and stared at Skinner. I thought he might do something foolish, but even Luther was smart enough to know Skinner was not a man to mess with. He mumbled under his breath as he dismounted his horse.

Carl stepped into the water, speaking gentle words to calm the team, as others showed up and pitched in to help. They had to unload nearly half the wagon before they finally got it and the team out of the creek. Then they all pitched in to put everything back.

Luther never bothered to tell anyone that he was grateful for the help. He drove his wagon in the circle, unhitched the team, and started yelling at his wife again. It was a hard thing to hear.

Later that night as we bedded down, Becca started crying while she was lying in my arms.

"I'm afraid of Luther," she whispered.

"He won't hurt you, Becca. I promise you that."

It wasn't until the next morning that we all discovered how dangerous Luther's temper was.

~ 38 ~

Rebecca's diary…

April 16, 1868—Luther Rangel is a despicable man. I can hardly wait until Nathan and I are on our own homestead.

Hannah…

I worried for Eunice the day she got stuck in the creek. When she come and set down on our wagon hitch she didn't say nothin' to me. She didn't talk to her girls either. And when her wagon was finally out of the creek she just kept settin' on our wagon hitch. Her girls brung her somethin' to eat but she didn't touch her supper. Luther was yellin' at her the whole time. Finally when it was dark she went back to her own wagon. I was afraid for her, but I knowed there was nothin' any of us could do to help her.

It was the next mornin' that I seen how bad Luther beat her. I didn't understand how a man could beat a woman like that. I felt my own fists clench tight when I seen she could hardly walk. Both her eyes were so swollen she only had little slits to see out of. I seen Carl's jaw muscles workin' on his face. He said nothin' and left to tend to our animals. We both knowed if we tried to help Eunice when Luther was 'round, we'd only make it worse for her.

Her girls did what they could. I watched out of the corner of my eye as Clara Beth and Minnie helped their mama with breakfast. Luther kept barking orders at the girls as they helped her climb into the back of their wagon. At least he didn't try to make her drive the team that day.

The girls didn't walk with me and Rebecca, but walked behind their own wagon where they could keep an eye on their mama.

Rebecca seen the sorry state Eunice was in too.

"I miss walking with the girls," she said. "Thanks, Hannah, for warning me about that man yesterday."

It was over our noon meal that Skinner rode up. He and my Carl walked off a little ways and talked. Carl looked at me, looked at the Rangel wagon, and then nodded.

As Carl walked back to me, Skinner walked to the Rangel wagon. I heard what he said to Luther and I thought it strange.

"Luther, I need you to saddle up and ride with me for a bit."

Luther's answer was slow. His face wore a puzzled look. "Eunice cain't drive today."

"Carl said he'd do your drivin' if you help me scout."

Luther looked at Carl. Carl nodded and added, "My Hannah can handle our team for a ways."

And so I drove that afternoon, not knowin' why, but trustin' there was a good reason.

It was a long time afore we seen Skinner and Luther return. They come ridin' back real slow and easy and Luther was bent over in his saddle. I stopped the team and waited as they rode up aside the wagon Carl was drivin'. Skinner was talkin' loud enough that I could hear, but I kinda figured it was for Eunice's benefit that he wanted others to hear too.

"Luther's had a bad accident. Fell off his horse and hurt hiself a little. But he's plenty good to drive his own team now."

Skinner waited 'til Luther got off his horse, tied his horse to the side of the wagon, and climbed onto his own wagon seat. It was a good long wait.

"Much obliged to you Carl," Skinner said. Then he rode off at a gallop to get to the front of the trail and lead his wagon train.

39

Rebecca's diary…

April 17, 1868—My mother would say that Mr. Rangel got his comeuppance today. He beat his wife last night, but he had a bad accident when he fell from his horse later in this day. The accident occurred when he and Mr. Skinner rode out of camp together.

Carl…

I didn't like to see any animal hurt—even one as low down as Luther Rangel. But I figured Skinner knowed what he was doin' that day he took Luther out to scout with him.

Skinner told me we'd be in Indian territory soon. He asked if I'd mind bein' the last wagon in line. It meant me and my Hannah would have to be the last to circle.

"I'd feel better knowin' you could keep an eye on him, too," Skinner said, as he tipped his head in the direction of where Luther was walkin'.

I didn't think his meanin' was for Luther's welfare.

I nodded.

"We'll switch in the mornin' then," Skinner said.

I nodded again.

Hannah…

I didn't mind at all that we was behind the Rangel wagon. It meant I could walk with Clara Beth and Minnie as company again. But walkin' with the girls was not near as pleasurable as it was afore their daddy had his accident.

Eunice wasn't able to keep up at walkin', so she spent her day bouncin' around in the back of their wagon. Clara Beth watched over her mama like a brood hen. The girl was so busy when we camped at night that I started milkin' Bossy myself, though we didn't mention that to her daddy. I had just set myself on my milkin' stool when Rebecca come up to Bossy and started gently strokin' her belly.

"Could I try again? It's something I want to learn to do better. Clara Beth showed me how, but I've only done it once."

Even though the chore was easier to do myself, I got up and handed her my stool. I could tell the ever'day things that needed doin', didn't come easy for her, but she kept tryin'. I seen her nose wrinkle when the horses did their business. I seen her fear when she saw a bull snake slither in the grass. But she tried hard and was doin' her best.

"You're doin' good," I told her, even though the milk was only comin' out in little squirts. It took a good slow time, so I set on the grass and watched. She worked hard at the task, talkin' to the cow like that might help. Bossy looked back at her, then turned her head away and chewed on her cud with a great deal of contentment.

40

Rebecca's diary...

April 18, 1868—Samuel, the man who drives the lead wagon, spotted a flock of wild turkeys today. Three of the birds were shot and roasted to make a wonderful supper for the entire camp. We were all in a joyous spirit until Mr. Skinner called for our attention after the feast. He told us we are going to be traveling through Indian territory for several days. I keep thinking of my mother's warnings and pray she will not be proven correct when she said we will all die from savages attacking us.

April 19, 1868—We only had Samuel's prayer to start our Sabbath this morning, before we were on our way. Everyone has their rifles ready and close to them at all times. Nathan has assured me that he has faith in Mr. Skinner's ability to deliver us to our destination safely.

Nathan...

I had changed my mind about going to Nebraska because I'd had fears of Indian troubles. Then I heard that the route we were traveling, the Smoky Hill River Trail, used to be an Indian trail. When Skinner gathered us all together it seemed like we might meet some Indians after all.

"When we passed near Topeka, I heard rumors that there's been some unrest with a couple of tribes in some of the area we have to cross," he explained. "I doubt there'll be any troubles, for I'm talkin' about the Kaw and the Cheyenne. Their fight is usually betwixt their tribes. However, I want ever' one of you to have your rifles loaded and ready just in case."

He let that soak in and picked his next words carefully. "Now, that means have them ready," he said. "That means you only shoot if I give the word or you see arrows flyin'. We're just taken some extra precautions.

"If I give the signal to circle, I want no delays. Move'm as fast as you can and get yourselves as protected as you can. Just don't nobody go off half-cocked, ya hear?"

I felt my skin crawl. I put my hand on Becca's shoulder. She was shaking. I gave her shoulder a little squeeze. There were a few murmurs amongst the crowd.

"What about the livestock?" someone said. "I heard stories how them redskins kin steal a horse right from under a man."

"They do like ponies, that's fer sure, but I've traded with a good many of the fellers we might meet up with, and they know me. Where'd you think I got this name from? My mama didn't give me the name Skinner."

There were nervous chuckles, before he went on. "I'm sayin' we need to be a little cautious and we won't have any trouble. We'll take turns on watch tonight. Now, get a good night's sleep 'cause we're headin' out at sunrise."

41

Carl...

The trail was becomin' more familiar to me the further we went. I'd followed it comin' from the west when I'd gone back home to Illinois. I'd met up with a couple of those fellers Skinner mentioned, but they'd found me no threat and they'd done me no harm. I must've looked a pitiful sight back then.

Now I had to keep my rifle at the ready again. Even killin' our food went against me now, so I sure was prayin' we wasn't gonna run into Indians. I'd shoot if I had to, but I figured this part of the country was their home and they was only tryin' to protect it.

Hannah...

Since we was in Indian territory, Skinner didn't let us stop but a short time to rest the animals at noon. We'd gone but 'bout three miles when we come on to a creek crossin'. He rode out and scouted around afore he said it was safe to let Samuel's wagon cross. As each wagon crossed, one by one, the rest of us all kept a sharp lookout for any trouble. We didn't know that we was bein' watched.

But Skinner knowed. He had the wagons circle up as soon as they crossed. We was the last in line now, and as soon as we joined the rest, the circle closed tight. Skinner spoke to all of us whilst two of the men stood on the perimeter with rifles ready.

"We're campin' here a little early, 'cause we're close to water and it's as safe a place as we'll find for a few miles," he explained. "I seen an Indian scout watchin' us cross the creek bed..."

As low murmurs of fear interrupted him, he held up both his hands to quiet them, and went on.

"He's done us no harm. We're in his land," he said. "If they wanted to attack, they'd a done it whilst we was crossin'.

"Now, we're not gonna tempt them to take our livestock. So we'll keep them inside the circle with us and pair up with a neighbor. Take turns when you water the animals."

"What're we supposed to do if we see that Indian?" someone asked.

"Depends on what he's doin'. If he's just watchin', then go on 'bout your business and let me know. His friends aren't far away, and there's more of them than there is of us. They need to know we're just passin' through."

No one said any more.

"Okay, then. Let's get the stock watered afore it gets dark," Skinner added.

Carl...

I felt a fear creepin' over most ever'one when we camped. I knowed it afore—in battles. I'd seen men do some stupid things if they let it take over their thinkin'. The animals sensed it too, so takin' them to the creek for water took more time, and it was dusk afore we was finishin' up the task. My team and Bossy was all that was left. Luther was the one watchin' over my shoulder.

When Bossy had her fill, I turned from the creek to lead her back into the safety of the camp. I seen Luther jump. I turned, looked back on the other side of the creek, and seen what had spooked him. It was an Indian standin' there, just watchin' the two of us. He must've been behind a clump of bushes, watchin' us the whole time, and we'd not heard or seen a thing.

I turned back to Luther just as he cocked his gun and raised its butt to his shoulder. He must've squeezed the trigger at the same time I grabbed the barrel of the gun and pointed it to the sky. The crack of the rifle got ever'one's attention.

"What the hell did ya do that fer! I had him dead in my sights," Luther was screamin' as he tried to pull the rifle free from my grip. I didn't know but what I was gonna have an arrow come into my back, but I couldn't let Luther shoot a man for just watchin'.

"He was doin' us no harm," I said.

Luther's face was red and twisted as he pulled the gun away from me.

"Water your stock by your own damned self next time." He looked back in the direction where the Indian had been standin'. There was only shadows there now.

Luther stomped off to camp. I could see where others had thought there was trouble and they was ready and waitin'. I knowed ever'one would have a long night ahead of them.

42

Rebecca's diary...

April 21, 1868—Yesterday there was conflict between Carl Taylor and Luther Rangel and because of that, Clara Beth and Minnie did not walk with Hannah and me today. Everyone is anxious because of the threat of Indians. I overheard Mr. Skinner tell Carl that the scout is still following us. I can think of little else.

April 22, 1868—I saw the Indian today. He was in the distance sitting astride a spotted pony. I was so frightened my feet would not carry me and I stood paralyzed like a statue. The whole train stopped while we all watched as Mr. Skinner rode out to where the Indian was. It appeared they were talking with each other, even though Carl has told Nathan that most of them do not speak our language. I thought I might faint when Mr. Skinner turned his horse back to the train and the Indian raised his rifle high in the air. Then Mr. Skinner turned back to him and raised his rifle too. It seemed to be some kind of salutation. The Indian turned and rode off, and tonight Mr. Skinner explained that we are out of their territory and the scout would no longer be following us.

Nathan...

I breathed easier when I saw that Indian scout ride away in the opposite direction of our travels. Skinner said he'd been following us for three days. With the exception of Luther saying he'd sighted him down by the creek, no one else except Skinner even knew he was there. We'd all heard the gunshot that day, and then saw

Carl and Luther wrestling over Luther's gun. Carl said nothing to me about the incident. Luther told everyone the Indian was there, and he would've *got him,* if it hadn't been for Carl. Maybe he did see the Indian scout, but I figured at the time that Luther had just seen shadows.

Whatever had happened that day caused a tension between the Taylor wagon and the Rangel wagon, and Carl and Luther weren't the only ones that suffered from it. The girls smiled and talked to Becca, but they walked close to their own wagon. Becca said Minnie didn't lead Bossy anymore and Clara Beth didn't milk her. But she also told me that she saw Hannah sneak Clara Beth some milk for her biscuits one night in camp.

"I miss walking with the chatter of Clara Beth to keep us company," Becca said.

Then the very next day Luther started riding his saddle horse again, and Eunice went back to driving the team. He always rode ahead of the wagons when he rode that horse, and we all knew it was so he didn't have to eat dust kicked up by everyone else. I don't think any of us in the last three wagons minded that Luther wasn't close by, and I suspect that included his wife and children. The girls started walking with both Becca and Hannah again. It was sweet to hear their laughter ever so once in awhile.

43

Hannah...

My Carl didn't say much about his ruckus with Luther, but it was plain to see that Luther held a grudge when he wouldn't even let his girls get milk from Bossy anymore. They stayed close to their wagon when their daddy drove and we didn't hear their usual laughter.

Rebecca fell back in line and walked with me. I found she had a great kindness for animals for she thought it cruel that Bossy had to be tied to the wagon. She took over leadin' the cow as we walked, just like Minnie had. Since Clara Beth wasn't fillin' the air with talk, Rebecca hummed a tune to Bossy as we walked. I'd never heard that tune afore, but it was a happy little sound and it filled up some of the quietness of the day. I never been much for talkin' just to hear myself. Guess it was the way my Sarah and I was raised.

"Seems like once a body says somethin', there's no need to keep repeatin' it," my daddy had said—more than one time.

We laughed ever' time he said it, but his words had stuck with us. Since we was both born on the same day, our thoughts had always seemed to run the same too, and we didn't see a need to say them in words. When we grew older, I knowed in my heart how she felt about Jacob and she knew my feelin's for my Carl. When we married the brothers we both lived with the Taylor family, and helped out as much as we could when our men both left for the war.

Then Sarah got the letter 'bout her Jacob and I felt her pain like it was happenin' to me. Shortly after the news come that both Jacob and his brother Robert died at the

Battle of Shiloh, she moved back to our daddy and mama's house. The Taylor family was grievin' for their sons and brothers, but Carl's sisters, Cora and Elizabeth, kept it all bearable. They was soon back to bein' full of chatter and cheerfulness—just like Clara Beth.

Luther didn't much like havin' to drive the team, and as soon as the threat of an Indian raid left, he rode out on his saddle horse the next day. It helped lift my spirits, 'cause Clara Beth and Minnie fell back to walkin' with me and Rebecca.

At first they acted as shy as the first day I met them, but Clara Beth couldn't help herself—she was prattlin' away in no time. It took my mind off what was past and put it back on lookin' forward.

Carl...

Skinner figured out what happened betwixt me and Luther afore he asked me about it.

"That fool jackass could a' got us all killed," he said. "I'm much obliged I got you to keep an eye on him fer me."

It was a chore I didn't like, and the sooner I didn't have to do it anymore the better it'd be for me. Fellers like Luther Rangel was one of the reasons I dreamed of a secluded place for my homestead.

It was odd to my thinkin' that this same trail that I traveled three years ago looked so different goin' west instead of east. It was only when we camped at night that it settled on me and felt a bit familiar. I seen where more settlers had moved onto the lands where there'd only been tall grasses afore. I was already tired of bein' on the road and didn't have no envy for those goin' further. It made me anxious to get to the place I'd found afore when I was in Kansas, so I could stake my own claim and make a place for me and my Hannah.

~ 44 ~

Rebecca's diary...

April 26, 1868— Sundays are the hardest day of the week for me, as we only hear Samuel's prayer and sing a few hymns before we start our travels. How I long to touch my fingers to the keyboard of a piano. I fear I may never see another piano, although Nathan has promised I will have one again someday. So today I started humming the happy song I composed for my mother. The Rangel girls are walking with Hannah and me again and Minnie started humming with me. Clara Beth said the song needs words and we all laughed. I wonder if Clara Beth could survive if she wasn't capable of putting words in her days. The girls make the days go so much easier. Mr. Skinner said we shall reach the town of Salina tomorrow and will have the opportunity to pick up needed supplies. Then he said we shall camp for most of the day and it will give us a good rest. I cannot understand his reluctance to rest on the Sabbath instead.

April 28, 1868—Yesterday was a good day of rest for the animals once we got across the river and made camp. Nathan went with most of the men into town to purchase supplies. I had him post a long letter for Mother and Father while he was there. My letter explained that we should soon be at our final destination and I shall then have an address for them to send their correspondence. I had the opportunity to visit with more of the women on the train and found out that most of the families are traveling much farther west than our travels will take us. We washed clothes and took advantage of having a cooking campfire most of the day. Every one of us cooked up a big pot of beans that should last us for several days and make meals easier as we travel. Then Hannah said she was going to make a pot of stewed apples. She said if I threw in half the apples we could divide them and have them for several days too. Nathan said they were the best he's ever had. I burned the griddle cakes I tried to make this morning so I served some of the left-over apples with them and they were not so hard to get down. Nathan is very understanding with my learning so many unfamiliar tasks. He said within a week we should be close to the place where Carl wants to homestead. I am of the mind that he wants to settle near there too.

April 29, 1868—We passed two abandon dugouts today. Hannah said people build them because there are not enough trees to build cabins. I cannot imagine living in one. There were five freshly dug graves near one of the dugouts. A half-starved dog was sitting beside the graves. As we passed by he started to follow the Taylor wagon. Luther Rangel said he should be put out of his misery, but he didn't want to waste a bullet. Hannah fed the poor creature tonight.

Nathan...

Longer hours between sunrise and sunset gave us the opportunity to make good miles. The land was taking on the looks that I heard Carl talk about and I knew it wouldn't be long before I'd need to make up my mind if we were going to follow him to the place he was headed. The day after we left the town called Salina, I decided it was time to talk to Becca.

I had some trouble swallowing the idea that there'd be no trees where I thought we'd settle. We'd finished supper and were getting ready to bed down for the night when I told Becca we might have to live in a dugout for a time. I didn't like the look she gave me. At first she didn't say anything. Then she asked me the question I couldn't answer.

"How long?"

She waited, while I was thinking of the best way to tell her I didn't know.

She finally said, "I thought we'd have a cabin."

"Sounds like there won't be enough trees for that," I said. "But I promise to build you a real house as soon as it's possible."

Pure disappointment showed on her face, but she said nothing more.

~ 45 ~

Hannah...

We was not far gone from Salina when we passed a couple of abandon dugouts. It appeared that a sickness might have struck one of the families as there was five graves near them. I wondered at whose task it might have been to dig the graves.

"Is that a dog?" I heard Rebecca ask, more to herself than to any of us 'round her.

The most pitiful dog I ever laid my eyes on was layin' by the graves. The critter looked up at us as we passed and then he got up real slow and started followin' our wagon. He kept lookin' back ever' so often, like maybe he shouldn't be leavin'. He must've stayed loyal for some time 'cause his ribs showed plain through his burr lined coat.

When we stopped for the night the poor thing flopped his tired body down and looked at me through matted eyes. It was then that Luther started walkin' to him with his rifle in hand. My Carl was eatin' his supper, but he stopped. He stood up and gave Luther a look that was a clear message. Luther gave back a look of pure hatefulness.

"Hell, he ain't worth wastin' a bullet on," he muttered, afore he went back to his wagon.

My Carl looked down at his supper, took one more bite of his beans, and asked, "Do we have somethin' we can feed that critter out of?"

I got him a pan and he scraped the rest of his beans and cornbread in it. I took another bite of my supper and did the same with what was left. My Carl's smile filled my heart. And when I set the food close to the dog, he gave me a pathetic wag of his tail afore he lifted his tired head to eat.

Carl...

I suppose I've always had a soft spot in me for any of God's creatures, although sometimes I found it hard to find it for humans. I'd seen men like Luther in the war. It seemed to me they didn't mind killin' so much and I wondered what had made them that way. I'd always tried to stay my distance from them, but Skinner wanted me to keep an eye on this one, so I did my best. I knowed I wouldn't miss him none when it was time to part our ways with the train.

Ever since we'd crossed over the Missouri, it worried me some that maybe the spot I'd picked for our claim would already be taken. But when my Hannah gave that old dog the rest of our supper I had no fears that wherever we landed, as long as we was together, we'd both make out fine.

I noted on our last couple days of travel, the greens of spring had started pushin' away the dull of winter. It made me even more anxious to get to where we was goin' to plant ourselves. My daddy had told me that when I was away, it was my Hannah who raised the best garden he'd ever seen in the state of Illinois. I was hopin' someday to brag that she could raise the best garden I ever seen in Kansas.

Rebecca's diary…

April 30, 1868—Nathan has said we will leave the train with Carl and Hannah and seek a homestead near them. I have grown very fond of Hannah and I know I will learn a lot more from her. It means our journey will soon be over. How I will miss Clara Beth and Minnie. The stray dog has not left Hannah's side. She has named him Corky.

May 1, 1868—Everyone on the train, with the exception of Luther, has bid us a farewell tonight. When Mr. Skinner played his harmonica after supper, Minnie went over to where he was sitting and hummed the happy song I taught her. He picked up the melody right away and played it as well as I had on the piano. I cannot imagine how much I shall miss the Rangel girls. I long to see my mother.

Nathan…

We had camped a few miles from Ellsworth the last night we were with the wagon train. The doubts about my dreams of having my own land always seemed to be with me at night. But by morning I was looking forward to seeing the spot of Kansas that Carl kept talking about. He said the way would be harder traveling after we left the main trail, but it would only be a couple of days until we'd get to the place.

Both Becca and Hannah stood watching as the wagon train left us that morning. The Rangel girls turned to look back over their shoulders once or twice. Then they raised their arms in a final farewell and looked back no more.

It hurt me greatly to see tears rolling down Becca's cheeks, but I was anxious to get started and I knew Carl was too. He waited until Hannah looked at him and nodded, before he slapped the reins on his team. Becca started walking with Hannah. She didn't look my way.

Carl...

When we parted ways with the wagon train, I waited for my Hannah so she could see the Rangel girls for the last time. Luther usually rode out afore the train started movin' for the day, but that day the mean old cuss stuck around his own wagon so the girls would be afraid to say their good-byes.

Seein' Hannah standin' there lookin' at them leave, reminded me of seein' her twin sister when we left Illinois. Sarah and Hannah was the spittin' image of each other. But Hannah was always easygoin' and uncomplainin' and Sarah was more quick-tempered.

"She's easy to rile, but she can't stay mad at me," Jacob told me, afore any of us married. "Your Hannah may be tolerant, but she holds a grudge forever."

I had to admit that if my Hannah went sour on me, I had to walk careful for a long time and it took her quite a spell afore I'd be forgiven.

She was a good woman though, and I probably didn't deserve her. She left ever'thing she knew in life to follow me and my dream. The closer we got, the more I was thinkin' how much I wanted her to love the spot I'd picked for us too.

Hannah...

My Carl told me the goin' would be harder, and it was, but only 'cause the grasses hadn't been trod down afore. Bossy kept wantin' to stop and graze and ever so often a jackrabbit would pop up and scare Rebecca. Corky would lift his ears and raise his head, then put his nose back close to the ground and keep on walkin'. I wondered if he'd ever get enough meat on his bones that he'd have the strength to chase a rabbit again.

I don't think Rebecca smiled once that mornin' and I sure don't think she was enjoyin' any of what she was seein'. When the day's end drew near and we camped, she finally talked a little, whilst we was fixin' our supper. Rebecca had just put a skillet of cornbread on the fire and I was fryin' up the rabbit Carl shot earlier.

As her eyes searched the darkness that surrounded the campfire, she whispered, "Hannah, does it worry you that we're alone? I mean just the two wagons?"

Just then the yip of a coyote made Rebecca jump and the hem of her dress touched the edge of the campfire.

I smelled singed wool and pushed her away from the fire afore she even knowed she was in danger. When I pushed her she fell backward and I stood above her and stomped the edge of her dress 'til I was sure it had stopped burnin'.

Rebecca let out a scream, and Nathan come runnin'. When he put his arms 'round her, she calmed down right away, but it near broke my heart when she took a deep breath and said, "I can't do anything right."

Later that night after we all bedded down inside our own wagons, my Carl asked me if Rebecca had burned herself at all.

"No, she was mostly just scared," I answered.

Then Carl said somethin' that gave me the goose bumps, for it wasn't just the words he used but the way he said them. "Fear will be that girl's undoin'."

47

Rebecca's diary…

May 2, 1868—There is no road to follow now. As far as one can see, there are only prairie grasses waving in the winds. Our day was of endless walking, and without the chatter of Clara Beth to break the monotony. Carl said our travels will soon end.

May 3, 1868—I cannot bring myself to share in the excitement that the others seem to have, now that we are almost at our destination. We came upon the homestead of Adam and Edna Walden. They have one small child and an infant. They invited us into their soddy, which Edna has tried to make comfortable, but there were bugs scurrying across the floor as we visited. She seemed desperate to hear any news we might share with her. I cannot help but hear my mother's warnings of what this land would be. Adam Walden said he knew of the place Carl is trying to find and they will be our closest neighbors. He told us that someone started a homestead not far from there but they are gone now. Edna asked if we are people of the Lord and should we be traveling on the Sabbath. She told us how much she misses attending church services and spoke very poorly of Ellsworth. She thinks it is an omen that Ellsworth suffered from a devastating flood last year. I felt pity for the woman's loneliness, and her words frightened me.

Nathan…

We'd been traveling on flat land since we'd left the camp at Ellsworth and I'd seen no hills in the distance, only the flat land of prairie grasses. When Carl told me we didn't have far to go, I began to doubt him. He'd told me there were soft hills on the land he'd seen and I couldn't fathom where they were. Then when we found the homestead of Adam Walden, Carl told him where we were headed, and the two of them started talking about the hills we'd have to travel.

"You'll need to take precautions on that first hill," Adam Walden said.

"I've been thinkin' on it," Carl replied. "I think Bill and Barney will do fine." He looked over at me. "We'll not let the women ride with us, and we'll go one at a time," he said. "We traveled over taller hills when we was with the train."

I nodded, though I surely didn't comprehend what he was saying.

As we left the Walden homestead, I finally understood. We'd not gone a quarter mile when Carl stopped his wagon. I did the same. I saw hills covered in a haze in the far distance, and before us lay a small valley with a cluster of rolling hills. It was a sight to see that far. I realized we were on the hill that Adam and Carl had talked of.

Carl was smiling as he got down from his wagon. When the women walked up to where we were standing, Carl put one arm around Hannah and pointed to an area several miles away.

"There, right after that bend in the creek down there, that's the place."

A look of pleasure and trust passed between Carl and Hannah.

It was an exciting feeling, standing on that ridge looking down upon land I might someday own a part of.

But when I looked at Becca I knew she didn't feel the joy the rest of us felt. She had no smile. She didn't look at me, but turned and walked back to the wagon where she sat down in its shade.

48

Rebecca's diary…

May 4, 1868—We are at the place where Carl and Hannah will homestead. How I wish I could feel the joy the others seem to have. Nathan will look for a place for our homestead tomorrow. I have faith that he will live up to his promise to build us a proper house as soon as he can, but I have a great sense of dread that it will take longer than he imagines. Sometimes the sadness I feel of not seeing our families until then is overwhelming and I think I should insist that we go back to Ellsworth and take a train home to civilization. I shall try to keep my thoughts contained in the words I write and not burden Nathan with them.

Nathan…

Once I stood at the top of the hill that Carl and Adam had talked about and looked down over that little valley, I was itching to find the place Carl had pointed to. But we talked it through, and we both thought maybe it was best that we camp for the day and get an early start in the morning.

I was so anxious that I woke up way before the sun did. And when the sun did finally rise, it cast a purple hue on those distant hills that I won't soon forget. Becca was still half asleep, as she was trying to get our breakfast cooked up. When I tried to point out the beauty of it all, she gave me a puzzled look and I knew she didn't see the same thing I saw.

Carl...

We took our time comin' down from the hills and had no problems with it. Once we was on level land, the women rode the rest of the way with us. My Hannah seemed happier than I'd seen her since we left Illinois.

"Any regrets?" I asked her.

She shook her head and smiled. "You look as happy as that twelve year old boy I first met when he was stealin' my daddy's apples," she said.

I laughed out loud. "I'm feelin' good, Hannah, we're almost there."

It took near half the day afore we finally got to the place I wanted to settle on, and we didn't talk much more 'til I stopped the wagon. I didn't tell her we was there—she just knowed. We set a bit and took it all in.

It's hard to put words to the way I felt when I seen the place again. I'd only been there one time afore, yet to have my Hannah by my side made me feel like I was really home.

Hannah...

Carl helped me down off the wagon. I followed him over to a place not far from the creek.

"How's this place right here?" he said.

"For the soddy?" I asked.

He nodded.

When I smiled and nodded back, Carl threw his hat in the air and did a little jig, grabbin' me and twirlin' me 'round in a circle. Corky had plopped his tired body down already, but he caught on to the excitement and set up and barked a couple of times. Oh, it felt so good to be part of it all.

We stopped dancin' and looked over at Nathan and Rebecca. They was settin' in their wagon, takin' it in. They both had smiles on their faces. Nathan's smile was almost as wide as Carl's, but Rebecca's smile didn't look true.

~ 49 ~

Rebecca's diary…

May 5—Carl and Nathan found the survey markers today, so they will leave to file claims tomorrow. Hannah doesn't seem to mind that she and I will be on our own. They also found a dugout that appears to have been abandoned. Nathan thinks it is the place Adam Walden spoke of. If there has been no claim filed on it, Nathan said it will be our home. I have written to Mother and given the letter to Nathan to post. I did not tell her we will be living in a hole in the ground. Hannah seems to think we are very fortunate, as she and Carl will have to live in their wagon until they can build a dugout or soddy. I cannot find the words to write of my displeasure that the men will be leaving Hannah and me to fend for ourselves.

Nathan…

Carl had no trouble finding the section corner stones for the place he wanted. Then we scouted around a little and saw where there'd been some sod busted on the land I liked. That was when we found an abandoned dugout. We figured it was the place Adam Walden had told us about a couple of days ago. He'd told us the two fellows that had lived there, just up and left one day.

"The missus didn't like Henry or Fritz too much," he'd said. I remember he lowered his voice so the women wouldn't hear what he was saying, "I got to admit, I myself thought they was nothin' but a couple of hooligans."

"Think they'll be back?" Carl asked.

"Nah!   I'm purty sure they was runnin' from somethin' and the somethin' found 'em." he'd said. "They left mighty quick."

Carl nodded when Adam had gone on to say he doubted they'd even filed a claim. I was hoping they hadn't. I knew Becca wouldn't be fond of the dugout, but we could make do with it until I could build her a proper house. And since the land was right next to Carl's homestead, it didn't take us long to find the quarter corner markers.

Carl and I decided the first thing we should do is file our claims. It would mean we'd be gone for a couple of days. I knew Becca wouldn't be too fond of that idea either.

It worried me some, because the Walden's place was the only homestead we'd seen since we'd left our camp at Ellsworth.

"You think the women will be safe with us leaving so soon?" I asked.

"Hannah's a real good shot with the rifle, if she hasta be," Carl said with pride.

I knew it needed to be done, but it was when I told Becca that I'd be gone for awhile that her eyes narrowed and her face went from soft to hard. I'd never seen her resemblance to her mother before that day, but I saw it then.

"You're just going to leave me?" she said between gritted teeth.

"No," I assured her. "I'm not leaving you. I've just got to attend to the business of filing a claim."

She turned her back on me then and I felt bad because I knew this part of our life was hard on her.

"Hannah doesn't seem to mind." I added.

I should have known better than to say that. It was a long night for both of us. I knew Becca didn't sleep well and by the morning I felt like she probably wasn't going to miss me so much after all.

50

Rebecca's diary...

May 6, 1868—Nathan and Carl have gone to file our claims. They unloaded our wagon before they left this morning and Hannah is helping me set up living quarters in the dugout. As I unpacked my trunk I had a most wonderful surprise. Mother had carefully wrapped two of her cups and saucers from her finest china in pretty tea towels and hidden them in my trunk. I burst into a flood of tears when I found them. She also put in a small tin of her finest tea and included a note that I shall treasure. Hannah said she'd never been one for tea, but we had tea today. I forgot I was on the prairie for a little while and we had a most delightful time.

Hannah...

My Carl and Nathan took the Carter's wagon when they left me and Rebecca. I knowed she was havin' a hard time with us bein' alone, but it wasn't practical for us to all leave. I knowed if Nathan couldn't get their claim for that piece of land, all our work of trying to make the dugout homey was for naught.

We was busy in the dugout, tryin' to find the right places to make things handy. I had my back to Rebecca when she gave a gasp and started sobbin'. She opened her trunk and found two teacups and saucers planted deep inside. When I went over to her, she was holdin' a note from her mama. She was cryin' so hard she couldn't read it, so she handed it to me.

"Hannah, read this for me," she begged between sobs.

With my poor eyesight we had to go outside in the daylight. The note was on the fanciest stationary I ever seen, and the handwritin' was a beautiful script. I read…

Dearest Daughter Rebecca,
You know I don't want you to leave, but Nathan seems determined to take you away. Maybe you will remember me when you have your afternoon tea.
Your loving mother

Rebecca was silent whilst I read the note to her, and when I finished she was quite hysterical. She paced back and forth in front of the doorway to the dugout, cryin' and mutterin' things I couldn't understand. I finally caught hold of her and held her like I did my Carl's sister, Elizabeth, when she found out her brothers, Jacob and Robert was killed in the war. I held her until she calmed herself. Then I let her talk whilst I listened.

"Why did we come to this barren land, Hannah?" she asked me.

I knowed why I had. It was for my Carl. I was about to say so when she went on.

"Mother warned me that the land would be uncivilized. She told me Nathan was being selfish to take me away from her. She wanted me to convince him to stay in Eaton." She stopped and caught her breath with a few shudders 'cause she'd cried so hard.

"I could have, you know. Nathan would have done anything for me. I didn't think it would be this hard. Hannah, there's nothing here!" she looked 'round the dugout. "There's no one around. I mean there are no people." Her eyes was wide, like she was searchin' for somethin'.

"The wagon train was hard, but there's no one out here. Nathan expects me to live in a hole in the ground."

She had to catch her breath again, 'cause the words was comin' out of her so fast. Then she stopped and looked at the note. She brought it to her bosom and held it close to her heart. She closed her eyes and started to speak real soft—almost in a whisper.

"The teacups are from my mother's finest set of china." She took a long breath of fresh air, gave another shudder, and opened her eyes.

"Hannah, let's have a cup of tea now. Will you have tea with me?" She smiled with the idea. Her mood had changed so quick that it scared me.

I nodded and said, "I'll get us a fire started. Maybe we can bake us some biscuits too."

We had our cup of tea. Of course we didn't have a fancy teapot or a tray to serve it on, but it didn't seem to matter. Rebecca made me feel like an elegant lady when she handed me that tea cup and saucer. We laughed and talked. She told me 'bout her days growin' up in Eaton, and I talked 'bout Sarah. We was havin' such a good time. Then it was like a cloud passed over her again and I didn't know what to expect next.

"How could you leave your twin sister, if you were that close to her heart?" she asked.

I thought on my answer for a bit afore I said, "My Carl."

All happiness left her eyes.

"Me and Carl was married afore the war. Sarah's Jacob never come back," I explained. "When Carl come back, he wasn't whole. It was when he told me 'bout this place he found, he was my Carl again. Sarah understood that."

Rebecca didn't say anything after that and I don't know if she got my meanin' of what I was tryin' to tell her. I got up from the trunk we was settin' on and gathered her teacups. Tea time was over. We had chores to do.

51

Rebecca's diary

May 7, 1868—I am trying not to despair. Hannah felt that the dugout would be a much safer place for us to spend the night than in her wagon. She told me I was lucky that I had a home already, for it needs little work done to it. I don't want to seem ungrateful, but I am now living with the worms. Who knows what other kind of varmints are here. The wind howled most of the night, keeping me awake, and when it finally died down, coyotes started yipping. Corky slept just outside the dugout and growled at them several times. In spite of my fatigue, I was so frightened that I could not sleep until nearly dawn.

Hannah...

I knowed it would take our men-folk more than a few days afore they'd get back to us. It was hard for me and Rebecca. Carl told me they'd hafta go all the way back to Junction City to file at the land office there

They was gonna go to Ellsworth, take the train to Junction City, file their claims, and then take a train back to Ellsworth. I knowed they'd be gone a while, but I don't think Nathan told Rebecca how long it might be.

"Hannah, don't you worry that something dreadful might happen to them? Or to us?" she asked me several times each day.

I tried to keep Rebecca's mind off us bein' alone, by keepin' busy. We managed to get her dugout nice and cozy that first day, and that's where we spent our nights. Then I hitched the wagon up and drove it back to my own place in the mornin' so I could work there. It was the middle of May already and I was itchin' to get my garden in the ground and my daddy's tree saplin's planted. The ground took some gettin' ready first though.

My Carl had hauled a sod cutter all the way from Illinois. It was a heavy thing for me to manage by myself, but I finally got it untied from the side of the wagon. Rebecca mostly stood and watched me, all the whilst askin' more questions than a child.

"What are you going to do with that thing?"

I was huffin' from gettin' it unlashed from the wagon when the thought come to me, that Rebecca was learnin' to be a lady, when I learned how to farm with my daddy-in-law. As much as I liked Nathan, I wondered what he was thinkin' to bring this delicate flower to the middle of a Kansas prairie.

"Rebecca, I'm gonna bust some sod," I said. "You can help me, or you can watch, but this is what needs to be done afore I can plant anything." I was determined I'd figure out how to do it whilst the men was gone.

She was lookin' at me like I'd gone daft.

"But Hannah, that's a man's chore."

It was clear she didn't think I was up to the task. So I explained how Sarah and I worked beside my Carl's daddy when all his boys 'cept Levi went off to war.

"Carl's family had a farm to run and we women did a fair job of helpin' him do it. His sisters was 'bout your size, and they learned too."

I seen her bite her lower lip as she turned her head away from me.

I walked to the place where Carl said we'd build our soddy. I tried to vision what a nice little orchard would look like down close by the creek. That's when Rebecca walked over aside me.

"Hannah, I really do want to learn," her voice was meek. "It's just so overwhelming." She looked back to where her dugout was. "I'm not sure I can do it, but I'll try."

"I'll help you when I can," I promised.

We worked hard all that day. I harnessed up Barney to pull the sod cutter. It took us some time and more than one try afore we made any progress. I couldn't figure out how to guide Barney whilst holdin' onto the cutter too.

"Why don't I try leading him for you?" Rebecca suggested.

Together we made it work. When we got two rows of strips cut, I took a spade and cut the strips into blocks. They was only half the size of the ones the Walden soddy was made of, but if they was any bigger, we wouldn't have been able to move them out of the way.

"If my Carl can't use them for our soddy, maybe I can make a chair," I said.

Rebecca frowned.

I started laughin' then. She did too when she figured out I was teasin' her. It felt good to laugh and to see her laugh. I knowed we only did a bit of what the men would have done if they'd been doin' the job, but we was proud of our day's work.

We decided we had enough sod bustin' for a while, so I hitched up Bill and Barney to take the wagon back to the dugout with us. The seat on that wagon felt mighty hard as we bounced along the path we had started to make betwixt the two places. I was bone tired, but Rebecca wanted to talk.

"Hannah," she looked ahead to where the dugout was, "why did we set up everything in the dugout already? What if it already has a claim filed on it?"

I didn't have an answer for her afore she finished her thought.

"Maybe Nathan would give it all up and move back home," she said. Then she started hummin' a tune.

She stopped, long enough to add, "I finally know what to title my song."

"What might that be?" I asked

"*Hope*." She started hummin' again, with a smile this time.

52

Rebecca's diary...

May 8, 1868—I was so fatigued last night that I fell instantly asleep, but was awakened before the first light of morning by a terrible nightmare. Nathan and Carl were coming home to us when they were attacked by a band of savages. I could see them coming across the prairie, and I tried to warn them. A multitude of Indians rode toward them and surrounded them. I could not see Nathan anymore, only the Indians. I woke up screaming. Hannah rushed to my side. I was nearly hysterical with fear because the dream seemed so real. I have been angry with Nathan for leaving me here. Now all I pray for is his safe return.

Hannah...

Rebecca scared me near to death when she started screamin' in her sleep. I didn't know whether to grab her or the rifle first. She had herself worked in such a state that she was shakin' with fear and wet with sweat.

"Oh, Hannah, I'm so sorry," she said over and over. "I want no harm to come to them. I just want Nathan to be safe."

I finally grabbed her arms and shook her hard.

"Rebecca, get a hold of yourself," I said. "It was a dream."

It was too dark to see Corky, but we both heard him give a deep growl from the doorway.

Rebecca grabbed hold of me so tight, I could hardly move.

"I'm gonna get the gun," I whispered in her ear. "You have to stay calm."

She let out a really big breath of air and let go of me. I felt around in the dark for the rifle. As soon as my hand found it, I grabbed it. Holdin' it in one hand, I hugged her with my other arm. She clung onto me again, and we set huddled like that 'til the sun showed up to start the day.

When we stepped out of the dugout Rebecca's eyes was wide with fear and searchin' across the prairie grasses. It was like she had to convince herself that her husband wasn't layin' out half dead on the prairie.

"They're gonna be fine," I told her. "They'll be back in a week or so to…"

"What do you mean, a week or so?" she said afore I'd finished my words.

"Didn't Nathan tell you they had to go all the way to Junction City?"

She frowned and shook her head slowly.

"With the wagon?" she asked.

"They was goin' on the train—from Ellsworth."

She said nothin' more right then. Finally I asked her if she'd be okay whilst I went to milk Bossy. She nodded. I thought somethin' else might be on her mind, but I left her to get a mornin' fire goin'. I went to get started on the chores.

When I come back from tendin' the horses and milkin' Bossy, Rebecca had fixed us a *tea time* breakfast. The biscuits was plain from the day afore, but she had her fancy little cups out. She was hummin' her song of *Hope* as she motioned for me to set myself down. She served me a cup of tea like we was back in her parlor at her mama's house.

"I feel a little foolish," she said. "I was upset with Nathan when he told me he was leaving right away to file a claim. I really didn't listen to much of what he had to say about it." She stopped talkin' long enough to look at the colors dancin' across the mornin' sky. She looked at me, smiled like she was the happiest woman in the land, and said, "It's going to be a lovely day to plant your saplings, Hannah."

~ 53 ~

Rebecca's diary...

May 9, 1868—Hannah and I are doing the work of farm hands. It helps me to keep my mind off the reality that we are truly alone in the middle of nowhere. I hate coming back to this dreary lodging that is supposed to be my home now, but I am so tired that I can at least sleep for part of the night. This morning I awakened early again with a dread in my heart, but I managed to stay quiet so that I didn't wake Hannah. I am praying that this land already has a claim on it. When Nathan gets back and I tell him how unhappy I am here, maybe he will see that it's not what he thought it would be. Surely he will agree that we don't belong in this place that God has seemed to have forgotten.

Hannah...

I was ready for my Carl to come back and take over on the sod bustin' part of my garden, but I was mighty proud of what me and Rebecca had done. I could see that workin' the ground into cropland was gonna be a lot different than doin' the farmin' I'd done on my daddy-in-law's land. But the earth looked rich under all those grass roots, and I was ready to get some seeds in the ground.

I'd planted my daddy's saplin's already. They survived our travels and was already startin' to bud when I put them in the Kansas soil. My hopes was high that they'd bear us some fine fruit one day.

Rebecca was really good at helpin' me with the work I was doin', and I knowed she was learnin' a lot from me. I was learnin' a lot from her too.

Ever' night afore we'd lay our tired bodies down, she would brush her hair.

"One hundred," I'd hear her say. Then she'd finally put her head down for the night. She was proud of her hair and told me she brushed it ever' night since she was old enough to hold a brush. "It's one of the things Nathan says he likes to watch me do," she said.

And ever' mornin' she'd fix us a 'tea breakfast' whilst I tended to the animals.

It made me feel like a real lady to drink out of her fancy cups and saucers, and it seemed to give her much pleasure. Then we'd hitch the wagon up and go back to my place and work on that little patch of ground I was diggin' on.

"I do have a distaste for this chore of farming," she said many times in the day whilst we worked in the dirt. The only time she didn't complain was when Corky come to her, or she was leadin' one of the animals. Then she seemed to forget where she was and she'd put a smile on her face or start hummin' her *Hope* song.

We must've made a strange lookin' couple as we worked together—she bein' careful to wear a bonnet whenever she went into the sun—me carin' only 'bout the chores at hand. I knowed how hard the work was gonna be to make Carl's dream come true. I thought it to be true, that Rebecca didn't see it the same as me.

Rebecca's diary…

May 10, 1868—We were caught in a horrible storm last night. It hailed and the wind blew so hard that part of the cover on Hannah's wagon was ripped. With the wind came buckets of rain. Some of the ceiling of the dugout fell on us and the floor was slick with mud, but we were grateful we had the dugout for shelter. Hannah and I were going to have a day of rest for the Sabbath today. Instead, we spent the day trying to dry things out. The creek is still raging. Surely Nathan will not expect me to live under these conditions. I pray he will have changed his mind about living on this land when he comes back.

Hannah…

It was early in the evenin' when me and Rebecca finished stakin' the animals a little ways from the wagon. She looked up at the sky.

"Oh Hannah, look at the pretty green. It's the same shade of a dress my mother made for me."

With no trees 'round, sky was easy to see on the prairie. When I turned to look, a flash of lightenin' come from out of nowhere. I could feel the hairs on my head stand up. That purty green Rebecca seen, turned dark and ugly. I never seen a sky change so fast afore. Bill, Barney, and Bossy, was all stompin' on the ground and tryin' to pull up their picket lines.

"Whoa, whoa," I was sayin' with no luck at calmin' any of them. The breeze had been gentle just a minute afore, and in a southern direction. Then the winds shifted. They was swirlin' so that I didn't know where they was comin' from next. And the air turned cold.

When another flash of lightenin' lit up the sky and thunder cracked, poor Barney pulled free from his stake. His eyes was wide, as he started runnin' sideways, draggin' his tether aside him. I started to go after him when I seen the first piece of hail bounce off the grass in front of me. I turned back to Rebecca.

"Head for the dugout," I screamed.

We both started runnin'. Corky had already taken cover under the wagon. The hailstones was only as big as peas, but they stung like bees when they hit us.

When we got to the dugout we both stood by the open door and watched as my wagon rocked back and forth in the wind. It finally stopped hailin', but the wind caught a corner of the canvas on the wagon's cover. It was flappin' and tryin' to pull loose from the bow.

Whilst we was standin' there wonderin' if my wagon was gonna sail off, a chunk of the dugout's ceilin' fell at our feet. Mud come rainin' down on me and Rebecca. We moved our mattress over to the far corner and hoped that part of the ceilin' would stay put.

I ain't never seen it rain like that afore. I suppose it didn't go on for all that long, but it sure seemed like it did. When it let up just a bit, I thought the worst was over. Then I seen another worry, as our peaceful little creek was comin' up fast to meet my wagon.

"Hannah, what are we going to do?" Rebecca gasped. Her eyes was as big as Barney's was, when he pulled up his stake and ran.

"We're gonna be fine," I said, not knowin' it to be true. I grabbed her hand and held on tight, "We're gonna be fine," I repeated.

The rain stopped as fast as it had started, and a streak of golden sunshine busted out from behind the clouds. Rebecca sighed, like she'd been holdin' her breath. I looked at her and we both smiled. Her hair had globs of mud and grass in it. I suppose mine did too.

"Let's step outside and get ourselves cleaned up a bit," I suggested.

She nodded. But as soon as we stepped out into the fresh air, I seen our worries wasn't over yet. The rain had stopped, but the creek was still risin'.

"Must've been even more rain upstream," I said. I heard rumbles in the hills to the south of us, where there was still lightenin' flashes and a dark sky. Then I heard a welcome sound—a very loud snort from Barney. He was standin' on the other side of the creek that had gone wild. His rope was still hooked onto his halter. Me and Rebecca smiled at each other again.

"How did he ever get across?" Rebecca asked.
I couldn't answer. I didn't care as to the how, I was thankful for the fact.

"You sorry old horse, you're gonna have to stay put for a while," I yelled at him.

He answered with another snort, put his head down, and started munchin' on wet grass. Bill snorted back at him from our side of the creek, then he started munchin' on wet grass too.

The thunder rumbles was growin' softer as the storm moved on. The creek was ragin' but it didn't appear to be gettin' any closer to the wagon. Not takin' any more chances, we respected its anger and cleaned ourselves up as best we could with only the wet grasses.

There was nothin' dry to make a fire with, so we ate some cold biscuits for supper. At least our mattress was mostly dry, so we went to bed with the fadin' daylight.

Our Sunday was anything but a day of rest. Rebecca read out of her Bible as soon as we woke up.

"Would you like to sing a hymn," I asked, knowin' how important music was to her. She turned her head from side to side real slow, and her lips started to pucker up, but no tears fell.

"I suppose we'd better get busy," I said. "We've got a lot to do today."

Half the floor of the dugout was a slimy mess, and I needed to see to how much damage was done to my wagon.

"I'll get started in here, while you start on your wagon," Rebecca said.

I nodded.

I spent most of the day repairin' the canvas and layin' things out on the grasses to dry in the sun, whilst Rebecca scooped mud out of her house. The creek tamed enough that we could get water to scrub with. I walked a ways upstream and found a spot to cross, so that I could bring Barney back on our side.

Since we had no more biscuits, I used a little of our precious kerosene to get a fire started. Then I made us a proper meal of bacon and cornbread to warm our tired achin' bodies. Tired as she was, Rebecca made us a cup of tea, and insisted we drink from her china cups.

"Maybe tomorrow, we can clean ourselves up," she said as she brought the teacup to her lips. I looked down at my filthy clothes and thought it to be a fine idea.

55

Rebecca's diary…

May 11, 1868—Hannah and I had a day for ourselves. It was a beautiful day but I long to be back home in Eaton. I fight off the pain of my homesickness every day.

May 12, 1868—Nathan has returned. Although I am grateful that he is safe, I cannot share in his happiness that he now has a claim filed for this land. He is filled with plans for our future that I cannot comprehend. As disappointed as I am, I was delighted that he brought the Walden's dog, Rusty, home as a companion for me. I hope Rusty will be as well behaved as Hannah's dog, Corky is. I have promised to keep him away from the two chickens Carl brought for Hannah, as Adam Walden said he chases chickens. I am hoping instead of chickens, he keeps the varmints out of our dugout. Nathan promises a grand house someday and predicts we shall soon have more neighbors than we will be able to count. He has such high expectations for this land and thinks we are at a great advantage of being the first to settle here. I hope I will someday see the reality of his dream.

Hannah…

After tendin' to the animals and eatin' our own breakfast, me and Rebecca spent the mornin' cleanin' ourselves up. It was a day to pamper ourselves a little, and it was plain to see how much it meant to Rebecca.

"Mother used to brush my hair for me after I'd washed it," she said whilst she held the brush out for me to take.

"My Sarah and I used to do the same," I said as I took the brush from her and started brushin' her hair.

That day we talked about our families we'd left. Then we cooked up a big mess of beans and cornbread and talked about our new life.

"Hannah, I don't know if I can do this," she said to me. "I want to be around people, and there are no neighbors for miles around us. Aren't you afraid?"

I thought careful afore I gave her my answer. "It's my Carl's dream."

"Don't our dreams count?"

I didn't answer her.

By the next mornin' I was itchin' to get back to the saplin's I'd planted. I needed to see how they'd fared the storm. I was happy to see only one of them was layin' on its side and washed out of the place where I'd planted it. I picked it up and planted it again with little hope that it'd ever grow. Rebecca watched me whilst I did it.

"Hannah, do you really think they'll ever be the orchard that you envision?" she was lookin' at me like she couldn't even imagine it.

I straightened up when the tree was where I wanted it again. "My daddy started his orchard with saplin's. We didn't have a farm like Carl's family, but my daddy's orchard was his pride. I know there won't be no orchard here unless someone plants the trees for one."

Later that day, Rebecca led the horses whilst we worked together bustin' more sod. The rain made the job a lot easier. We'd cut enough strips to finish a good sized patch of ground for the start of my garden when we decided to eat our noon meal. It was when we finished our cornbread that Corky's ears perked up and his tail started waggin'. I looked to where he was lookin' and seen the Carter wagon headin' in our direction.

"They're back," I said as I stood and waved.

My Carl took off his hat and waved back at me.

When the men reached us, the wagon had hardly stopped afore my Carl jumped off and had me in his arms, twirlin' me 'round and plantin' kisses on me.

"We was worried 'bout you, with the rain, and all," he said. "We got us a claim filed though. And look at this, he said as he swept his arm in the direction of the new planted saplin's. "My Hannah's started her orchard already. Look Nathan, we'll have apples to share with our neighbors."

Nathan's eyes was dancin' with excitement. "It's going to be ours, Becca," he said as he looked to where the dugout was in the distance. He turned back and looked at Rebecca, who had half a smile on her lips. I noticed her eyes didn't hold any happiness though.

56

Carl...

I felt like a kid again when I seen that Hannah and Rebecca was safe and doin' fine. And when I seen that Hannah had broken sod for a garden and for her saplin's, I thought I would bust with pride. I was whoopin' and hollerin' so loud, I near covered up the squawkin' that was comin' from the back of Nathan's wagon.

Both me and Nathan had surprises for our women. All the travelin' we'd done gave us lots of time to plan things out for our plantin' and bustin' sod. We bought some supplies in Junction City, 'cause we found the prices not as high as they was in Ellsworth. Then we took time to stop at the Walden place on our way back to our new claims.

When we first met Adam, he told us he'd sell us a couple of his chickens to help us get started. I bought a couple for Hannah. They was raisin' such a ruckus in the back of the wagon that they wasn't much of a surprise though.

"Fresh eggs of our own?" Hannah asked, a big smile on her face.

I nodded. "Adam told me Edna will soon have some chicks to sell too, but I figured I'd let you women-folk figure that one out," I said.

"There's another surprise," Nathan said. A loud "yip" come out from inside the wagon as soon as he said it.

Nathan climbed up onto the wagon and worked under the seat, untyin' Rebecca's surprise. A furry head popped up over the front bench.

"He sure wants those chickens of yours, Carl," Nathan said as he untied the mutt he'd got from Adam.

When Rusty figured out he was free, he jumped the rest of hiself onto the wagon bench. He looked 'round and started pacin' back and forth on the seat.

"Oh, Nathan, is that the Walden's dog?" Rebecca asked. She no sooner said the words than she started runnin' to him with outstretched arms.

The dog was near waggin' his tail off, when he seen her friendly face. He took a giant leap off the wagon—right into her arms. But Rebecca didn't take time to brace herself. Both her and that dog went stem windin' across the grasses.

We all hurried to see the damage done. Rebecca was on the ground with the dog on top of her. He was lickin' her face out of gratitude for the soft landin'. Her eyes was shinin' with laughter and she was gigglin' like a schoolgirl whilst the two of them tried to untangle themselves from each other.

Rusty finally got free, but thought it was all a game. He kept jumpin' back and forth against Rebecca.

"Adam told me the pup hadn't learned all his manners yet," Nathan said. He grabbed Rusty and held him whilst Rebecca got on her feet. Then he let go of him so he and Corky could get acquainted again. They was soon headed off together in the direction of the creek.

Nathan...

When we stopped at the Walden place, and Carl bought a couple of chickens from Adam, I happened to spy an unhappy dog tied up under their buckboard. Adam's little girl, Lizzie, was sitting beside him, stroking his fur, and looking sadder than a little girl should ever look.

"I'll sell you a couple of chickens real cheap. Might help to get you folks started," Adam told Carl. "Don't know as you'll get any eggs from 'em though. Damned dog was chasin' Edna's chickens earlier." Adam spit a stream of tobacco juice across the yard.

"Chickens would make my Hannah happy," Carl said.

"Cain't guarantee any eggs, like I said, the dog…" he nodded to where Lizzie and the animal were sitting. Lizzie's lower lip puckered out. "You wouldn't happen to want a good fer nothin' dog would ya?"

That's when Carl looked at me, as I looked the situation over.

"I wouldn't want to take your child's pet," I said.

"My Edna's raisin' chickens. We cain't have a chicken chaser around," he looked at his little girl. Then he turned his back to her and spoke low enough that Lizzie couldn't hear him. "If you could take the dog and put it down fer me, I'd be much obliged." He looked back over his shoulder with a tenderness for his daughter. Then he turned back to us again, "Lizzie wouldn't have to know that you put him down."

I'd seen the way Becca watched Hannah and Corky. She'd never had a dog of her own, but she had a fondness for any kind of animal, so I thought it might be a good opportunity for her. "I think Becca would like to have a dog,"

"Fer sure?"

"I think she would."

"He'll chase those chickens, given a chance," Adam warned one more time.

When I nodded, he went over to where his child sat. I couldn't hear what he told Lizzie, but she started crying and hugging the dog. She finally got up, looked my way with a stare I couldn't read, and ran to her mother who was standing at the doorway. Adam brought the dog over to me and handed me his rope.

"His name's Rusty," he said.

"Maybe Lizzie can come visit him," I offered.

When I saw Becca's reaction to Rusty, it made the memory of Lizzie's sadness a little easier to take. She stood smiling as she watched the dogs take a swim in the creek. When the dogs tired of the swim they climbed up the creek bank and shook the water out of their coats. Rusty paused and looked to the south— the direction of the Walden place.

"He'll probably try goin' back to his old home," Carl cautioned.

Becca didn't appear to like that idea. "Rusty, come here boy," she whistled. The dog came to her right away.

57

Rebecca's diary...

May 17, 1868—There was nearly a tragedy yesterday when Rusty caught one of Hannah's chickens. We were at the Taylor homestead. Nathan was helping Carl build their soddy. I was helping Hannah in the garden when we heard one of her chickens squawking. When I saw what had happened I feared the chicken was dead, as Rusty had her head in his mouth when I screamed at him. He looked up, opened his mouth, and the chicken made her escape. Rusty hung his head in shame and I tied him up for the rest of the day. I apologized, but Hannah said not a word about the incident. I can't imagine how I would survive this place if Hannah and I were no longer friends over the loss of a chicken. She is teaching me how to plant a garden. Today she and Carl came to our house for a Bible reading and singing of a hymn. It seems strange to have no church to attend and it is on Sundays that I miss my music the most.

Hannah...

My Carl didn't use his special compensation for his years in the service when he filed his claim. He didn't have to let me know his decisions as to why, but he always took my feelin's into account when he could.

"I'd have to pay taxes on the land and I figure it will take us a couple of years to get on our feet with crop money," he explained.

"If you think that's best," I agreed.

"We'll live here five years afore we can call it our own though." He looked to me to see if I thought that was a good idea.

"Then we best get busy with makin' it ours," I said.

Carl laughed at that. He'd done lots of plannin' when he'd been gone. I'd done the same. One thing we disagreed on was where to put the soddy. My experience with the storm when my Carl was gone put me in favor of not bein' close to the creek.

"It'll be a longer ways for you to carry water, but I suppose you know that," he said.

I nodded. I didn't want our things washed downstream if it flooded again.

The Carters was turnin' out to be good friends to me and Carl, and we was happy to have them as such close neighbors. My Carl had a sod cutter and Nathan had a new plow, so we traded the use of our implements and worked with each other.

We all worked together bustin' sod that first day, and after we cleared enough for a garden, Nathan brought his plow over and worked up the soil.

The smell of the fresh turned earth made me anxious to get the garden started. Rebecca was helpin' me break up big clumps of dirt. She was tryin' her best to learn all she could. The men had gone to the Carter's dugout to repair its roof with some of the sod, when we heard an awful ruckus. Rebecca started screamin' and near scared me half to death.

"Rusty! Bad dog! Rusty! Leave that chicken alone!" She was scoldin' the dog and runnin' to him. I looked up to see one of my hens runnin' away lickety-split.

Rebecca was near tears when she got to where Rusty set with his head hung low. She turned back 'round and looked at me like she didn't know what to do. I never seen whatever it was that Rebecca seen, but I figured her dog was chasin' my chickens. I held my tongue, but got her Corky's rope.

"I'm so sorry, Hannah," she apologized. She took the rope and tied Rusty up.

Later that day when I was at the wagon gettin' our supper ready, and Rebecca was fetchin' water from the creek, I watched one of my fool chickens go up to Rusty and peck him on the nose. The dog gave a little yip, looked over at me with pitiful eyes, and hung his head whilst the fowl quickly danced far enough away that Rusty couldn't touch her. It was hard to believe, but my eyes was showin' me the truth. I wondered if that dog really chased chickens, or if that dog chased one particular chicken. Either way, I couldn't take a chance with the only two chickens I had, so I never did tell Rebecca what I seen that day.

58

Rebecca's diary...

May 24, 1868—I find my heart confused. I've wanted to marry Nathan since I was ten years of age, yet I have no understanding of why he chose for us to live here in this desert of grasses and nothingness. I've written a letter to Mother and Father and told them we are in our home. I did not tell them it was a hole dug out of the side of a hill. Mother will be pleased when she reads that I think of her whenever I have my tea. This is the truth, but I omitted telling her that I don't have tea every day like she and I did. How I miss everyone. I asked Hannah how she deals with homesickness. She told me that wanting what cannot be is a wasted energy. Here, where there is so little of everything, I shall try not to waste my energies.

Hannah...

Me and Carl was standin' watchin' the western sky at end of the day. It was streaked with colors that I figured only God could make and if we looked away for only a bit, those colors changed into somethin' even purtier. Tired as we both was, he put his arm 'round me and we enjoyed the sight afore us as the day faded away.

"I'm a contented man, Hannah," he said. He turned and looked over at the ground he'd worked on all day. "I know it's not all bottom land, but where I want the crops is rich and black under all that sod. I figure the hills to the east will make us a fine pasture."

I could tell he had more to say by the way he kept lookin' first at me, and then back up to the hills. But my Carl had his own way and time in sayin' his mind, so I waited. We turned back to see the last light of day when ever'thing turned deep purple. Then as we was walkin' back to the wagon he told me the rest of what he had on his mind.

"I found somethin', up by the buffalo wallow, near where the hill starts to raise." He stopped and looked that way again.

"Is it a good find?' I asked.

"I think it might be limestone." He got a slow smile on his face. "If I can figure how to quarry it, we can use it for buildin', instead of sod." He talked his hopes out loud, as we come to the wagon and laid our tired bodies down. It was like hearin' sweet music to me when he shared his plans. The last thing I heard afore I went to sleep was, "Course that'll be a couple years down the way."

Carl...

I figured I'd have plenty of time in the winter months to study on how to quarry and mason that limestone. I could build my Hannah a fine home some day. On my walk home from the war I'd seen some grand houses made out of stone. Course, my mind wasn't clear then. Now I wished I'd paid them more notice, for what I seen on our hill looked to be the same kind of stone.

I started to tell Hannah 'bout them when she started snorin' real soft and gentle like. It gave me a joy deep inside to hear it. Tomorrow I'd work on buildin' our soddy and clearin' more land for crops. It was a long way afore we'd have time to quarry any stone, but it made for a good dream.

59

Rebecca's diary…

June 7, 1868—I've hardly had time to journal my thoughts, as I've found that we are toiling every day from the time the sun comes up until it fades in the western sky. Hannah has shown me how to appreciate some of the beauty in this land. She sees it everywhere, but I have to search, and I find it fleeting. If it were not for Hannah, I think I would beg Nathan to return to Ohio, for I cannot get accustomed to the constant winds. The heat is unbearable in the middle of the day. The only escape is in the dugout, but it is always dank and crawling with varmints. The men have finished the Taylor's soddy and Hannah is quite pleased with it all. Since we have no church to attend, we do try to make our Sundays special with Bible readings. I try to also lead everyone in singing hymns. I may not have a piano, but my voice is strong. How I miss the music of my mother's piano.

Nathan…

I'd never worked harder than that first month after I staked my claim and I'd never before felt so accomplished. I was no longer trying to please anyone but myself. I knew the life was hard on Becca. I promised her we would soon be surrounded by neighbors. I was filled with hope for the future. I could see that she hated the dugout, but during some of those hot windy days, it provided a pleasant cool respite from the prairie heat.

Carl and I worked together most days. He was a quiet man who thought things through before he spoke. How I envied what he had grown up with in his family, for when he talked of them it was with mutual respect and love. Somehow we got to talking about the war one day and when I mentioned what it did to my father, he nodded like he understood. We worked, each silent with our own thoughts for a bit. We were laying up sod for my stock stable, and when we sat in the shade for a rest, he told me that his family had split sides on the war.

"We don't know if my brothers survived or not, as no one in the family heard anything from them since the day they left." He took off his hat and fanned his face. I did the same.

"I know it was hard on my mama... my daddy too, but I can see how Theodor and Philipp did what they thought was right." He stopped and pulled a stem of dried grass out of a sod brick. Sticking it in his mouth to chew on, he continued on with his memories.

"I try to remember the good times though. Like when me and my brothers was walkin' in the creek behind our farm. I was a little tyke at the time. I walked right into a hole and went under. I was sputterin' and flayin' my arms. I was drownin'. And then I felt a great pain when Theodor grabbed me by my hair and yanked me outa that hole."

When he caught me looking at his bald head, he chuckled.

"Oh, I had a head full of hair back then—red too," he said. "I coughed up a mouthful of that creek, whilst the brothers all laughed at me. Truth was, they'd all been scared too. I never had a doubt that Theodor and Philipp loved all my family."

It was almost like he'd forgotten I was there when he started his recollection. He finished his thought out loud.

"Don't know why we felt so different 'bout men ownin' other men. Never could figure that out."

We got busy again without any conversation. Carl stopped for a minute, took off his hat and wiped the sweat from his head with his kerchief. "There's somethin' I been meanin' to ask you," he said.

Rusty and Corky started barking just then. We both looked to see what had them excited, when we saw Adam Walden riding hard in our direction. We knew his message must hold importance because a man surely wouldn't drive his horse like that without good reason.

~ 60 ~

Carl...

Adam Walden was in a sorry state when he come ridin' in that day with his disturbin' news. His horse was lathered slick with sweat, for it was a hot day, and he'd rode the animal hard all the way from his place. When he got down off that poor critter it was plain he was havin' trouble puttin' what he wanted to say into words. He looked down like he was ashamed when he finally spoke.

"It's my Edna. I've busted my arse fer the last year. Now I'm supposed to leave it all behind? But I'll have no family if she takes the children." He turned his face away from us. It was twisted in defeat and frustration.

"I'm here fer two reasons," his words come out so fast then, I wasn't sure we was hearin' him right.

"You want to buy our stock? Not the horses, we need the horses fer travelin'. She's packin' up the wagon now. Think it was the Injun scare that made her get stubborn on me. That letter, too, from her mama sayin' we need to go back, and then little Walter and the rattlesnake—it was all too much fer her." He had started pacin' back and forth and words tumbled out of him. He stopped. "You want our stock or not?" he asked.

"Let's sit in the shade and talk about it," Nathan offered.

Adam's shoulders slumped as he nodded his agreement, and walked over to the little shade the half-finished wall of the stable provided. His horse had cooled enough that I led him to the creek for a sip of water and by the time I got back to the two men, Adam had calmed a bit. I asked him 'bout his son.

"Oh, he's fine. Lizzie seen a rattler headin' Walter's way. She screamed and the thing slithered off. But it scared her and Edna."

"And Edna's folks?" I asked him.

"Her mama's homesick fer her, that's all. Then when I went in to Ellsworth yesterday, I heard the Injuns are all riled up agin, but it's all way east of here and sounds to me like they're fightin' each other. I mentioned it. I shouldn't said nothin' to her. She said she's had enough and she's goin' home. She don't want nothin' to do with this place ever agin."

"So you're leaving?" Nathan asked.

"Got to, the ways I see it. She won't stay." He ran his hand through his hair. He looked older than his years.

"I can't take the stock with me. Molly's ready to calf soon, and Edna wants to get rid of most all her chickens. Says she doesn't care 'bout them no more." He caught his breath and went on. "I got a pig too. I figured he'd grow some and be ready to butcher 'fore winter gets here."

We talked more and settled on a fair price for Adam's cow, pig, and chickens. Then Nathan asked him 'bout the Indians again.

"Should a never said a thing 'bout 'em to her. She's always had a mighty fear of 'em."

As he mounted his horse, he shook his head back and forth slow, like he didn't believe what he was tellin' us. "We'll be headin' out early in the mornin'. Better come today to pick up the critters." He started to head back to his place when he pulled up his horse one last time. Without lookin' our way he said, "If the antelope don't eat the crops, you're welcome to 'em." He started walkin' his horse back home. This time his horse was about as slow as a horse can go and still be walkin'.

Hannah...

Carl was later than usual when he come to the soddy at noon and told me 'bout the Waldens leavin'. I was happy to be gettin' a pig and chickens, but it was hard to think we'd be losin' the Waldens as neighbors.

"Nathan said he would just as soon his Rebecca doesn't know 'bout the Indian scare," Carl said.

I nodded. Carl knowed I wouldn't say nothin' unless Rebecca asked me. He knowed I couldn't lie though, if she did.

"I'd like to go with you when you pick up the stock, so I can bid farewell to Edna."

"I think that's a fine thing to do."

"I baked extra biscuits this mornin' too. At least it'll give them breakfast to start off their travels.

My Carl smiled and repeated his words. "I think that's a fine thing to do."

61

Nathan...

Carl and I didn't say much to each other as we finished unloading the sod bricks out of the wagon. Once again I was uncertain that I'd made the right decision of where my homestead should be. I'd decided to come to Kansas because I'd heard of Indian raids in Nebraska. Now I was hearing of Indian raids in Kansas. By the time we laid the last of the sod onto the wall of the stable, I'd made up my mind that I had to face my fears. I wanted this place more than anything I'd ever wanted before—except for Becca.

Becca had a power over me since that day in the store when I first recognized she had become a woman. Whenever I looked into her eyes, I'd go weak with the desire to make her happy. But when I told her the Walden's were leaving and we were going to buy their cow, I surely was surprised by her reaction.

"Leaving? Why are they leaving? Where are they going?"

"Back to her folks, I suppose. Adam said something about a letter from her mother," I said.

Becca had just dished out some beans on my plate. She'd turned away from me to put the ladle back in the pot. She stopped and swung around to face me again. Her beautiful eyes were dancing. I'd seen that look before. It was the look of hope and planning.

"Nathan, can't we go with them? We could go back to Independence. I'm sure you could find work there."

When I realized what she'd said, I sat there with my mouth open, ready to spoon some beans inside. I put the spoon down and looked at her. I knew she'd been fighting off some homesick feelings, but I thought she wanted the same things I wanted. Now she was asking me if we could leave. Maybe she didn't know how important it was for me to own my own place. The land was free if I was willing to work it and improve it. And I was.

I don't know how long I sat there, saying nothing, looking at my lovely wife and feeling bewildered. My innards were so conflicted I surely couldn't eat anything right then. My dream was just starting and I was so proud of everything I'd accomplished on our claim. I still hadn't found anything to say, when I picked myself up and walked outside to where I could breathe again. I stood there looking over what I'd done since we'd arrived at our claim. I didn't even know Becca had followed me until her small voice came from behind me.

"We'll have no neighbors at all if the Walden's leave," she said.

I turned around and faced her. "Carl and Hannah aren't leaving."

"I'm lonely, Nathan. I've always been around people."

"Becca, I've always been around people too. And we will be again. I'm sure of that. We can't wait for there to be people first—there may be no land left then."

She looked away from me. I couldn't see why she couldn't understand.   It made me angry because I didn't think she was trying to see it. I needed to be away from her just then.

"I'm going to water the horses and then Carl and I are going to the Walden's to pick up the animals. Do you want to say good-bye to them?" I waited for an answer.

"I want us to leave with them." Her voice was no longer soft and gentle. When I turned to face her there was defiance in her eyes. My stomach churned again.

"I'm staying. If you want to leave, I'll not stop you," I said.

We stood staring at each other until I saw tears well up in her beautiful eyes. I wanted to take her in my arms and tell her everything would work itself out. Instead I walked away.

The whole time I was tending to Polly and Jake, I prayed she wasn't packing her trunk.

62

Rebecca's diary...

June 14, 1868—I have had little patience with Nathan this week, for when he told me the Walden family was going back East and giving up their claim, I expressed my wishes to join them. I only succeeded in making Nathan angry with me and we've not spoken about the subject since. He does not understand my longing for the company of others and I cannot comprehend his love for this barren land. We bid the Walden family farewell and acquired their cow, Molly. Edna was in such an agitated state that she sat down on the dirt floor of her soddy and started weeping when Hannah asked her if she might help her. Seeing how this upset poor little Lizzie, who was left with the task of caring for her brother, I took both of the children outside. But when she heard her father and Nathan discussing the exchange for Molly, she too started crying. I promised her I would take good care of Molly. I nearly wept when I saw her hug the gentle cow and tell her good-bye. It has been such an unhappy week for me. More than one time I found myself telling Rusty and Molly my concerns. I am of the opinion they understand me better than my own husband.

Hannah...

There was a mighty difference in Edna Walden from the day we first met up and the day we said good-bye. Rebecca took the children outside, and as soon as they was out the door, Edna confided her true feelin's to me.

"Hannah, I could put up with almost anything, but those Injun raids put the fear of God in me," she said in a loud whisper. She kept lookin' to make sure Lizzie wasn't comin' back into earshot. She let out a big sigh and continued, "I know I hurt Adam, fer it's always been his dream to own his own land."

I could tell there was part of her that didn't want to leave. She looked out the door to where her little ones was and continued. "I got the children to think of. I seen what those savages can do—I seen it with my own eyes."

Her face twisted. "When we come out here, we passed by another wagon train that got attacked. I hid Lizzie inside the wagon so she wouldn't have to see." She shook her head like that would erase the memories she seen there. "I wish you well, Hannah. I'll be prayin' fer you all."

I'd not knowed her long, but I liked her. "I'll pray for your safe return to your folks too," I said. I helped her carry some things to their wagon, and then it was time for us to go. We hugged each other like we was kin, all the time knowin' we'd never meet up again.

The men-folk had ever'thing ready to go in short time. All of Edna's chickens, except the two they would take on their journey, was in a good sized crate Adam had made out of willow branches.

"This here crate's too big to fit on our wagon, and coyotes sure do like chickens if 'n you're not careful with 'em at night," he warned. "Didn't want fowl in the house with me and the crate worked purty good."

He looked over to the garden. "Ya all might as well have anything the critters don't git." It was plain to see how upset he was, 'cause he was talkin' so much. It was time to leave.

I drove the wagon. Rebecca could've rode with me, but she wanted to walk and lead Molly. The wagon was loaded with the chickens, Adam's plow for Carl, Edna's cookin' stove for Rebecca and Nathan, and some boards Edna used for a table. My Carl and Nathan was herdin' the pig.

Lizzie stood alone, watchin' us leave. Rebecca turned and waved one more time. Lizzie didn't wave back.

63

Rebecca's diary...

June 24, 1868—I try to get the majority of my chores accomplished before the harsh heat of the day saps all of my energies and takes over my thoughts. It gives me time to journal when I escape to the dugout, where it is cooler. However, even in the dugout I cannot escape the unceasing wind. Hannah said the crops will not dry unless there is wind to blow the dew off them. How I envy her outlook on nature. She embraces the wind. It is true that when the wind is not present, the air is filled with a dampness that makes it hard to breathe. But when it comes, I feel no breezes. It roars in like the buffalo I saw yesterday. Two riders were chasing the animal. I could hear the poor thing snorting and pounding the earth with his hooves. Nathan and Carl were on the hill east of the Taylor soddy and the buffalo was racing toward them. The riders caught up with the buffalo. As they rode beside him, I heard the crack of their rifles. But the huge beast ran on. It took some time before he finally succumbed to his wounds. He stumbled and fell. Nathan and Carl were not far away when all this happened. When they approached the men, they had already started skinning the buffalo. Nathan said little about the men. He said they were going to leave the carcass to rot after they removed its hide, so he and Carl got the buckboard and brought part of the animal home. Hannah had buffalo chips ready. She roasted some of the meat for a rich delicious feast for our supper. She said she will also jerk some of the meat. I am constantly learning from her.

Nathan...

Carl and I were standing on the hillside on the eastern part of his claim. He'd just showed me his find of limestone that was buried in the hill.

"I've been meanin' to ask you if your hill has anything like this?" he said.

"I've not seen any, but I've not looked for it either."

We were both sitting on our haunches, getting a closer look at the stone and discussing the possibilities of learning how to quarry it, when we heard an awful ruckus. The dogs, down by the creek, started barking. When we stood up we saw a buffalo headed toward us with two riders in hot pursuit. The buffalo was running one way and then another and Carl and I didn't know but that he might run our way. The riders caught up with him and fired several shots into him before he came crashing down. Then they jumped off their horses and brandished knives. The buffalo was thrashing around on the ground when one of the men plunged his knife deep into the animal's heart.

By the time Carl and I got to them, they already had the animal half skinned. They seemed to be enjoying the task too much for my taste, and I could see the act wasn't settling well with Carl either. The fellows weren't any too friendly when Carl and I walked up to them.

"This your claim?" the tallest man asked us. He never looked our way, he just kept on with his task.

"It is," Carl answered.

"We been chasing this 'un fer a while. His hide's ours, fair and square," the shorter man with an ugly scar running across his face stated. He stopped skinning long enough to stand up and puff out his chest. He brought his bloody knife up to the tip of his hat in a mock salute to Carl.

"I'm not arguing the fact," Carl finally said.

The man bent back to the animal and once more started separating the hide from the flesh.

"You takin' the meat?" Carl asked.

"Prime part is all." The man quit cutting on the hide. He reached over the hump of the buffalo and sliced off a huge chunk of meat. "We get fresh near ever day." He sneered, "You're welcome to what's left."

Carl never said another word. He looked the man in his eyes for an uncomfortable amount of time, in my opinion. Those two had rifles and knives. Carl had a spade. Without saying a word, he turned away and started walking toward his soddy. I followed him, all the time wondering if those two fellows might shoot us in the back.

By the time we got back up the hill with the buckboard, the men were riding off to the south. Carl was saying no words against them, but I could surely feel his dislike for them. Carl's rifle was near his side now. The dogs had followed us back up the hill. They were cautious and didn't go close to that dead beast until Carl went up to it. Carl's patience with animals always impressed me. That day he snapped at them.

"Go on you two. Git for home," he yelled. His mood was foul.

Both dogs ran back toward home a ways before they stopped. They sat and watched Carl and me as we loaded a good deal of the meat onto the buckboard. When we started to leave they went closer to the carcass, sniffed around it, but then followed us back to Carl's place.

Becca had gone to the Taylor place too, so we stayed there and helped with the meat. We had a mighty good supper that night. We were enjoying our meal when Hannah asked Carl about the buffalo hunters. He gave her a look that somehow told her how he felt without saying any words. She asked no more questions. I could tell she didn't find the need. Becca asked me about that when we were walking home after supper and I found that I couldn't put into words how I felt either. I just knew that there was something more to those two that I didn't like—something more than I'd witnessed that day.

64

Carl...

I never cared much for greedy men. That day I seen those two buffalo hunters kill for the price of a hide, I felt an anger rise in me like I'd not felt since I'd seen the atrocities of the war. The Waldens left on the rumors that Indians was raidin' again. To my way of thinkin', the Indians had a good reason to be upset, if someone was killin' off their food supply.

People called them redskin savages. Yet what I seen that day was two dirty white-skin savages. If they'd a needed food or even if they'd a needed that hide for themselves, I could've understood, but it appeared to me that they enjoyed the killin'. It was a natural thing for buffalo to roam free on the land, but those two had no respect for that. They didn't appear to have respect for much of anything.

Funny, I thought back to Skinner. He said he'd got his name from his trade afore he become a wagon master. Yet I seen him bein' nothin' like those who'd skinned that buffalo whilst me and Nathan stood there watchin'. There was somethin' more 'bout the two that got under my skin, though I couldn't think what it was. And it was after that day that my Hannah said I was thrashing around in my sleep at night again.

Hannah...

Carl had been free from his nightmares ever since we'd planted ourselves on our claim. Then he started havin' unrest at night again. It was after the killin' of that buffalo. Though we'd prospered from it with a feast, I knowed it upset my Carl more than he was sayin'.

"Hannah, take caution if you see those two good for nothin's ridin' our way. They've got their camp somewhere close, maybe at the Walden place."

I heard a bunch of gunshots one day when the air was still. They sounded far off, and I wondered if another buffalo died. I never seen any riders, and when the winds picked up again I never heard any more shots.

Quiet days on the prairie didn't come very often. Rebecca hated the wind and found complaint with it. But the heat was near unbearable when there wasn't wind to cool the sweat. It was one of those insufferable hot days when we near lost my Carl.

Him and Nathan was tryin' to cut sod for our barn. We'd had no rain for some time, and it made hard labor for the chore of breakin' new ground. Me and Rebecca was in the soddy when we heard Corky and Rusty raisin' a ruckus. As soon as we both went outside, we seen the reason why. Nathan was callin' for us to come help him.

"Hannah! Hannah!" he was yellin'.

My Carl was down on his knees. He had a hold on the handles of the sod cutter. Nathan was beside him tryin' to help him up. Me and Rebecca started runnin' to them. It was a short distance, but I felt I'd never get there. When I did, I could see Carl was in trouble.

"We need to get him inside the soddy," Nathan said. Carl's hands let go of the handles then, and he fell back into Nathan's arms.

"We need to get him out of the sun," Nathan said, and I didn't question him. Nathan lifted his top half and I grabbed one of his legs. Rebecca grabbed the other. I don't recall it now, but Rebecca told me later that I was prayin' out loud the whole time we was carryin' my Carl.

As soon as we got him into the cool soddy, Rebecca went to fetch some water and Nathan grabbed my dishpan and started fannin' him. His skin was clammy and his color was off, and his eyes kept rollin' back in his head. I don't know how long it took for him to come back to me, but he finally did. That's when I felt tears slidin' down my face as I gave him little sips of water.

"You gave me a scare." I said, half whisperin' and half cryin'.

He gave me a weak smile and nodded just a bit. His eyes lookin' back at me was the best thing I ever seen. They was the cool blue color of clear sky. We looked at each other for a long while until I seen one lone tear slip out of one of his eyes. Then he closed them both and rested for the rest of that day.

65

Rebecca's diary...

July 5, 1868—Today is the first time I've felt like journaling for a long time, as there is little but heat and wind to write about. The wind is merciless. It's either constant with its howling, or it stops completely and makes it impossible to draw a fair breath. Yesterday there was not a blade of grass moving when Carl was overtaken with the heat. It gave us all a great amount of fright. The men have decided it's necessary to take more precaution in midday, so they rest then and work later in the evening until they can no longer see from lack of daylight. Nathan practically falls into bed when he comes home. His dream of having a prosperous crop keeps him going. I find myself hoping he fails so that we have to leave this desolate land. Carl has discovered limestone on his claim and Nathan thinks it is a promising building material. There are still only the four of us in this place and I have seen no newcomers flocking to make claims near us. I wonder who we will entertain in our grand house that Nathan promises to build for me.

July 10, 1868—Again there is no breeze of any kind today. The stillness is as miserable as the roaring wind. How I wish we could have gone back East with the Waldens. It is almost unbearable that I have no correspondence with my mother, as the men are unwilling to take even one day off from their fieldwork to travel into town. My requests seem to fall on deaf ears. I will keep asking until Nathan relents.

July 11, 1868—Carl and Hannah have agreed to make a trip into town tomorrow to see if we have letters. I was hoping to go too, but Nathan offered us to take care of the Taylor stock while they are away. Because of Carl's spell the other day, Nathan says it makes more sense for Carl to go and have a good day's rest from heavy labor. I've had a long letter for Mother and Father written for a month. I do not mention how Mother's foreboding about this land was correct. Instead I wrote using Nathan's optimistic dreams, pretending they are also mine.

Hannah...

I hafta admit I was lookin' forward to goin' with my Carl to see if we all had letters. I knowed how much Rebecca wanted to go too, but I had to think of what was best for my Carl. We all needed letters from home and when Carl said he could take a day off to go to town, we all thought it a good idea. He could use a rest from workin' in the heat.

Nathan gave us a list of some supplies to pick up. Then when Rebecca couldn't hear him, he whispered somethin' to me. "Hannah, if there's any to be found, would you pick up some horehound for Rebecca?" His eyes kinda twinkled. He winked and smiled like he was a schoolboy buyin' somethin' for his best girl. Rebecca had told me the story of how Nathan won her mother over with horehound candy.

I smiled and promised I would try to find some.

Carl...

The first thing me and Hannah did, when we got to town, was to see if we had letters. We did. We found us a shade tree, parked our wagon, and read them. All the news from my family was sweet, but Sarah's letter to Hannah had some disturbin' news that her mama and her daddy was in ill health.

"Sarah's a strong woman, and she'll take good care of them," I told Hannah.

She nodded, but she couldn't hide the sadness that crawled over her face. Hannah's eyesight is poor when it comes to readin', so I read Sarah's letter to her again. She set quiet in her own thoughts for a bit afore she got up.

"We'd best get our tradin' done and be gettin' back," she said. "I'm gonna try to find some horehound. Rebecca will have a fine day with letters and somethin' for her sweet tooth too." She smiled, but I knowed she was holdin' a homesickness inside herself.

Me and Nathan thought we'd share in the cost of buyin' a scythe, so whilst Hannah did her tradin' in the general store, I went on to the blacksmith's shop. I had to walk past one of the saloons on my way, and I no sooner was past the swingin' doors when I wished I was somewhere else.

I recognized their smell afore I seen their faces, though now the smell was mixed with rotten whiskey. It was the two scoundrel buffalo hunters that had passed our way earlier in the summer. They almost stumbled into my arms. Two others that looked to be of the same kind was with them. They was all four talkin' loud and comparin' the kills they'd made and the hides they'd taken. My thinkin' was that they was too liquored up to recognize me and I was happy for that. But just as I was walkin' away, their talk stopped me. I wish I hadn't heard the words they was sayin', but I did. I was grateful my Hannah wasn't beside me, hearin' it too.

"Tain't nuff of 'em ugly critters left 'round these parts anymore," the tall one said.

"We had it good whilst we was camped at that Walden claim though," the one with the scar face boasted. He let out a snort. "Hell, that place tain't never doin' that family no good ever agin, but we sure thank the fact they told us 'bout it 'fore they all got scalped."

My skin felt like somethin' evil was crawlin' on it. I had my back to them, but I clearly pictured that ugly face sayin' those words. I felt sick. I wanted to walk away and not hear anymore, but I couldn't make my legs move me.

"How ya know they was scalped?" asked one of the others.

"Seen it. Weren't nothin' we could do to help. There was too damned many of em."

My legs still wouldn't carry me away from them. I didn't want to listen to anymore of it, but they kept talkin'. One of the others bumped into me and near knocked me over as they tried to walk past me. He just kept on stumblin' around with his feet and his words.

The story they told, was that they met the Waldens as they was headin' west and the Waldens was goin' east. They all camped at the same place and learned of the Walden's claim. The next mornin' they left earlier than the Waldens and headed on their way west. They'd not gone far when they heard gunshots, so they rode back and watched a band of Indians surround the lone wagon.

The Indians massacred the entire family.

"We high-tailed it outa there," the scarred man said. He finished with, "It was a damned bloody mess, but we had ta save our own skins."

I still couldn't get my legs to move. Even durin' the war, I never hated men the way I hated those two just then. I don't know how long I stood there. My ears was ringin' with the last words, "Had ta save our own skins."

66

Hannah...

Our trip to town was bittersweet. The letters from home helped lift our spirits, but on the ride home Carl told me the Indian raids that chased the Waldens back East was worse than he first thought.

"I guess maybe Edna was right for takin' her children out of harm's way," I said.

Carl got a strained look on his face. When his eyes turned away from me and he slowly shook his head, I knew there was more.

"Did you hear 'bout them?"

He nodded and he drew a big sigh. He didn't say anything.

"All of them?" I asked.

He nodded again, still not lookin' my way.

I didn't ask more.

It musta been a mile afore either of us said anything else. Finally Carl found his voice again.

"We could try goin' back too," he said. He was lookin' deep into my face. It sounded like a question, and when I said nothin', he added, "Train might be a safer way to travel."

Now it was me who couldn't find words. I knowed how much Carl needed the place he'd put in for his own claim. Hard as our life was, we both loved the land we lived on. I figured God would take care of us if we took care of the place he took us to. As bad as I wanted to see my family, I knowed in my heart how much Carl didn't want to leave.

"This is our home now," I said. I hoped my voice sounded strong, cause I have to admit I felt a fear I'd not felt afore. "I don't want to leave it."

Carl's face looked like a big burden was taken away when I said it.

"I'll hafta tell Nathan."

"Rebecca will want to go," I said.

"Can you manage without another woman 'round for miles?"

Thinkin' on that scared me almost as much as seein' Indians. I swallowed and nodded.

67

Rebecca's diary…

July 13, 1868—At last, I have letters from home, two from Mother and one from Martha. Mother has no understanding of our circumstances—that we are not able to post letters more often. She has heard rumors of terrible Indian raids in Kansas and told me she is near frantic with worry. I'm glad my letter to her didn't mention the reason of the Walden's departure from this area. How I wish Nathan would have agreed to go back East with them. I also had a letter from Martha. I miss her, so. She and William are engaged to be married in September. I am so desperately homesick for everyone.

Nathan…

Becca had been miffed at me the whole time the Taylors were gone. I knew she wanted to go into town too, so I promised her the next time we'd not wait so long to check on our mail. We'd finished up our chores, when the evening turned quiet. The wind died down for an unexpected calm, and the sun was giving us a glorious show before it left us for the day. While sitting outside watching the gold and orange colors streak across the sky, we heard Corky barking in the distance.

"I'll bet they're back," Becca said as she jumped up. She was standing on her tiptoes, trying to give a look-see.

"Don't you think we should probably wait until the morning?" I teased.

"Nathan, I've waited all day. I'm going to go see." Becca gave me a frustrated glance, then looked over at

Rusty. His ears had perked up with the sound of Corky's bark. "You'll go, won't you boy?" she asked.

Rusty's tail wagged at the opportunity. The two started walking.

"I fear we've lost our sensibilities," I said. "It'll be dark before we get back." I grabbed a lantern. The daylight was already fading, but Becca and Rusty didn't seem to care the least bit, and I had to hurry to catch them.

Carl was unhitching the horses when we reached their place. He smiled and handed us four letters. Three were for Becca and one was for me. I knew Becca needed to hear from her family in the worst kind of way, but I didn't realize how much a letter from home would mean to me, until I saw my letter from my mother and William.

"Better read them quick, afore it gets any darker out," Carl said.

I read my letter while there was a bit of daylight left. But Becca was still trying to read hers, so I lit the lantern for her. Carl tugged on my shirt sleeve and pulled me to the side.

"Mind helpin' me water the horses?" he asked.

I knew he had something of importance to say. So as Hannah went into the soddy to rustle up something to eat, and Becca finished reading her letters, I walked to the creek with him. The night was so quiet that Carl brought his voice to a whisper when he told me what he'd heard from the buffalo hunters. I was grateful Becca couldn't hear it.

I was sick to my stomach when he said they left the Walden family to fend for themselves. I couldn't speak until the shock of it all wore down just a bit. He said nothing for a while either. Then, with his voice low he started talking about our own situation.

"I'm thinkin' we need to be extra careful, for our own selves."

I felt a chill, though the air was still warm from the day. I tried to think of what I would tell Becca. I tried to think of what I would do if a band of Indians came for us. We talked of several possible ways we could make a defense for ourselves.

Then I heard Becca's voice. "I wonder what's takin' the men so long to water the horses?" she said.

"Does Hannah know?" I whispered.

"Some of it," he said.

The evening darkness kept me from seeing his face, but I knew Carl well enough to know he was deeply upset. We staked the horses for the night and walked back toward the soddy. Becca was chattering like I hadn't heard for some time.

"We need to leave these folks get some supper and we need to head for home," I said as I grabbed the lantern, wishing I'd brought my rifle with me.

As we walked, moonlight shone bright enough that we no longer needed the lantern lit. The heat of the day was gone and the night was beautiful. Becca was happier than I'd seen her in a long time. I couldn't bring myself to talk about Indians with her just then. I felt bad enough that the prairie life was hard on her and I didn't want to worry her more than necessary.

"I can hardly wait for the morning, so I can read the letters again," she said. She started humming the tune of her 'happy song'. Every so once in a while she'd stop and tell me something Martha or her mother had written about. "Aren't you thrilled for William and Martha?" she asked.

"I am," I said. "William sounded real happy in his letter too." I tried to make my voice light. I tried to think of all the good things my letter had said. But I didn't feel the peace that the prairie usually brought to me. I'd have to tell Becca to keep watch for Indians. I figured I'd tell her in the morning. Then she'd harp on me about how we should've gone with the Waldens again and I knew I couldn't tell her what Carl had just told me about them.

When we finally got home and went to bed, Becca seemed content to lie in my arms. She went to sleep in the middle of talking about William and Martha. But, tired as I was, it took me a long time to find sleep myself. I was haunted by the innocent faces of the Walden children, Lizzie and little Walter.

Rebecca's diary…

July 14, 1868—Hannah came calling today. She surprised me with a gift of horehound candy. Nathan had asked her to buy it when she went to town. I insisted that we have a proper tea. It was then I confessed to her that my mother loved horehound and I only pretended to like it to please mother and to get Nathan's attention. We laughed so hard at the irony of it all, that we both had tears come to our eyes. She happens to like horehound, so I sent it home with her. Later I thanked Nathan for his consideration of asking her to buy me something sweet. He found great amusement in my admission of eating the candy to woo him.

July 23, 1868—My letters are the only thing I have to sustain me now. I feel like I can trust no one here, not Hannah and certainly not my own husband. I have been betrayed by them all. No one told me about the Indians being on a warpath, until Mr. Skinner came back into our lives. I so wish I would have left with the Waldens. I will find a way to leave, for I fear my own sanity if I stay in this barren place. I am so angry I cannot think with a clear mind. The wind is relentless, the heat is unbearable. I have flea and bedbug bites from living in a hole in the ground. Yesterday there was a snake in the dugout again. Nathan tells me the bull snakes are harmless. He will never convince me of that. I asked him if he thought Adam and Eve had a discussion about the danger of snakes. I think I must convince him to change his mind about living here. If Edna could convince her husband to leave, why won't Nathan at least listen to my requests when he sees how desperate I am to go?

Nathan...

After we got our letters, Becca seemed very content for several days. We even had a great laugh over the horehound candy Hannah brought her. I didn't want to ruin Becca's happiness with worry about Indians, and I didn't have the heart to tell her the bad news that Carl had overheard. Then early one morning about a week after we got our letters, Carl and I were hoeing in my cornfield between our two claims. Corky started barking at a lone rider headed our way. Rusty's ears perked up and he raced off to join Corky. Carl and I watched as the rider stopped where Hannah was working in her garden.

"Maybe I best get home and see who's callin' on us," Carl said. He laid his hoe down and started walking toward his soddy, but stopped when the rider mounted his horse again and rode our way. When he got closer Carl added, "Well, I'll be. That sure looks like Skinner's horse."

I stopped hoeing. Carl and I waved. Skinner waved back. I didn't notice that Becca had walked out to the cornfield too.

"Is that Mr. Skinner?" she asked.

"Sure looks like the old cuss," Carl said with a smile spread across his face.

Skinner called out when he got a little closer, "Howdy folks." He looked all around and complimented our hard work. "Looks like you've got yourselves some purty decent claims here." He pulled his horse up and dismounted.

"Welcome friend," Carl said as he and Skinner shook hands. Skinner shook my hand and tipped his hat to Becca, "Ma'am."

"What brings you back to these parts?" Carl asked.

"Well," he started off slow, looking Carl in the eye. "You all heard 'bout the Indian dust up?" He looked to each of us in turn. Then he explained, "The United States Army's got me for a while, cause of me knowin' the Cheyenne's ways."

Carl seemed to understand.

"I made sure they got a good man to take over the train for me."

I glanced at Becca. Right then I knew it had been a mistake not to tell her about the danger we were in. Her brows furrowed and her eyes questioned as Skinner went on. He told us how he was staying in the Walden soddy.

"Gul-darned those buffalo hunters left it a mess," he said. I held my breath that he'd say nothing more about the Waldens and was thankful when he didn't. He talked for some time before Carl looked at the sun that was hanging straight above us.

"Hannah will be expecting me for dinner. Will you stay and eat with us?"

"Hannah already asked when I seen her up by the soddy. I wouldn't miss her cookin' fer nothin'."

"I've our dinner waiting too." Becca added, "Good-day Mr. Skinner." She turned and started walking back to the dugout. I knew she was not happy with me. I said my good-bye and ran to catch up with her. When I did, she started in on me.

"Carl didn't seem very surprised that there is more Indian trouble." She spoke through gritted teeth.

"He heard about it when he and Hannah went into town," I explained.

"You mean you've known about it." It was an accusation.

I knew what was coming next. I'd been hearing about it for days. I knew what she was going to ask me before she even said it. I knew this was not the life like she had known, but I also knew we had a good future if she would just believe in me. She stopped walking so suddenly that I nearly ran into her.

"I'm not a child anymore Nathan," she said, while she stood there with her back to me. "What if I put my foot down like Edna did?"

"Becca, I have to tell you…"

"I'm too angry to listen to anything you have to tell me. I told you we should have left with the Waldens, but you wouldn't listen to me." She turned and looked me in the eye, "Do I mean nothing to you anymore?"

I started to reach out to her, to hold her in my arms, to tell her how much I loved her, but she turned back around and stomped off toward the dugout.

69

Rebecca's diary…

July 24, 1868—I had the most unpleasant encounter with a skunk today. I'm certain the varmint would have attacked me if it hadn't been for Rusty fighting him off. Nathan heard my screams and came running with his rifle. At first I feared Rusty was hit when the shot rang out, but Nathan's aim was true and the detestable animal was killed. Unfortunately Rusty was sprayed with such an offending odor, that it brought tears to my eyes. Nathan has quarantined my best friend downwind and far away from the dugout.

July 25, 1868—I have cried until there are no more tears. Today Nathan told me the Walden family all perished at the hand of the Indians. Do they all think I am a child? Hannah knew too, and she didn't tell me. I have never felt so alone. They do not tell me their secrets, I will not tell anyone mine either.

Nathan…

Becca had been sick for a couple of days, and I thought maybe it was because she was so angry. She wouldn't let it go. She had to keep telling me that we should have left with the Waldens. I loved her so much, but in my anger I was cruel in what I told her.

"Nathan, it's still not too late. We could pack up and find a claim somewhere east of here, where there is at least some civilization."

"Becca, have you seen any Indians around here?"

"I see no one around here—no one except Hannah and Carl. If we had left with the Waldens…"

"Becca! The Waldens are all dead!" I knew as soon as I said it that it was harsh, but a man can only take so much nagging.

Becca looked at me like I was a stranger, "What? What did you just say?"

"Look Becca, I tried to tell you the other day when Skinner showed up. But you stomped off and wouldn't talk to me."

We were both sitting down, or I think she might've fainted. Her sigh was so deep, I didn't think she had any breath left in her. Then I watched as her face turned red. Her fists were clenched when she got up suddenly, ran outside, and started vomiting. I followed her, but I kept my distance. It was plain to see she didn't want me too close.

When she finished, she wiped her mouth with the back of her hand and stared at me.

"Tell me what happened," she demanded. "I want to know it all. I want to know how long you've known it." She stopped talking and stood with her hands on her hips.

"Carl told me after he and Hannah went to town for our letters."

"Go on."

"They were massacred by a band of Indians. That's where the Indians have been. They've been attacking east of us. Becca, if we'd have been with them…" I couldn't say it. I thought she should be able to see it.

"Does Hannah know?"

"Carl said she knew some of it."

"But we laughed, we had such a good time, and she didn't say anything."

"I…"

"Stop. Don't say anything else right now, unless you have more secrets you've been keeping from me?"

I shook my head.

Becca didn't look well. The color was gone from her face. She was so angry she was shaking. I knew how much I'd hurt her when tears started rolling down her cheeks. I wanted to comfort her. I started toward her.

"Don't touch me!" she screamed, before she turned and walked toward the creek.

70

Rebecca's diary…

July 29, 1868—I am ill every morning now. I've entrusted no one but the animals with my secret. I miss Rusty so much, but Nathan says his odor will take a long time to fade away. I know my stomach cannot tolerate the odor right now. At least the wind calmed last night and I can enjoy a morning without its constant roar.

Hannah…

The wind and heat was takin' its toll on ever'thing. I was glad my garden and the saplin's was close to the creek, for I had to haul water to them ever' day. It was 'specially hard workin' against the wind. But I learned the wind was God's way of makin' the summer sun bearable, as one day it quieted. It was so still, even the thinnest blades of grass didn't move.

My chickens wandered around the yard with their beaks hangin' open and their wings draggin' on the ground. The poor things had near quit given us much in the way of eggs anyway, and that day I found none at all.

Bossy was hardly givin' us any milk either. That day when I milked her there was no wind to give her relief from the flies, and they was bitin' her so bad that she kept swishin' her tail and hittin' me square in the face. I thought I'd be smart, so I grabbed her tail and held it in the bend of my knee whilst I milked her. I was just 'bout finished when she lifted her back leg to kick a horse fly off her belly. As her leg came back down, she kicked the bucket and I jumped back so fast I went over backwards.

I was layin' there on the ground, wonderin' if I broke any of my bones when I heard Rebecca's voice callin' in the distance.

"Hannah!"

Somethin' was wrong. I got myself up off the ground and seen her walkin' fast to the soddy.

"Over here," I yelled.

We hurried to meet each other. She was all out of breath, her face was tear stained, and her eyes was wild with fear.

"Where are the men?" she asked as she gasped for air. "I have to find Nathan—it's Molly—I think it's her time, and something's not right."

71

Rebecca's diary…

July 30, 1868—I named Molly's calf Patches. He is strong and healthy, but I found Molly's suffering almost impossible to watch. I am fraught with fear. What if there is no one near when my own time comes?

Hannah…

Only minutes afore, there was no wind. But when Rebecca come racin' to fetch me, the wind picked up. By the time she told me what was wrong, it was blowin' strong. It helped to give some relief from the blisterin' heat, but when me and Rebecca hollered at the men, our voices was carried away.

The men was cuttin' prairie hay up on the hill.

"Let's go help Molly," I said.

"But Hannah, I don't know what to do," Rebecca said.

"I'll tell you." I looked at where the men was workin'. "It'll take too long to fetch them. Sounds like Molly needs a hand now."

Molly's pitiful bellows was growin' weaker by the time we got to her side. I helped my Carl's daddy with deliverin' a calf once. We lost the little heifer that time, and I was determined Molly wouldn't have the same fate.

"Rebecca," I said, whilst tryin' to catch my breath. "I need a rope."

Rebecca didn't move. It was like she was paralyzed as she stared at the poor cow.

"Rebecca!" I screamed. "Get me a rope. Hurry!"

She moved then, and when she come back with a rope, she turned her head away as she held it out to me.

I got off my knees and grabbed her by the shoulders. "Rebecca, I'm gonna need help. Either you help me, or you've got to fetch the men."

Her eyes looked down to where Molly was layin' on the ground. The calf's front hooves and part of its legs was stickin' out of Molly's rear-end. Rebecca looked sick.

"Tell me what to do," she muttered.

"Look at me, not at Molly," I said, as I tied the rope around the slippery legs of the calf. "We need to pull when Molly's belly moves."

"Won't we hurt her?"

"Rebecca, trust me and just do like I say. We have to help her get her calf out."

She nodded, swallowed hard, and picked up the rope. I got in front of her and told her when we needed to pull. It was slow, but whenever Molly's belly got tight, we pulled and worked with her.

"I see a nose," Rebecca yelled over my shoulder.

Molly bellowed. Corky had been standin' back, watchin' us. He started to bark.

"Hush, Corky," I said. He set back on his haunches and waited.

"Pull... pull."

As we pulled, the head came out a little further. I reached up and pulled back some of the goo from the calf's face. Molly's belly gave a good push and the calf slid out onto the grass.

Rebecca was standin' behind me. She gave a little holler, then she turned her head and vomited.

"We did it, Rebecca," I said.

She nodded, still bent over, and as soon as she was done, she stood up and gave me a weak smile.

I wiped more slime off the calf's nose and stuck my fingers in his mouth. He opened his eyes and started to suck on my fingers. I wanted to celebrate the victory, but I knowed there was more to do.

"Rebecca, we have to get Molly up," I said.

"Can't she rest a while?"

"She's got to get up right away or she'll hurt herself and keep on tightenin' her belly."

But try as we might, Molly didn't want to get up. Corky's started whinin'. It gave me an idea.

"Corky, sic em," I yelled. I pointed to the calf.

He jumped at the newborn and started barkin'. That got Molly's attention. She was up and standin' over her baby as fast as I called Corky off. She started lickin' the slime off her calf right away, and I finally took a deep breath and relaxed.

I looked over at Rebecca, thinkin' she'd be pleased with it all. A deep frown crossed her pale face. She looked down at her hands, and then at mine. Her nose crinkled up.

"I've got to get cleaned up," she said, as she turned away from me and headed for the creek.

72

Rebecca's diary…

July 31, 1868—The wind is back again. There is no escape from it. Even in the dugout, it whistles and roars all day. How I hate it. How I hate this place.

August 1, 1868—I've hidden my diary. I must find some way to convince Nathan to let me leave. I cannot live here much longer.

August 2, 1868—I found the most beautiful little patch of wildflowers today. I picked some and put them in my hair, but they wilted to nothing by the time I got home. Nothing of beauty can last long on the prairie.

Carl…

I seen Rebecca settin' on the ground on a little knoll, not far from where she'd staked Molly for the day. I thought maybe she was sick at first. But when I walked closer, I could hear her hummin' the tune that my Hannah talked 'bout. When I got up aside her, I seen she was settin' in the middle of a patch of wildflowers.

"Oh, hello Carl," she said. "You must be looking for Nathan."

"Are you feelin' alright, Rebecca?"

"Why of course, Carl. Aren't these the loveliest flowers?" She smiled and swept her arm out over them. Her hair blew over her face and when she reached up and pulled it out of her eyes, I didn't like the look I seen there. It was like she'd took off a mask. Her face had turned hard.

"Out here where no one can appreciate their beauty. How wasteful," she said.

She stopped talkin' then and stared down at the flowers. I told her I was gonna talk to Nathan, but she didn't look up at me. It was like I wasn't there, standin' right aside her.

Nathan was in the far corner of his claim, cuttin' hay to lay up for the winter. I helped him for a bit, and when we took a little rest, I told him where I seen Rebecca. He took off his hat and wiped the sweat from his forehead.

"I'm worried, Carl," he said. "I'm thinking maybe it's been a mistake to think Becca's strong enough to live out here."

"You thinkin' on goin' back?"

It took a while afore he answered. "I don't know what I'm thinking," he said. He picked up the scythe and started sweepin' it on the prairie grass like he'd find the answer hidden there.

73

Rebecca's diary…

It's August, but I'm not sure what the day is. It's not important to me anymore.

I had Mother and Martha for tea today. Nathan walked in and spoiled the lovely party, but then he gave me a gift.

Nathan…

When I saw that Becca hadn't milked Molly that morning, I thought something was surely wrong. I walked back to the dugout to get the milk pail and what I saw, scared me. I knew I had to do something, even if it meant altering my own dream.

I heard Becca talking inside. I went in, thinking I'd tease her about talking to herself. It wasn't funny when I realized she was doing just that. She was pouring tea into the cups her mother had sent with her, smiling and talking like there were people on the other side of those tea cups.

"Would you like another cake?" she asked. She reached over and placed a biscuit on the table beside one of the teacups.

"Becca, what are you doing?" I startled her when I spoke.

She looked over to where I was standing. First she frowned, and then smiled. "Nathan, I have guests," she said. "Mother and Martha have joined me for tea."

Was she teasing me? There was no fun in the joke if she was. I waited. I was wishing I hadn't come in just then. I was considering what I should do, when she suddenly changed back into reality.

"I thought maybe Hannah was coming this morning," she said. "It looks like she won't. Now I'll have no one to help me drink the tea I've prepared."

Chills were running down my back, in spite of the heat of the day. Had she been teasing me? I didn't think she was. I said the first thing that came to my mind.

"Becca, would you like to go see your mother?"

First I saw a sparkle in her eyes that I hadn't seen for a long time. Then she smiled and ran into my arms.

"Oh, Nathan, how I've waited for you to say that."

~ 74 ~

Rebecca's diary…

Nathan has finally come to his senses. We are going home.

Nathan…

I got my Becca back the day I asked her if she'd like to see her mother. I'd not told her about the money her father had given me and I had a small cache left. It was meant for hard times, but I figured a visit to her mother might help her get through her rough times.

She misunderstood my intentions, and talked on and on of future plans when we moved home. I told her several times that I couldn't leave right then, that we would buy her a train ticket in Ellsworth, and she could see her mother while I stayed here and made improvements on our claim. She was packing things in her trunk as I spoke.

It was as though she didn't hear anything I was saying. She went about her chores that day, with no complaint. In fact, she was humming her song, over and over. I stopped explaining things to her and went about my chores too, ready for her anger when she realized what I'd been saying. It didn't come that day.

We laid in silence for a while when we went to bed that night. I thought surely Becca would see things different in the morning. Then right before she fell asleep, she yawned and said more to herself than to me, "I'm going to Hannah's in the morning to tell her she can have my stove. Hannah has always admired it."

Sleep was a long time in coming for me. I knew I had to make Becca understand I wasn't going to give up my claim. Hard as the work was, I loved working the land and knew our future was here. How could I convince my lovely wife?

As usual, I was awake before Becca. She stirred in my arms and woke up with a smile.

"Good morning," she said. "I had the best dream. I dreamed we were back home. Your father was so happy you came back that he gave the store over to you and William."

"Becca, I need to talk with you," I said.

"When are we leaving, Nathan?"

"Becca, when I asked you if you wanted to see your mother…" I hesitated, searching for the right words, "I meant only for a *visit*."

"But, I thought…" She didn't finish whatever she was going to say. I could feel her body tense. She lay there for a minute in cold silence before she flung herself out of bed.

I had emphasized the word visit. Had I spoken too harshly?

"Becca, we need to talk about this," I pleaded.

She turned back toward me. The morning light was dim, but I could see her face turn hard as stone. Staring, saying nothing, she stood for a long time, looking at me like I was an animal that might attack her.

"Becca," I tried again.

She turned and marched out of the dugout. I thought it best she work off her anger at me.

Hannah...

It was early in the mornin' when Rebecca come over. The sun hadn't chased away all the shadows yet. It had been a quiet night. The wind was just startin' to pick up a little, but the dew was still heavy. Corky's ears perked up and when he seen Rebecca his tail started waggin'. He barked once, then raced off to meet her.

It was when I seen how fast Rebecca was walkin', that I knowed somethin' wasn't right. I let the chickens out of their pen and hurried her way.

I never seen her in such a state of mind afore. She was talkin' afore I even got to where I could hear what it was she was sayin'. Her words come out so fast I couldn't make much sense of them.

"I can't do it anymore, Hannah. You'll have my stove. Martha and Mother didn't see how he is. They were here you know. We had tea yesterday. It was so lovely. Then he said I could see Mother. Now he says I can *visit*. Visit! I want to go home. Will you take care of Rusty for me? And Molly too? Martha is so happy now."

I didn't know what to do with her. Her words was so confused. She was walkin' in little circles as she talked. I was scared for her. Carl heard her too. He come up by her side. Whilst she was spittin' out words, Carl started talkin' to her in the same voice he uses for the animals when they get riled.

He kept talkin' that way and leadin' her to the soddy. We'd not ate our breakfast yet, so he stayed by her side whilst I cooked. Then I seen somethin' I'll never forget. She calmed right down, ate breakfast, and started actin' like herself again.

After we ate, she thanked me for breakfast and said she needed to get home and milk Molly.

"Mind if I walk along?" Carl asked her. "Me and Nathan need to talk."

Carl...

I walked with Rebecca back to the Carter place. She stopped suddenly and vomited. When I asked her if she was alright, she straightened and started walkin' again.

"I'm fine," she said, and then she smiled. She seemed to be fit and in her normal state when we reached the dugout. She glanced inside and said, "I don't know where Nathan is." Without even a so-long, she grabbed the milk pail and took off to where Molly was grazin'.

I went to find Nathan, though I wasn't sure what I was gonna tell him.

75

Rebecca's diary...

It is the first or second week of August, I think. I don't know why I cannot comprehend what day in August. I am sure of nothing. Nathan has said I may visit my mother. He treats me like a child. I must be careful of my words now. If I am able to find a way to escape from this life, I shall never come back. I can trust no one. Carl came to talk with Nathan this morning, but he didn't tell me anything. Why am I, always the last to know what is going on?

Carl...

It was a job findin' Nathan that day. He was a long ways from the dugout, settin' on the creek bank, starin' at some bushes. He didn't even look up at me when I got close, he just kept starin' at the bushes. The wind had picked up enough to carry the noise away from me until I got up close. Then I heard and seen a pitiful sight. I set down aside Nathan and stared too. I noticed he had his rifle by his side.

"It happened a couple weeks ago," he said without lookin' my way. "He tangled with a skunk."

"I seen it afore. It ain't a purty thing."

"I've kept him away from Becca the last couple of days. I used the excuse that he still had the odor on him. She's so angry at me, I don't think she even suspected anything else."

I was thinkin' she was more than angry, but I couldn't lay that on my friend's shoulders right then. "You need me to do the particulars?" I asked.

"No. I can at least do that for him."

He got up like an old man and walked slow, over to where he'd tied the animal up. Rusty was snarlin' and had near choked hiself tryin' to pull free. There was foam drippin' from his mouth. I had to turn my head away when Nathan did the deed. I jumped at the crack of the rifle. Words couldn't help much, but I got up, put my arm on Nathan's shoulders, and said them anyway.

"He had to be put down."

Nathan nodded. "I don't know how Becca's gonna take this."

"I'll help you bury him."

76

Nathan…

When Carl and I got back to the dugout Becca was writing in her journal. She closed it quick when I went inside. Carl didn't come in with me, but went to fetch my shovel. I'd told him where I wanted to bury Rusty.

"Becca, I need to tell you something," I said.

"I'm going to visit my mother," she replied.

"Yes. Yes, I think that's a very good idea, but…"

"I'm going to do it soon, if I have to walk to Ellsworth by myself."

"Becca, this isn't about that." The eyes that I'd always loved to look into were cold and there was no trust in them. I continued, "It's about that skunk that took after you a couple weeks ago."

"Rusty saved me, you know. If it hadn't been for Rusty, that nasty creature would have attacked me," she said. Her words were defiant. "I know you said he still smells, but surely it's not that bad. I want to see him before I leave. I've written a letter to Mother. Do you think I might arrive back in Eaton before the letter does?"

"Becca, I…"

"You shot that nasty varmint, didn't you?"

"Becca, that nasty animal had rabies," I said.

"Yes, and you killed it."

"Becca, Rusty was bitten. He had rabies too," I said. Her face twisted as she took in my words. She shook her head to clear her thoughts. I started toward her, to try to comfort her in some way.

"No!" she screamed. "No! No! No!"

I grabbed her then and held on to her. I expected tears, but there were none. She took long hard breaths and pulled away from me.

"I don't believe you. I have to see him."

"I had to put him down, Becca. He was suffering."

She looked at me like I'd gone mad.

"I have to see him!" she demanded.

"Carl's here," I said. "He's digging a grave for him."

She threw her journal down and walked out the door. She saw Carl off in the distance and started screaming at him to stop as she ran in his direction.

Carl...

I had part of the dog's grave dug when I heard Rebecca's voice. She was runnin' my way. By the time she got to where I was, she had that wild look in her eyes that I seen earlier that mornin'. I held my arm out to stop her from goin' closer to the dog.

"Rebecca, you can't touch him. Rabies is a dangerous thing."

She fell down on her knees aside me. Real slow like, she looked up at me. I seen that look afore—in the eyes from men at war.

"You helped Nathan, didn't you," she accused me.

"There was nothin' he could do, Rebecca."

"You helped Nathan keep him away from me. You helped Nathan take away my best friend."

Nathan stood aside her, lookin' helpless.

"He'll not be buried here," she said. "I want him to be over there, where the wildflowers are."

Nathan shook his head real slow and shrugged.

"He'll be buried with the wildflowers," Rebecca said again.

"Can you show me where?" I asked.

She nodded and stood up. Lookin' ahead, she led the way to the little knoll where no sod was yet broken. It was the patch of flowers that I'd seen her settin' in afore. She marched to the middle of the flowers and pointed down.

"Here," she said.

It's where we buried him. And when we was done, she asked us to leave. I didn't think she should be alone, but Nathan turned and walked away. I followed him. He never looked back, but I did. Rebecca was layin' on top of the ground where we'd buried her friend.

77

Hannah...

My Carl come back that day and told me all that happened at the Carter place. He shook his head at the sadness of it all and said he thought maybe Rebecca needed another woman to talk to. As soon as we finished our noon meal, I went to see her.

As I got closer I seen her at the place Carl said they'd buried the dog, but Nathan was settin' outside the dugout with his head in his hands.

"Hannah, I don't know what to do," he said to me as I walked up. "She won't come back in now, but she was here."

"I'll go talk to her," I said.

"You need to see inside first." He nodded his head at the dugout.

I went inside the dark dugout and stood for a minute to let my eyes get used to the change.

"I found her in here," Nathan said. He was standin' in the doorway, blockin' any sun that might come in. "She came back for awhile, and after she did this, she ran back out to the grave. I can't get her to come back."

He moved the rest of the way inside. As the sunlight come in, I seen things I didn't want to see. There was big chunks of sod chopped out of the walls. Dirt and grass covered almost ever'thing inside. Rebecca's mendin' basket was chopped into little pieces. Her trunk was open and the insides was spilled onto the mess on the floor. The fine little tea towels that Rebecca's mother had wrapped her special tea cups in, was there in the dirt, all hacked up. The wood shelf that had been above the stove, was layin' in splintered pieces on the floor. Near ever'thing in the dugout was destroyed.

It was pitiful to watch Nathan, as he bent down and picked up a piece of broken china from one of Rebecca's teacups. His face was full of pain. He looked out the doorway where he could see Rebecca still layin' on Rusty's grave.

"Hannah, I don't know what to do," he uttered.

78

Nathan...

Hannah went with me to bring Becca back to the dugout. She didn't fight Hannah like she had me, but I don't think she could have resisted anyone just then. She'd been lying on that mound of fresh dirt for hours. Her dress was torn, her lips were cracked and bleeding, and her hair was tangled and filled with dirt.

Hannah was ever so gentle with her.

"Rebecca dear, you must come in from out of the sun," she said. Hannah then reached down and helped her up. Becca got up and let Hannah guide her back home. I felt helpless to know what to do. A fear like I'd never known was growing inside of me when I looked into her eyes. There was no light there. The eyes that had always held me captive were gone, empty as a dried up locust shell.

Hannah...

I cleaned her up as best I could, but try like I might, I couldn't get Rebecca to take even a sip of water.

"Maybe, if you could get me her brush, I could get some of these tangles and dirt out of her hair," I said.

Nathan nodded and poked 'round 'til he found her hairbrush half stickin' out of a hole in the wall where the shelf had been. He handed me the brush and whilst I was brushin' out Rebecca's hair he started to pick things up. I looked over at the bed in the corner of the room. It was full of dirt and had holes chopped in it. I knew it was none of my business to say so, but I did anyway.

"Nathan, maybe she could stay with me and my Carl tonight," I said.

He looked around the room like he couldn't believe what he was seein'. "I'd be much obliged," he said. "I'm not sure where to start here."

"She needs to see a doctor, Nathan."

"I know." He sighed real deep. His shoulders drooped like an old man's. "It's getting to be late in the day. I'll get the buckboard and take you up on your offer for the night."

Carl...

It was late in the day when I seen the buckboard comin'. Corky started barkin' different than his normal bark. It was like he could sense somethin' wrong.

"Okay, you old hound, go meet them," I said. The dog hesitated a bit afore he took off.

I had a feelin' it was gonna be bad news when I seen it was my Hannah drivin' the buckboard with Rebecca settin' aside her. Nathan was walkin' behind them, leadin' Molly. Still, it was a shock to see how bad off Rebecca was.

Whilst Hannah got our supper, Rebecca set outside the soddy, not movin' a bit. She looked like a statute settin' there.

Whilst me and Nathan tended the animals, I didn't say much. I let him tell me at his own pace, how Rebecca tore up the dugout.

"She must have been in a terrible rage," he said.

I said nothin'. The man was hurtin' for his wife.

"I'd be much obliged to you if you'd take over the care of Molly," he said. "I'm gonna see what the doctor in Ellsworth says first. I may need to take her back to...hell, I don't know what I'm gonna do." He looked off to his claim and shook his head and muttered, "It may be a long while."

He didn't need to say more. I understood.

"Anything I got on the place, just use it if you want, and feel free to any crops that might be coming in while I'm gone."

"Maybe it won't come to that," I said.

79

Nathan...

It surely was a fact that we were all feeling low. I know how much Carl and Hannah loved Becca too. So I didn't argue with Hannah when she offered to have Becca stay with her in the soddy that night. Carl said he'd be fine sleeping under the stars again. I made a bed for the two of us under the buckboard.

The wind died down when the sun left for the day and the night turned peaceful. Carl wasn't a big talker, but he was a mighty fine listener, and lying there under the stars with the beauty of the prairie night all around us, I talked to him like I used to talk to my brothers when I was a child. I even told him how Becca always reminded me of an angel.

"She is a fine lookin' woman," Carl murmured.

He started snoring a little right after he said that, but I kept on talking. A cloud moved out of the moon's way and a coyote yipped in the distance. Corky was lying over by the soddy's doorway and he gave a little woof.

"She doesn't see what I see out here," I said. I knew Carl wasn't listening anymore, but I needed to say the words out loud. I needed to try to understand without blaming myself for what happened to her. I thought of Rusty. I couldn't watch him suffer the way he was before I pulled that trigger, and now my Becca had the same look in her eyes. I didn't know what I would do if the doctor couldn't help her.

"I hate to see Becca suffer so," I said.

I guess I was all talked out. I finally fell asleep.

Hannah...

I fed the men, and I ate a bite, but Rebecca clamped her lips tight for both food and water. I got her to lay down, but I don't think she closed her eyes even once. I finally went to bed too and dozed off. I'd been asleep for a bit when I realized Becca was settin' up in bed. I set up aside her.

"Rebecca?" I said.

I don't remember anything then 'til my Carl was aside me. I was laying on the dirt floor and my head hurt.

Carl...

Corky's yelp woke me up. Then there was a deep growlin' that made me knock my noggin on the bottom of the buckboard. It was like no sound I'd ever heard afore.

My first thought was, it was Indians. It wasn't Indians. It was Rebecca. The moon was bright enough to let me see her runnin' straight for the buckboard. Her arms was raised over her head. Then I seen it—she had an axe in her hands. I scrambled out from under the other side of the wagon. I got a good hold of Nathan's overalls and I pulled. The axe come down where he'd been layin'. It stuck into the ground and whilst Rebecca was workin' it back out, I ran around the side of the wagon. She had the axe raised again. When she seen me, she come my way.

Nathan had woke hiself up enough that he run around the other end of the wagon and grabbed her from behind. How that little bitty woman had so much strength, I couldn't figure, but it took the two of us to wrestle the axe away from her. I don't know how she could make any noise after havin' no water all day, but there was a deep growl comin' from deep inside her.

When I seen that Nathan had a good hold on her, I let go. Corky was raisin' a ruckus inside the soddy.

"I got to see to Hannah," I said.

I stumbled over my Hannah when I went inside. She moaned as I fumbled around gettin' the lantern lit, and by the time I could see where she was, she was settin' up on the floor.

"Carl," she said. "What happened?"

I grabbed both of her hands in mine. "Are you okay?" I asked.

"My head hurts, but…"

I looked her over. I seen no blood. "Thank the Lord, my Hannah's safe," I said.

"Carl, what happened?"

I shook my head. "It's Rebecca."

I helped Hannah up. She was unsteady on her feet, and she had a big old goose egg on her head, but otherwise she seemed to have no wounds.

"I need to see about Nathan," I said.

"I'm comin' too," Hannah said.

We walked outside together, with me holdin' on to her so she might not fall. Nathan and Rebecca was on the ground together. He was holdin' her in his arms, rockin' back and forth. As we got closer, Nathan just kept on rockin'. There was no fight in Rebecca anymore, and there wasn't nothin' any of us could do for her. Hannah started weepin' real soft then. Rebecca was gone.

THE PRICE PAID

✛✛✛✛✛

There were only three mourners that came to the grave to help lay Rebecca in her final resting place that day.   They recited the 23rd Psalm before they covered her with prairie soil. She had no coffin.

✛✛✛✛✛

Rebecca Louise (Martin) Carter
born on September 9, 1851
died on August 10, 1868

✛✛✛✛✛

80

Nathan...

I remember very little of the day I buried Becca. If she had died back in Ohio, she could've had a proper funeral. I remember thinking that I never should've brought her into this land. If only I could've gotten her to a doctor, maybe then...

I think I told Carl I needed some time alone. I thought maybe if I was alone that I could weep. I wanted to. But the lump in my throat couldn't be swallowed. I had no tears. I thought maybe I would go mad like Becca had.

Hannah...

My mama always taught me and Sarah that tears was not to be wasted. She also said they was needed when a loved one passes. She said they helped wash away some of the grief. I had always heeded Mama's words and had never been one to weep when things didn't go my way, so tears never come easy for me. I shed a few when Rebecca passed, but for some reason they didn't come when we buried her.

"She'll be put to rest beside Rusty," Nathan said.

"She'd like that," was the only words I could find.

So whilst the men was diggin' her a proper grave, I went to the dugout where Nathan took her body. I found the quilt Rebecca had folded away on the corner of where her bed was. It was covered in dirt, but only had one little place where she had chopped on it. I wrapped it 'round her and waited with her 'til Nathan come and carried her out to her grave.

"I'll help you, Nathan," Carl offered. But Nathan shook his head and picked her up by hiself and carried her all the way without stoppin' once. When he laid her in the grave, I started in with sayin' a Psalm. Nathan and Carl said it too. When we finished, Nathan covered her with prairie soil.

"I never got to tell her good-bye," Nathan said. "I need some time to tell her that."

We left Nathan to grieve by hiself. We walked past the dugout and I tried to think of all the good times I spent with Rebecca since I knowed her. We hadn't said much to each other. Then my Carl started talkin'.

"I don't think Rebecca ever liked this land," he said.

I didn't tell him what I knowed to be a fact. Rebecca had told me many times how much she hated the land. I never told Carl that she'd wished her and Nathan had stayed in Ohio. She even told me that sometimes she wished she'd not married him.

"I had lots of beaus that my mother would have liked me to marry," she'd said.

It would've served no purpose to tell anyone that now. The men took pride in makin' a go of it on our homesteads. I guess maybe I should've told Rebecca that. I remember thinkin' at the time of her complainin' that she would feel different after she was here for awhile. It was harder for her than it was for me though. Maybe her roots was all back in Ohio and she just couldn't transplant.

I was glad I didn't say more 'bout Rebecca's feelin's that day. Carl usually keeps things inside hiself, but that day he told me things I don't think he ever told anyone afore.

Mostly I just listened as he told me why he picked the land we was on. He didn't like to talk of the war. But that day he told me 'bout a boy named Lucas that he held in his arms when the boy was dyin'. And he said he come to this place because of him.

I guess I have that boy to thank for my life out here on the prairie, 'cause I love Carl and this is where Carl has to be. It was a strange feelin' to know how Rebecca felt—like this land was against us all, and then to know how Carl felt—like this land saved him.

81

Carl...

When I told my Hannah I didn't think Rebecca ever liked the land, she didn't say nothin' at first. Then she finally asked, "Do you think Nathan will make it on his own?"

"I do," I told her. "I think he's strong."

I was just as worried about Hannah as I was Nathan. The prairie was a lonely place for her, even though she never complained. I looked over at her as we walked side by side, and thought how she had total trust in me to make all the right decisions. She left her family to follow me to where I wanted to go and she never once questioned me 'bout it. I understood how much Hannah had given up to be with me.

Maybe my Hannah didn't love the land so much either. I'd never forgive myself if Hannah would ever come to the same fate as Nathan's Rebecca. Maybe it was time for me to tell my wife why I had picked this part of Kansas to homestead on.

We both slowed our steps, and I told her what was in my heart. I shared some ugly memories with her that day, 'cause I couldn't explain it without tellin' her some of the bad with the good. After I'd said my piece and we was close to the soddy, Hannah kept walkin' 'til we ended up down by the creek. We set down to rest ourselves and listened to the water trickle over the stones in the creek, afore she said anything.

"I won't lie to you Carl, it's hard sometimes. And I miss Sarah, and Mama, and Daddy something fierce.

And now with Rebecca gone it's gonna be even lonelier."

Then she went on with a real soft voice, and what she said made me near bust with love for her.

"But I seen the look on your face when we stopped our wagon at this very spot, and the first time since you come back from fightin' in the war, you looked at peace. I seen this land did somethin' good for you. You looked whole again."

Hannah took a deep breath and went on. "When Jacob didn't come back to Sarah, I felt blessed to have you come back. But you wasn't the same man that you was afore you went. The only time you didn't have that pained look on your face was when you talked about this place you found out in the middle of Kansas."

We set there for a long time thinkin' on each other's words. When we got up and walked back to the soddy, we both looked north to Nathan's place and seen we had a new worry Much further north of there, we seen five different patches of smoke curlin' into the sky.

82

Hannah...

It wasn't long afore we learned where the fires come from. Skinner come ridin' in from the north. As soon as he got close enough I seen his face, I knowed the news he brung wasn't good.

"How-do, Hannah," he said whilst still settin' in the saddle. "I need to talk to Carl."

"He took the corn knife with him," I said. We both looked to the corn field.

"Sure enough, I see his hat," Skinner tried for a smile then, but it didn't look right. He got down off his horse and added, "I think you'd best hear what I have to say too."

We walked over to where Carl was tyin' corn stalks into a bundle. When he seen us both walkin' his way, he stopped his chore and met us.

"What brings you our way, Skinner?"

"I'll not waste your time Carl. I know you have a fresh hurt, as I talked to Nathan and seen Rebecca's grave."

Carl nodded.

"I've not done much in the way of talkin' peace with the Indians." He stopped and looked in the direction he come from.

"We seen all the smoke yesterday," Carl said.

"It was them livin' on the Spillman Creek. Cheyenne warriors raided 'em yesterday, burnin' ever'thing those people built. They captured a couple women and they killed ever' white man they could find." Skinner was lookin' at the ground.

A cold fear set inside me. My mouth was dry as prairie hay and my stomach churned. I was grateful when I felt my Carl's arm come 'round me.

"Some are goin' to Fort Harker for protection, but I'd not advise tryin' to get to Lincoln Center, as most of the raids are takin' place north and east of here."

We was walkin' as we talked, and as soon as we got back to the soddy, Skinner said he had business in Fort Harker hiself.

Carl...

Whilst Skinner ate supper with us we made plans to go to Fort Harker with him. Hannah was beside herself with worry for the animals.

"We'll be no good to them if we're raided too," I said. "If all goes well, we'll be back in a couple days. They can survive that long without us."

After supper me and Skinner went to tell Nathan of our plans, but we couldn't convince him to come with us.

Nathan...

I suppose I lost all reasoning those first couple of days after Becca was gone. I couldn't get past the grief of losing her. I remember telling Carl I'd watch over his animals while he and Hannah went to Fort Harker for safety. If Becca was alive we would have gone with them, but without her, what difference did it make? I couldn't leave her now—I couldn't leave her all alone because I was afraid of an Indian raid. I think I would have welcomed an Indian putting an arrow in me. Anything would have been better than reliving the night my own wife tried to kill me with an axe. I couldn't get the image out of my mind.

I had to force myself to go back into the dugout. Somewhere in the chaos, Becca had a tin print of the two of us together. I needed it to remember her as the lovely bride she was. Her trunk was overturned. When I set it back up I was disappointed that it was empty. I carried it outside. Then I carried anything still usable outside, putting the smaller things into the trunk. When there was nothing left to salvage, I sifted through all the bits and pieces again. My search was in vain. I found no print. I hadn't seen her diary she wrote in every day either. She had some precious stationary and her pen that had been ground into the floor, but where was the tin print and her diary? And where was her Bible? And then a thought struck me.

I unhooked the stovepipe and wrestled the stove outside. Would she have burned the things that reminded her of me? The tin type wouldn't have burned up completely. I dug in the ashes. There was nothing there either.

83

Hannah…

Skinner no more than got us to Fort Harker than I seen him ridin' out again with a bunch of soldiers. We heard of the atrocities the Indians had done to people, but the Army was tellin' us the Indians had moved on east. Other settlers had come to the fort too. They told how they had escaped with their lives, but nothin' else. Some said there was nothin' to go back to. One of the women had the same look we seen in Rebecca—afore she left us.

I seen a change come over my Carl. It wasn't the fear I seen in most people's eyes, it was the way he was lookin' at the people 'round us—like he seen all this afore. When he walked off by hiself, I followed him. He was lookin' out to the prairie in the direction of our claim. I walked up behind him and thought hard afore I said what I did.

"I want to go back," I told him. He turned around and looked at me.

"To Illinois?" he asked.

I shook my head real slow, and Carl got my meanin'. He nodded. Then he looked into my face like he'd find the true answer there, and he asked me, "You sure?"

"I'm sure."

We packed up early the next mornin', stoppin' in Ellsworth only long enough to post letter's to our folks back home, and to pick up letters that was waitin' for us. We'd left our place in such haste, that both of us forgot to get our spectacles, and the wagon jostled us 'round so, that it was not possible for me or Carl to read our letters. We'd not have much of a chance of survivin' an attack, if we got caught out in open prairie, so Carl drove Bill and Barney hard.

When they slowed a bit, Carl slapped the reins and said, "I'm much relieved we don't see any signs of fires anywhere 'round today, but I'm mighty anxious to get home."

It seemed a long day, but we made it home afore dark. Corky was there to greet us and ever'thing looked the same as afore we left, 'cept Rebecca's cook stove was settin' inside the soddy.

We hurried as we tended the animals. Then afore we ate, we both got our spectacles and opened our letters. Carl read his letter first. It was filled with good news and the handwritin' told us his sisters had took turns with the writin'. I could almost see them settin' with their heads together, arguin' over who could write the best news.

Carl smiled at me when he finished. Then he seen the difficulty I was havin' and asked if he should read my letter. I reached up and carefully took off my spectacles. They didn't seem to help much anymore.

Carl took the letter and read to me.

My Dearest Sister Hannah,

> *I hope you are well. I want desperately to hear from you but it concerns me that maybe your eyesight has gotten worse, though I pray you can still write letters. The Taylor family has been ever so kind to me. They helped move me back into town so that I can be with our daddy and our mama.*

The cough Daddy developed last winter has not ceased, and the doctor said he can do no more for him. Mama gives no mention of her own complaints, but is now frail in her worries over Daddy. How we all miss you and pray for you and Carl ever' day. Carl's sisters come by to help me ever' week. I am grateful for the happiness they bring with them. Me, Mama, and Daddy all send our love with this letter to you.
    Sarah

Carl put his arm 'round me when he finished readin' and we both set in the quiet for a long time. We'd been so excited to read our letters that we missed seein' the brightest colors of the day's end, and darkness started to settle in for the night.

"I'll go over to Nathan's in the mornin'," Carl said, as he patted the place on his overalls where he had two more letters. One was from Rebecca's best friend, and the other was from her mama.

84

Nathan...

I didn't ever want to go back into the dugout again. I slept outside under the wagon bed at night and cooked my meals over an open campfire. The cooking stove sat in front of the dugout, reminding me of how I'd failed Becca. When she thought we were going back to Ohio she had said she wanted Hannah to have it, so I took it with me to the Taylor claim when I cared for their animals.

I wasn't sure what I would do if Hannah and Carl didn't come back. I even thought about going west, maybe as far as California, but then I looked over at Becca's grave, and I knew I couldn't ever leave her alone on the prairie. I vowed to make my claim work, or die at the attempt.

It wasn't the right time of the year to cut sod. The sun had baked the prairie all summer and there had been little rain to soften the soil, making it highly impractical to slice off slabs of earth. I did it anyway. I welcomed the pain it inflicted on my body, though it didn't help much with my sorrow.

It was late in the day when Corky let me know the Taylors were coming back. He barked when he heard what I couldn't hear, then he started off toward their place. He stopped and looked back in my direction. I suppose he was waiting for me to follow him.

"Go on," I said. "Go on home."

He took off lickety-split, not giving me another thought. I guess I hadn't given him much in the way of companionship while Hannah was gone.

It was almost dark by the time I ate some beans and bedded my aching body under the wagon. Tired as I was, it was long into the night before I went to sleep. I woke up just as the sun's first rays started the day.

Since I didn't have the Taylor's chores to do, I hitched up Jake and went to work cutting sod. It was mid-morning when Carl came by. My muscles were already causing me pain for the day, but instead of stopping and talking with my friend, I kept right on working. Carl walked along side me and we talked some. He told me all he'd heard about the Indians at Fort Harker.

"I've not had much time to worry about them," I said, finally stopping to catch my breath. I wasn't ready to talk with anyone just yet, so I turned and slapped the reins on Jake. He didn't move.

"Nathan…" Carl started to say more, but I ignored him and slapped the reins harder on Jake. He didn't move. That's when Carl had enough.

"Nathan, what the hell you gonna do when Old Jake drops dead? You gonna pull that sod cutter all by yourself?"

"Why should that be any of your concern?" I said before I thought.

"You want to kill yourself, that's your business, but that's a mighty faithful horse you're workin' to death."

My fist doubled up and took aim at Carl's face. If I hadn't got all tangled up in the reins, I might have made a real fool out of myself that day. I wanted to hit something so bad, that I almost hit the best man I knew.

My fist was doubled up when I got it loose from the reins. I punched it hard into the palm of my other hand.

I couldn't look at Carl after I did that. We both stood there with the sun beating down on us until Jake snorted. Carl went over to the animal and patted his neck. Something had just happened that I didn't understand. I felt like a real jackass, but for some reason the lump in my chest wasn't there anymore.

"Reckon I should be the one to show him some comfort," I said.

"Yeah, I reckon." Carl looked me in the eye and asked, "You feelin' any better now?"

I nodded.

He helped me unhook Jake's harness and we walked back to where I'd set up my camp. I told him why I'd given the cook stove to Hannah and why I couldn't go back into the dugout. I could tell that he understood. He promised we'd make a sturdy soddy for me before the winter set in. Then he looked uncomfortable and reached into his pocket.

"I've got somethin' for you," he said. He pulled out two letters. The lump came back and settled in my chest again.

85

Nathan…

When Carl went back to his place I pampered Jake and Polly. I tethered them and ran a currycomb over both of them. Becca had always been the one to do that. She loved those horses. She'd loved Rusty. She'd loved me once too. I'd turned that love into desperation. I asked too much from her. I couldn't picture the lovely face I'd once known. I could only see her coming at me with an ax. I could only see her when she was suffering. I didn't know if I would ever be able to forgive myself for what I'd done to her.

The lump in my chest was back, and the letters were making it grow harder until I couldn't get my breath. I finally went over and sat in the shade of the wagon bed. I pulled the letters out of my pocket and opened the one from Martha first. It was addressed to Mr. and Mrs. Nathan Carter. It was filled with happiness and plans that she and William were making for their wedding in September. I read that letter three times before I got up the courage to open the letter from Becca's mother, which was addressed to Mrs. Rebecca Martin Carter. It read…

> *My dear daughter Rebecca,*
> *I am frantic with worry as to whether you are still with the living. Your father had a copy of 'Kansas State Record' that he had hidden so that he thought I might not see it. The article of which I am speaking stated almost 200 people had been left destitute of provisions of clothing and*

bedding. It told of many atrocities the Indians have committed toward the white man.

If Nathan insists on staying in that uncivilized and barren place, I implore him to come to his senses and send you back to live with us until he can guarantee your safety. I pray daily for you.

Your Loving Mother

The lump grew until I thought my chest would bust wide open. I didn't even know I'd walked to Becca's grave until I realized I was reading the letter again, out loud, to her. I finished the letter and fell to my knees on her grave and I cried. Then I cursed God for my stupidity. I cursed my father for driving me away from my family. I cried some more.

When there were no tears left, I stood up and remembered the day Becca had mourned like I just had. It had been for Rusty, and I hadn't understood her pain. If I had understood her, maybe...

I knew I had to stop thinking that way, or Carl and Hannah would find me wandering the prairie, howling at the moon. I had to be a man again. I had a letter to write. How was I going to tell the Martins that their only daughter was never coming back to them? I couldn't tell them what had really happened to her—that she'd gone insane. Why should I hurt them more than necessary? I walked back to my camp wondering what I would say. The lump had finally been washed away with tears. There were no feelings in me anymore. There was only a great emptiness.

86

Hannah...

I missed the companionship of Rebecca. I tried to fill some loneliness for her, by readin' my Bible more. But my eyesight only let me read a bit, when there was plenty of light in the day, afore I had to give it up.

It was heartbreakin' to see what the loss of Rebecca was doin' to Nathan. I made extra biscuits and cornbread, and sent them home with him, 'cause he was thin as a stalk of corn. Now that I had Rebecca's stove, bakin' was made a lot easier for me.

When the days started gettin' cooler it turned our thoughts to our needs for our first winter on the prairie. We got enough from our crops that we wouldn't go hungry, but I worried 'bout having enough fuel to keep us warm. I gathered buffalo chips and worked at makin' twists near ever' day, whilst Carl and Nathan finished the walls of Nathan's soddy.

It was when Nathan set out in the buckboard to find ridge poles for the ceilin', that he met a neighbor that was only five miles from us. But it was a great disappointment to me to hear the man's wife was lost to a fever when their wagon train come out West.

"He does have a bull, though," Nathan said.

Our Bossy was past due for the needs of a bull, so my Carl took her and headed out to where the man told Nathan he lived. His name was Herman Tinkerman. Carl left our Bossy with him, and when he come back late in the day, he had stories 'bout the man.

"I can tell by his place that he's a hard worker," Carl said. "He said his friends call him Tinker, 'cause he likes to tinker with new things. He even dug a well for hiself already. He said he witched for the water."

I didn't like that. It sounded not quite right, but I trusted my Carl to be a good judge of a man's character, so I held my tongue.

Carl went to Nathan's the next mornin' to help him finish his soddy. When the men come home at noon to eat, they brung Molly with them.

"Keep her while Bossy is gone," Nathan explained. "I know you like to have milk to make your biscuits."

I was happy for it, but I wondered if Nathan would get so skinny he might blow away if he didn't have Molly's milk for his breakfast.

87

Nathan…

The nights were surely getting longer and colder by the time I got the soddy all done. I moved into the shelter, but without Becca beside me I was so lonely I could hardly wait for the sun to rise in the morning. Ever since that day I wept at Becca's grave, I started my day by going there to talk to her. Somehow it made me feel better and I wondered why I'd always been too busy to listen to her when she was alive.

In the last days of September, Carl brought Molly back. He was on his way to fetch Bossy. We talked about the man named Tinker. Carl said he'd promised to bust some sod for him, in payment for the use of his bull. He asked if I wanted to do the same. Then he changed the talk to that of family, and I got a pit in my stomach again.

"Hannah wants me to take a day off, afore winter sets in, to go to Ellsworth and see if there's mail," he said. "Her folks have been ill and I know she worries for them."

I had a chore to do. I could put it off no longer. "I need some supplies," I said. "I'd be more than willing to pick up your mail and any supplies you might need."

It was past time for me to do the task I'd been pushing away. "I'll go first thing in the morning," I said. "Do you have any stationery I might use to write a letter to the Martins?"

Carl looked down at his boots and said, "I'm sure my Hannah does."

When I saw Carl come home late in the day, I walked to his place. I ate supper with him and Hannah, got some writing paper from Hannah, and went straight home and wrote two letters. I started with a letter to my mother and William. I only told them that Becca had passed. I prayed they'd never ask me how it happened. Then I sat for a long time, summoning courage to write Fred and Carrie Martin a letter. Everything I wrote them was a lie, except for the part that their daughter was dead. I told them she had fallen and struck her head.

When I got back from Ellsworth two days later, Skinner was at the Taylor place. I gave Carl the letters I'd picked up for them. I'd also bought some fine tobacco, so Skinner and I stepped outside to smoke and give the Taylors some privacy while they read their letters. When I was in Ellsworth, I'd heard the news of the raid east of Lincoln Center on the Solomon River, so when Skinner told me the Indians had since broken up into small groups and made winter camps, relief washed over me.

"I'm thinkin' they won't be out raidin' agin in any great numbers 'til the spring," Skinner said. "I'll be your neighbor fer awhile. I'm beddin' myself down at the Walden claim fer the winter, unless I'm figurin' wrong and there's more trouble."

Carl came out of the soddy then. I asked him if the news was any better from Hannah's sister. He looked down and shook his head. We all stood quiet for a bit, until I offered him some of my tobacco.

"Hannah's dishin' up some beans, how 'bout we eat first? Then I'd sure enjoy it," he said.

Skinner left right after supper, Carl went outside to have his smoke, and I talked with Hannah until Carl came back into the soddy.

"I best be getting home, "I said. "Thanks for supper."

"You're welcome anytime," Hannah said. "I thank you for the sugar and the flour you bought us. We might treat ourselves with a cake one of these days. "

An awkward silence fell between us. Becca had been the one who always talked about making cakes.

"I'd like that," I finally said.

Hannah's eyes told me how much she missed Becca too.

"That'd be a really fine treat," I added.

88

Hannah...

When Nathan thanked me for supper, I felt bad I couldn't find the words to talk 'bout Rebecca. The hurt of losin' her was too fresh for all of us, but it didn't mean we wasn't thinkin' of her.

There was no need for him to thank me, for he brung me the gifts of some flour, sugar, and precious letters from our kin. But my heart was heavy with the news Sarah's letter contained. I couldn't read it in the dim lamplight, so Carl read it to me afore he went outside with Skinner and Nathan.

> *My Dearest Sister Hannah,*
> *I got your letter yesterday, and am sorry to hear of your friend's death. I imagine you must be lonely with no other women for neighbors. I remember how much you liked to listen to Cora and Elizabeth when we all worked together. They are both busy with their own families now, but they still take time to call on me and Mama. It gives a great lift to our spirits when they visit. Mama has succumbed to a great depression, for which I blame her constant worry over the health of Daddy. The doctor found a wheelchair for Daddy, that lets us get him into the fresh air much easier. Levi come one day too and helped me wheel him to his beloved*

orchard. I fear it may be the last time for him to see it, for his body gets weaker ever' day. His spirits are stronger than Mama's though, and he was pleased when your last letter told us that the saplin's he sent with you greened up. He's proud that you had such good fortune with your first year's garden too. With this letter we all send our love.
    Sarah

I busied myself again with gettin' supper on. I wanted to weep and wash some of the hurt away for my mama and daddy's poor health. It was a hard thing to understand that Mama was suffering from depression, for she was always so strong. She was the one that never approved of wastin' tears.

When Nathan and Skinner left and Carl come back inside, I asked him to read his sister's letter again. He asked if he should read Sarah's letter too. As much as I wanted to hear Sarah's words again, I didn't think my heart could take any more sadness that night. I shook my head and got ready for bed whilst he read the letter from Cora and Elizabeth. They was the ones that always wrote the Taylor news. I missed them near as much as I missed Sarah and my folks. The letter was filled with the good news of Cora and Elizabeth, as their houses would soon be overflowin' with children. It was such a blessin' to have Carl's family all well.

Me and Carl was both happy for them, but it made me long for a family that I knowed I'd never have. I said a silent prayer for all of them. Then I prayed my Carl would have no regrets of marryin' me, for I knowed I was barren.

89

Carl...

Skinner told us one of the Indian's winter camps was only ten miles distance from us. It was a place we'd not go near whilst they was there, and we hoped they'd not wander our way. It eased my mind some to think they'd not bother us durin' the winter.

We had some cold days of drizzle afore we had our first severe frost, and it made the chore of fall harvest an unpleasant one. Nathan shared his huntin' skills, by bringin' Hannah fresh meat. She fixed us some sturdy stews to warm our achin' bodies at supper time. It worked out good for us and for Nathan.

Both Nathan and Skinner was so much like family that I sometimes forgot they wasn't. And it wasn't unusual for Skinner to drop by at noon for some dinner. My Hannah was always prepared with enough for all of us. She never complained.

"When we're blessed to have enough to go 'round, it's no trouble to cook for more," she said. "Though I'd sure enjoy a woman's company now and then. Ain't much you men-folk talk 'bout that concerns me."

But I knew it to be untrue. I started talkin' on how to quarry limestone one day when both Skinner and Nathan was there sharin' a meal.

"I used to know a stone mason," Skinner said.

I wondered who he didn't know at one time or the other. He went on to answer some of the questions I had, and seemed knowledgeable on the subject. I seen Hannah was listenin' close to us men-folk that day.

Nathan hadn't said much whilst me and Skinner talked. He just nodded once in a while and seemed to be thinkin' hard on somethin'. When Skinner left to go back to his place, Nathan set for a bit longer. He was lookin' in Hannah's direction, but I don't think he was seein' her. His eyes was glistenin' in the lamplight.

"It was my dream for Becca." His voice cracked, "I promised her a fine house some day."

Hannah nodded but couldn't bring herself to look at Nathan.

We was all rememberin' a night we'd ruther have forgot. Nathan hadn't bothered to shave since Rebecca was gone and his beard grew wild. He'd been workin' hiself near to death ever' day, and he looked like he had eighty years on him instead of twenty. I knowed there was no words that would comfort him. I said nothin' as he raised his tired body up and shuffled to the door.

Hannah…

The day my Carl and Nathan picked for butcherin' the pig, we had our first snowflakes. They was workin' hard at the job when Skinner rode in with gifts for all of us.

"Got somethin' I think you'll like when you're holed up inside this winter," he said with a grin. Corky had his nose sniffin' in the air. When Skinner got off his horse and pulled three buffalo robes with him, Corky growled at him.

We laughed at the dog.

"Where'd you manage to get those?" I asked.

"The army brought me back here 'cause I know the Indians. Ain't nobody can work those hides like an Indian squaw. Course the army doesn't have to know where I got 'em," he added with a wink.

I didn't like that part of Skinner 'cause I didn't always know where he was comin' from, but when I put my cold hands inside that warm robe, I knew I'd be grateful for the gift. Skinner helped me carry the robes inside.

"These might help make up fer some of the meals you been cookin' fer me," he explained.

"There'll be fresh pork for supper," I said. "The men could use a hand though."

He laughed in the way I hadn't heard since we'd been on the wagon train. Then he went outside to help Carl and Nathan with the butcherin'.

It was a long day. By the time supper was over there was more snow on the ground and more was comin' down.

"I'd better get home and see to my animals," Nathan said. He wrapped hiself in one of the robes and headed out.

"I'd be much obliged if I could spend the night," Skinner said to me.

Carl winked at me whilst he said to Skinner, "You got a nice soft robe to lay yourself down on."

We all bedded down for the night. We figured we was as ready for the winter as we could be. Skinner threw one of the robes on the floor. In no time he was snorin' louder than I thought a man could snore. Me and Carl had ourselves a good laugh whilst we snuggled up in the other robe.

90

Nathan…

When the weather kept me from tiring my body with hard work, my nights were either sleepless, or filled with dreams of a Becca gone mad. I often woke up in a cold sweat, fighting with the ugly images—my fists striking into the darkness. My father found his way into my nightmares too, and I feared I would succumb to the same bitterness that plagued him. I lived a constant struggle with myself.

No matter how bleak and gray the days were, the animals had to wait for their care until I talked to Becca at her grave every morning. Then I'd chop ice at the creek, give them their feed, and milk Molly. I took milk to Hannah most every day, even though it often froze before I'd walk the three-quarter mile. I didn't realize how much I'd come to depend on Carl and Hannah for company, until it snowed enough to keep me at my own place for three days. I spent the time shelling corn, greasing Jake and Polly's harness, patching clothes, and cooking up a big mess of beans.

When I couldn't find anything else to occupy myself, I started talking to the walls. I knew I had to have someone for company. I wrapped myself in my buffalo robe and trudged through the deep snow to see Carl and Hannah.

Carl…

Daylight was short, but the days was mighty long. Some days the wind was so bitter cold it felt like needles jabbin' into bare skin. But no matter how cold it got, my

Hannah said she had to get outside ever' day. Whilst I tended the stock, Hannah took care of her chickens.

Hannah was missin' her family, but the only thing I ever heard her complain of was not havin' enough to do whilst we was cooped up inside. The light was often too poor for her to see, and though she tried to write letters to her sister, it become more and more troublesome to do the task.

She tried to read from the Bible too, but her eyes would blur, so she asked me to do the readin'. She liked the Psalms, her favorite bein' the 23rd, and I never understood why I should have to read it, for she knowed it by heart.

Bible' readin' was how we spent much of our time inside on those winter days. When I read the book of Jeremiah in the 29th Chapter and the 11th verse, I stopped, and I told her again how I thought God led me to this place.

"Maybe it was His plan for me," I said, "It gave me a future and a hope."

I looked over at my independent wife who was mendin' my pair of overalls whilst she listened to the passage I'd just read. The light was dim and she was squintin', but she just kept right on workin' until she poked herself with the needle. She stuck her finger in her mouth to suck the blood. I chuckled, and her eyes shot me the look that said I might mend my own clothes if I laughed at her.

"Woman," I said. "I'm sure of one thing 'bout God."

Her eyes narrowed. She took her finger out of her mouth and asked, "What's that?"

"I'm sure he blessed me the day you become my wife."

Hannah was settin' in a humble soddy. I knowed she was homesick for family. I knowed it was a hard life for her. Yet, she looked over to me and smiled, never seemin' to find fault with me. I felt like no man could be richer.

Hannah...

When Carl read the Bible, and we discussed its meanin', it reminded me of home, when our daddy read to us. Me and Sarah seen things so different sometimes, 'specially Bible readin'. But we was encouraged to talk things out. Even when we was little girls, both Mama and Daddy taught us to think for ourselves.

Ever'one we knowed said we was the spittin' image of one another, and we had much fun tryin' to fool people that Sarah was me and I was Sarah. Our differences come with our thinkin'. Most times we seen a different way on what Bible passages meant. So when Carl read and we talked on how we seen the meanin' of the Bible, it made me a bit homesick, but it helped to pass the long, lonely days of winter.

91

Carl...

Nathan come near ever' day that it was winter, and we never knowed when Skinner would show up. No matter how bad the weather, Nathan always went back to his place at night to tend to his stock, but Skinner made hiself at home with us, by sleepin' on one of the buffalo robes.

In spite of Skinner's raucous laugh, loud snorin', and gruff look, he was welcome company. Him and Nathan was our only visitors. Some of his stories wasn't made for a lady's ears, but my Hannah just shook her head at them. Instead of discouragin' his tellin' of them, her disapprovin' looks heartened him to tell more. I knowed if he went too far with his tales, she'd let him know how she felt.

When he'd leave, she'd shake her head and say, "I think he's got a good heart inside him."

Hannah...

Since my Carl hated killin' any livin' creature, it was Nathan that brought us meat for many a meal. On days when the weather was fair the men would take Bill and Barney and head for the quarry. It was the loneliness that I had a hard time with on those days. I went out to the quarry to watch them once and it set me to dreamin'. We'd have a fine house some day. I knowed it to be a long way off, but it was a good dream to have whilst I waited for the first signs of spring to show up.

It was one bitter cold day in February when Skinner come up with bad news of another Indian raid east of Lincoln Center by Mulberry Creek.

"I'd like to bed down with you folks for a day or two," he said. "There's safety in numbers, and it puts me a little closer to help you, if you need it."

Carl's eyes got a far-off look when they sought out his rifle by the doorway. He so hated the killin' done on both sides. Some of the settlers didn't think the Indians was anything but savages, yet Carl seen them as people who believed a different way.

We ate an early supper whilst the men talked 'bout what we'd do if we had a surprise visit from the Indians. Then Nathan went home alone to his place.

Nathan...

Carl thought it too bitter cold to work outside the day Skinner showed up with news of the Pawnee raid. Both Carl and Skinner were of the opinion that I should stay at the Taylor place that night too. But I had to tend to my stock. The truth I didn't tell them, was if there was trouble, I had to be where Becca was, even though I knew that thinking wasn't rational.

So when I went home and was lying in bed alone, I decided I was going to stay on my claim, make it work, and some day I'd build a fancy house in Becca's memory. Planning how I would build it and learning to quarry the stone, probably saved my life and my sanity. It was the only thing that got me through that first winter without Becca.

92

Hannah...

We heard no more 'bout Indian troubles for a while, though Carl stayed closer to the soddy. We was both gettin' restless with the winter days, and welcomed the mornin' we got up and seen the winds had shifted from the north to the south. There was a fresh smell of spring in the air, though the ground was winter cold. When I seen tiny buds beginnin' on my daddy's saplin's, I prayed there would be no more hard frosts.

Even the mice was venturin' out of their hidin' spots. One ran across the soddy floor and headed for the open door. I suppose he was checkin' out spring for hiself.

"Sic em," I yelled at Corky. But Corky paid me no heed, as he heard Skinner ridin' up just then.

What I seen next, struck my funny bone. Skinner jumped down from his saddle horse and ran after that varmint. He caught up with him and pounded his boot down on the top of the mouse.

It was the sight of seein' that big man go after that poor little creature. I couldn't remember the last time I laughed so hard.

"Damnation! I hate mice!" Skinner yelled out. Then he seen my look at his cuss word.

"I'm sorry for that Hannah, but I do hate those varmints."

I couldn't help myself, and I started laughin' again, 'til my sides hurt.

"Don't look like there's much left for Corky to munch on," I said with tears in my eyes. It was good to see that my cacklin' seemed to upset Skinner almost as much as his laughin' sometimes festered in me.

He finally reached in his pocket and pulled out letters. He held them in one hand as he crossed both arms over his chest.

"Don't suppose you can stop that ruckus long enough to see who these are fer?"

I stopped all gaiety. It was a long time since we'd gotten mail.

Carl...

Me and Nathan was up by the quarry when we heard Corky barkin' and seen that Skinner had come callin'. Since he showed up whenever there'd been trouble, we finished loadin' our wagon and hurried for home. When we got there we knew somethin' was wrong, as Skinner was down on one knee by Hannah's side. She was settin' on the ground lookin' poorly. I ran to where they was and seen the letter in her hands. She held the letter out for me to take, then set there, starin' straight ahead and lookin' at nothin'. I got my spectacles from inside the soddy. Then I read...

> *Dearest Sister Hannah,*
> *It is with a heavy heart that I write this news of Mama and Daddy's passing. Mama caught the consumption right after Christmas. She was better for a while. Then Daddy passed on and when I told Mama he was gone, I seen the light go from her eyes. She only lived ten days longer. I think she gave up. Mr. Jackson come to me the day of Mama's funeral. He offered me a*

*price for the house for only half of
what it is worth, but it was cash
money, so I accepted his offer. I've
had little time to mourn Mama and
Daddy, because Mr. Jackson's family
will be here from Philadelphia in the
early spring. He also wants most of
the furniture to stay with the house.
He is givin' me little money for it. I
argued that I would keep Mama's
rockin' chair and sewin' machine. I
will find some way to bring them with
me when I come to stay with you. I
hope I am welcome to stay with you
and Carl 'til I can find a place of my
own. Evert and Esther said I was
welcome to move back with them, but
I feel it is time to move on and care
for myself. I know you said the prairie
is hard and lonely, but I do so want to
be with you, sister. Maybe you will
not be so lonely for a woman's
companionship if I make Kansas my
home too.*
　　　　Your Loving Sister, Sarah

I read the letter to myself and when I finished I held
out my hand to Hannah and helped her off the cold
ground.

"Her mama and her daddy are both gone," I explained
to Skinner and Nathan as I lead Hannah inside. She set
down on the edge of our bed and wept. I held her in my
arms for a long time. I knowed her tears didn't come

often, but when they did, she had a hard time stoppin' them. When they did finally stop, she looked at me with a new thought.

"But my Sarah's comin'," she said. "My Sarah's comin' to live with us."

Lookin' past the tears, I seen a new hope in her eyes.

PERSERVERANCE

Strong family ties and an adventurous spirit gave
many women the courage to join their families on
the lonely prairie.

Sarah Ruth (Lucas) Taylor
born on February 16, 1846

93

Sarah...

I set my daddy's carpetbag down next to me. It was heavy with my travel needs and all the food the Taylor sisters had added for my journey. Levi made sure Mama's sewin' machine, Mama's rocker, and my trunk was loaded proper, whilst I got my seat on the train. By the time I got myself set down, he was standin' back on the station platform with Cora and Elizabeth. I waved a final farewell at them through the window and then turned so they couldn't see me wipe tears from my eyes. It was with great difficulty that I said my farewells to the Taylor family, and if I'd not had such a homesickness for my Hannah, I doubt I'd had the courage to leave them.

Mr. Jackson's family come earlier than anticipated, and the Taylors took me in whilst I finished up all our arrangements on my daddy's business. I'd never ventured far from Millersburg afore, so the Taylor family helped me arrange all my travels.

I didn't know what to expect in Kansas. Hannah said it was lonely and hard, but I'd felt lonely ever since I got the word my Jacob wasn't comin' home. And I knowed hard from when I watched Mama and Daddy fade away from life.

The train pulled out of the station and was startin' to move faster when a child in the seat across from me looked at his mother and asked "Is it the next stop, Mama?"

His mama looked too weary to answer. I wondered how long they'd been on the train. I smiled at the child. He returned no smile. Instead he buried his head close to his mama and brought back a memory of how safe I felt by my mama's skirts when I was his size. I swallowed the lump in my throat and tried to look forward to a new life on the Kansas prairies.

Hannah...

It took me some time to get used to the idea that Mama and Daddy was gone and that my Sarah was gonna be livin' with us. Carl wrote a letter back to Sarah the day her letter come to us. I wasn't thinkin' clear at the time and when I asked him what he'd told her in that letter, he turned to me and took me in his strong arms.

"I told her to write and let us know when she's comin'," he said whilst he was smilin' at me. "It'll be good to have more kin here."

He gave the letter to Skinner, who promised to post it on his next ride into Ellsworth, and ever' time Skinner come by after that, I thought he'd bring me a letter. He'd been by three times afore I finally got my letter from Sarah.

Carl...

Blessed with a couple of nice spring rains the ground was right for breakin' sod. Me and Nathan was a little south of the soddy workin' up another field for plantin' wheat, when Skinner rode up wavin' a letter in the air.

"From Sarah?" I asked.

"Looks to be," he answered.

"Hannah's busy bakin' the day's bread."

He rode to the soddy whilst me and Nathan stopped our work and went to see what the news was. By the time we got there, Hannah had her spectacles on and was outside in the daylight readin' her letter.

"No," she murmured. She held the letter close to her bosom as she ran back into the soddy for just a bit. When she come back outside she had my eye-glasses in one hand and the letter in her other. "Carl, I think my eyes didn't see right."

I put on my spectacles and read.

"Looks like we got a lot to do afore tomorrow," I said.

"The afternoon train," she said. "Carl, we have to leave today. I have to be there for her when the afternoon train comes in. Carl, we have to leave today," she said again.

94

Sarah...

I begin to question my decision to join Hannah and her Carl the longer I traveled. In one thought I was happy to be on this adventure, and in the next thought I seen myself as bein' foolish. I read Carl's letter several times to make sure I would be welcome with him and Hannah. Then I tucked it back inside my daddy's carpetbag where I had the three letters Hannah had written to me in the last year.

I looked out the window at the lay of the land and started seein' some of what her letters had described. Weary as I was at ridin' on the train, I thought how different my sister's journey to this same place must've been. It was hard to think a year had passed since her and Carl had left Millersburg in a covered wagon.

"Ellsworth, next stop ahead," the conductor said as he walked on to the next train car. I could feel the train start to slow.

Carl...

It was a thing of joy to see my Hannah and Sarah in their reunion. It reminded me of them when they was little girls and it felt right that they was together again. It was when Hannah seen her mama's sewin' machine and rockin' chair bein' unloaded off one of the train's cars that she got melancholy for a bit. She ran her hands over the fine wood on the sewin' machine and stood lookin' at the rocker like she seen her mama settin' there.

"We'd best be findin' a place to camp for the night," I said, as we was loadin' the buckboard with the sewin' machine, the rockin' chair, and the biggest trunk I ever seen.

Hannah found her voice again and was talkin' as fast as I ever heard her talk. It was like she was makin' up for not havin' another woman 'round for a while.

"So that's the machine our daddy bought for our mama. Oh…I'm gonna learn how to sew on it. Sarah, will you teach me?"

Sarah didn't get a word in to answer, whilst Hannah was goin' on.

"I wonder if we'll find any good material in the general store, and oh, my it's gonna be good to have nice furniture for the soddy," she said.

She kept on talkin' whilst I was tyin' the furniture down in the buckboard. I was wonderin' how we was gonna find room for it all.

Hannah…

I wanted to hold on to my sister and never let go when I seen her. I never wanted Carl to know how much I missed her, so I suppose I'd not let myself know either. I wanted to hear all 'bout ever'thing that she'd been doin' since we'd left Millersburg, but I didn't give her a chance to say anything. I couldn't stop talkin'.

I seen the looks my Carl and my Sarah was givin' each other, but it was like my mouth wouldn't stop movin'. As we rode home I told her 'bout all the good things on the prairie. I was so happy right then. I didn't want to mention any of the bad things, and I didn't want to scare my sister away.

95

Sarah…

As soon as I seen Hannah, I was certain I did the right thing to come live with her, but when we put our mama's trunk, sewin' machine, and rocker in the soddy, I couldn't see where there was room left for me.

I didn't appreciate how hard it must have been for Hannah the last year, 'til I had my first couple days livin' inside a house made of dirt. Hannah kept it clean as she could, but she told me there was no way to keep the bugs and mice out.

"And snakes, what about snakes?" I asked. It was not a secret to my sister that I've always had a great fear of snakes.

"We have to be careful for rattlers," she said. "But Carl won't let me kill a bull snake. They help keep the varmints down."

I shivered, in spite of the warmth of the day. "I don't know if I can get used to that," I said. And then I forgot 'bout snakes and any kind of varmint when I helped her do chores and work in her garden. I thought the prairie to be a beautiful place, though I missed havin' trees 'round. Carl said it was easier to prepare the ground for farmin' without them.

I watched Carl and his neighbor, Nathan, as they peeled the grasses off the earth. They told me how they made the sod bricks to build the shelters. And I listened to them talk 'bout the limestone they was quarryin' on the hill east of the soddy. It all sounded so promisin'.

I liked Nathan. I seen that Carl and him acted like brothers to each other. He had a sadness 'bout him, but I thought it to be a loneliness from his wife's death. I asked Hannah 'bout it one day.

"How did Nathan's wife die?" I asked. We was waterin' the little orchard Hannah had planted. I'd brung some peach stones and some cherry pits to add to that orchard. Hannah was pourin' water where we'd planted them. She stopped, still holdin' the bucket of water and looked over to where Nathan's place was.

"Rebecca is buried over on that little knoll by Nathan's soddy. She tried real hard at first...then..." She stopped talkin'. A pained look passed over her face, and when it finally faded, she went on, "She was ill...Nathan was gonna take her to the doctor in Ellsworth, but she died afore they got there."

She didn't say any more, and I didn't ask any more, but there was somethin' in the way she looked, that made me wonder. I thought of my Jacob and how I felt after I heard of his dyin'. I thought I knowed why Nathan always looked so sorrowful.

96

Nathan...

From the first time I saw Sarah I felt like she was a friend who I'd known a long time. I suppose it was because she looked so much like Hannah. I had trouble telling who was who sometimes. Both women stood tall, had a strong jawline, and their mouths turned down at the corners. They laughed often when they worked together. It was a pleasure to hear a woman's laughter again.

I still ate supper with Carl, Hannah, and now Sarah, almost every day. As I watched the two and listened to their chatter I started to see little differences. It was in their eyes. Both had hazel eyes, but while Hannah's took on a gray tone, I saw little gold flecks in Sarah's, especially if she got excited. And Sarah was quick to excite, while Hannah took most things calm and sensible.

It was only a couple weeks after Sarah arrived that I was working up a new field with Carl when we heard a scream. We looked over to where the women were. Hannah was chopping hard at the earth while Sarah kept screaming. Hannah was raising her hoe high in the air over her head and bringing it down, again and again.

"Must be a rat," Carl said.

"Or a rattler," I said.

We took off running. By the time we got to where the women were working in Hannah's garden, Hannah had a rattlesnake all chopped up in little pieces at the feet of Sarah, who was still screaming. Carl ran to Hannah and I ran to Sarah. I grabbed hold of her and turned her around to face me.

"Where did he get you?" I asked.

Her face was white and her eyes were wide. She stopped screaming and fell into my arms, inhaling gulps of air. I pulled her away from where the offending creature lay in pieces, and I started to lift her skirts. She flung her arms at me.

"Stop!" she screamed.

"Sarah, we have to see where he bit you," I said.

"He didn't bite me," she gasped, "he rattled at me."

I looked over at Hannah.

"I didn't ask first, afore I let him have it," she explained.

That was the day I noticed the gold flecks in Sarah's eyes. They were as bright as stars on a cloudless night. I hadn't looked into a woman's eyes in a long time. A quick memory of Becca's eyes made me take my hands off Sarah and back away from her. I didn't see her as Hannah's sister just then. I saw her as the woman she was, and I wasn't ready for that.

97

Carl...

The day Sarah near died from the fright of a rattlesnake, I seen a look pass betwixt her and Nathan. It was when Nathan mistook her scare for an actual bite, and he tried to lift her skirts to see the damage done.

I recognized the fire that shot from Sarah's eyes at the misundertandin'. I knowed how quick Sarah's temper could be. Nathan backed away from Sarah so fast he near fell over backwards, but there was somethin' else there. It was the way he was lookin' into her eyes.

He made excuses to go home for his own meals for a couple days, but was back to our place for dinner on Sunday. Tinker showed up that day too.

Hannah...

The first time I met Tinker was when he come callin' on a Sunday close to our dinner time. My Carl always had a way of tellin' if a man had a good heart. I knowed he liked Tinker, but that day I wasn't sure what he seen in the man.

He rode up to our place wavin' a willow stick in the air as a greetin'. When he got down off the mule he was ridin', I was surprised that he was at least half a foot shorter than me and Sarah. He had no beard, but wore a long mustache. Ever so once in a while he reached up and twisted its ends into curls.

Carl seemed pleased to see him and invited him to eat dinner with us. When he introduced us all, Tinker's eyes kept twitchin' back and forth betwixt me and Sarah. I wondered if he'd never seen twins afore.

When Nathan asked Tinker if he could take Molly over to meet his bull, me and Sarah went inside to get dinner on the table.

"Why does Tinker carry a willow stick with him?" Sarah asked me.

The men come inside just then. Carl heard Sarah's question and answered.

"Tinker can witch for water. He said he's come to witch for us. Said he'd witch for Nathan too."

I held my tongue. I didn't believe the things Carl had told me 'bout Tinker's talent to find water.

Sarah...

"There's somethin' not right 'bout what that man is doin'." Hannah said to me as we watched Tinker. He was walkin' real slow, back and forth across the ground Carl said would make a nice place for a well.

Tinker held onto the forked ends of his long willow stick. He started on the west side of the soddy, but nothin' happened as he walked. He walked for a long time, then stopped for a bit, looked at Carl and shook his head. Without sayin' anything he moved to the east side of the soddy and started his walk back and forth again. Hannah shook her head.

"I think it's an evil act. And on a Sunday, too," she complained.

Carl and Nathan was a ways away from us, talkin' in low tones, but Tinker just kept on walkin' back and forth. I watched his face, starin' at his stick, like it had a power over him. When I seen the corners of his mustache move, I looked at the end of the stick. It was wavin' up and down. Tinker walked real slow then, until the stick pointed straight down.

"Here." Tinker shouted. "Here, is water."

Carl and Nathan both had smiles on their faces, but Hannah sighed real hard. I knowed she was not believin' what the rest of us seen. Carl went over and marked the spot.

Hannah kept shakin' her head. Tinker looked over at her. He walked to where we was standin' and held his stick in front of her.

"You try," he said. "Sometimes others have the gift."

Hannah looked at the man like she thought he was daft. She closed her eyes and shook her head again. Tinker seemed to take no offense. He turned to me.

"No, I am wrong," he said. He held the stick out for me. I swallowed the lump in my throat. I wanted to try. I seen Hannah didn't want me to, but I stood up and let Tinker show me how to hold the willow stick. I went to the place where he'd started and I walked the same path he'd taken. At first I felt foolish, but the closer I got to the place Carl marked, the more trouble I had holdin' the stick straight. Soon it was wavin' up and down so hard I could hardly hold on to it, and when I was over the marked place, the point of the stick went down. I couldn't make it point any other way.

"Sarah has the gift," Tinker said as his head bobbed up and down. He stood twistin' the ends of his mustache, wearin' a satisfied grin on his face.

I looked over at my sister. Hannah was not easy to anger, but her look told me she was not happy with me. It was the same look I'd gotten many times when we was little girls. My daddy told me I had a gift then, too. He told me I had to keep it a secret, and secrets was always hard for me. It was 'specially hard to not tell Hannah when the gift would come. She always knowed when somethin' wasn't right though.

"Sarah, what's wrong today?" she'd always ask.

But I never told her 'bout the gift I carried. I was not sure it was a good thing to have.

98

Nathan...

When I asked Tinker to water-witch for me too, he said he'd do it that day. I knew Carl believed in his abilities, so Tinker and I left the Taylors and went straight to my place. Once again, Tinker walked back and forth until his witching stick pointed down to the place he said there would be water.

"You can dig here," he decreed with certainty. "Now I must get back to take care of my stock. Is your cow ready to go?" he asked.

It made sense. Carl and I had agreed to cut sod for Tinker. If he took Molly now, Carl and I could pay our debt to Tinker when it was time to pick her up. I went to fetch her. Tinker was in deep thought when I came back. He was staring at Becca's gravesite.

"Your wife is gone, no?" he asked.

I nodded.

"Mine too," he said. "I had to bury her alone, along the trail when I come out here." He tilted his head to one side and studied my face. "You are young. You need a wife and children." I heard a soft spot in the crotchety old man's voice, though I couldn't look at him just then. "I think maybe Sarah needs a husband, too," he added, and without another word he got on his mule and rode off.

I stood there thinking about what Tinker had just said. I watched him ride away, until all I could see was the rear end of Molly disappearing over the hill to the east.

I had that same empty feeling inside that I'd had last winter when I'd been stuck in the snowstorm and couldn't get to Carl and Hannah's place. I could never leave Becca all alone out here on the prairie—I owed her that. Yet, I wasn't for sure that I could spend another winter by myself either.

Every morning I visited Becca's grave that next week, I found myself talking to her about Sarah. I'd not shaved since Becca had died. My beard was long and shaggy. I looked down at my pitiful looking clothes. They needed patching. I hadn't bothered myself with taking a bath in a long time either. I wondered if Sarah would want me in the condition I was in.

I walked back to the soddy and found my razor.

99

Sarah…

It was a week after Tinker had come, that Hannah tried to shame me for usin' the witchin' stick.

"What harm does it do if it helps to find water?" I asked.

Hannah was one, that when she got somethin' in her head, she didn't want to let it go. Me and her never did agree when it come to what was right and wrong, and there was many times when our daddy read from the Bible that we couldn't agree on what the meanin' was. Our daddy encouraged us to talk over our differences. Our mama said it was because he could leave the house and not listen to us.

"You girls go outside with your arguments," she always said. Then she would smile and tell us how proud she was that we stayed with what we believed. I was confused by what that meant when I was young, but I understood its importance when I become a woman.

I thought how good it was to be with Hannah and Carl, but it took some gettin' used to—to live with my sister again. We couldn't agree 'bout the water witchin'.

"I'm gonna do what our mama always told us," I said. "I'm gonna take this argument outside with me. I'll go water your orchard."

Hannah put both her hands on her hips, but she wore a smile as she said, "And, I suppose you're gonna stay with what you believe."

"I see no harm in it," I said as I walked out the door.

By the time I got to the creek I was in a different way of thinkin'. Though I couldn't see what harm witchin' for water could do, I tried to understand Hannah's lookin' on it as a blasphemy. I filled my bucket and was thinkin' so hard 'bout it, that I jumped a little when I looked up and seen a man standin' on the creek bank watchin' me.

"I didn't want to scare you," he said. He come up aside me and held out his hand for the bucket. "Here, I'll take that. I...uh...I'd like to talk with you."

"Nathan?" I asked.

He laughed. He looked different as a clean shaven man. He looked much younger than I first thought him to be. And he was quite handsome. The way he'd been standing there lookin' at me, made me feel ill at ease, but in a good way.

"Hannah's orchard needs some water on the seeds we planted," I said.

He carried the bucket of water for me. We walked together, sayin' nothin'. When we got to the orchard, he set the bucket down. When I started to reach for it, he took hold of my hands real gentle, and he looked straight into my eyes.

"I don't know how to say this, Sarah," he said. "I need to know how you feel about...about the prairie?"

I must've had a real funny look on my face. He let go of my hands, and took off his hat. He worked it 'round and 'round in his hands. Then he looked at his boots and started to talk.

"You...you know I was married," he said. He quick looked up at me.

I nodded.

He looked down again, and said, "Becca didn't like the prairie, and I never should have brought her here until

I had a proper house, and …well, I guess I should've come out here ahead of her, and…I…I…I need a wife."

I didn't help him out none, even though I knowed he was distressed. I wasn't sure what he was gettin' at.

"I didn't say that right," he said as he sighed real heavy. "What I mean is… I know your husband, Jacob, was lost to the war. Carl told me that. And I know you just lost your parents. Life isn't easy out here, but this is where I'm going to stay. I can't leave this place, not with Becca all alone on the prairie." He looked off to his place. "What I'm saying is, if you think you could take to this kind of life, I'm offering to make you my wife."

He turned and looked at me again. Then I found my eyes lookin' down at his boots. It took me a long bit of time afore I found I could look up. When I did, he went on.

"I like you Sarah, and I know it'd be for practical reasons if we married."

His askin' come as a surprise to me and all I could think of was my mama's words, *"Stay with what you believe."* His offer seemed sensible to me and a good solution for both of us, but I knowed I had to make one thing clear to him.

"I have to be a partner. Any man I marry has to treat me as an equal." I said. "And…I need to think a bit afore I give you my answer."

He smiled and nodded. "I have a dream for my place. It's important that you like the prairie."

"I do," I said. "I…well…'cept for the snakes."

We both laughed at that.

He helped me finish waterin' the seeds and cherry pits I'd planted. Then he went off to find Carl. I went back to the creek to set by myself and think.

Ever since I'd lost Jacob, I'd been lonely. Then Sarah left. Then my mama and my daddy died. I didn't plan for my future. I come to live with Hannah 'cause I wanted to be close to her. I would be close to Hannah if I married Nathan, and I thought him to be a good man. I could see his dream.

I set there for quite a while tryin' to think of a good reason to not marry Nathan, and nothin' come to me.

It was noon afore I finally went back to the soddy. Hannah had our dinner ready. When Nathan and Carl come in to eat, and Nathan looked my way, I nodded. He swallowed hard. "Hannah and Carl," he said. "Sarah and I have something we want to tell you."

100

Carl...

When I seen Nathan had shaved his winter's beard, it come as no surprise to me that he would pursue Sarah's affections, but it was a bit of a shock that he did it with such speed. Hannah was dishin' out our dinner when Nathan started talkin'. She stopped dishin' out and held a spoonful of stew over my plate.

"Sarah's agreed to be my wife," Nathan announced.

The spoon stayed over my plate, whilst Hannah frowned a little, like maybe she'd not heard right. She turned to Sarah, who nodded, but never said a word. I'd seen it happen afore. The two sisters started communicatin' without talkin'. They looked so much alike right then, that it was hard to tell which one was my Hannah and which one was Sarah.

Nathan looked first at Sarah, and then at Hannah. No words was spoken, but clearly things was bein' worked out betwixt the two. Nathan looked at me like I could explain what was happenin'. I chuckled with the memory of seein' those two sisters in their younger years and I knowed Nathan had to be confused. He tried to smile, but it didn't come out that way until Hannah finally broke the silence.

"We ain't seen no preacher in these parts since we come out here."

Nathan was quick to answer, "I can talk to Skinner the next time he comes by."

Hannah's eyebrows raised.

"He should know where we can get wed."

"It should be a preacher that does it," Hannah said. She'd not took her eyes off Sarah since Nathan had started talkin'.

"That'd be nice," Sarah said. She reached over and took the spoon that Hannah held over my plate. "Is anybody hungry?"

Hannah...

'Cause it was a Sunday, we took our time with our dinner that day. Whilst we was eatin', I did my thinkin'. My recollection of Sarah bein' happy with Jacob come back to me, and also of her sadness when we got the letter of his passin'. I didn't think Sarah would ever feel for a man like that again. Then I thought 'bout how Nathan was when Rebecca died. Both Sarah and Nathan suffered a big loss. Maybe they could help each other heal, and I was grateful that they'd be livin' so close to me and Carl. The hardest part of livin' on the prairie was a loneliness for family. Now I was blessed with my sister bein' here, and if she married Nathan I felt we could always be close.

After we ate, Carl and Nathan went outside to have a smoke. I knowed I didn't have to say it in words, but I wanted Sarah to know how I felt.

"Sarah, I think it's a ..." I was interrupted when I heard a loud profanity come from Carl. Cussin' was not somethin' Carl did very often, 'specially on a Sunday. I went outside to see for myself what had him upset. Both men was lookin' off to the north.

"What is it?" Sarah said when she come up aside me.

Skinner was ridin' hard in our direction. Behind him in the far distance we seen smoke. It was hot outside for the last Sunday of May, yet a cold fear passed through me.

"Looks like another raid," I answered.

101

Sarah...

I felt my Hannah's fear when the man they all called Skinner rode up and I heard the words from Carl.

"Skinner's got a good reason if he's ridin' his horse that hard."

The man slid off the poor animal that was heavin' and covered in froth.

"Another raid?" Carl asked.

Skinner nodded as he gasped to catch his own breath, "North of here, 'bout fifteen miles or so." He jerked his hat off and wiped the sweat from his forehead with the sleeve of his shirt afore he told us the horror he'd heard of.

"Man named Parsons said they massacred a family, but they also got a woman and her little one. Said he seen it with his own eyes and they was headed south."

"Tell us what needs to be done," Carl said.

"Parsons is tryin' to warn the settlers north of the river. I'm on my way to the fort. I don't think they'll come this far today, but ya might not be safe here," he stopped talkin' and looked at me for the first time. He turned back to Carl and added, "I got to rest my horse a bit too, or he'll not make it."

"I wished I had a saddle horse to lend you," Carl said. "It's for sure that Bill or Barney can't outrun Indian ponies."

Skinner patted his wet horse, "He'll be fine with just a bit of rest."

"Can I get you somethin' for 'your' belly?" Hannah asked.

"I'd be much obliged, Hannah."

Nathan seen to the needs of Skinner's horse whilst Skinner and Carl talked of us goin' to the Walden place.

"You can a see a long ways from up on that hill. It'd give you a head start if they move this way," Skinner said.

Carl looked over at Hannah, she nodded, then ever'body started movin' fast, 'cept me. I started to shake. I had no idea what to do. I stood outside the soddy door, with a fear wellin' up inside. Hannah seen it. She grabbed hold of my shoulders and looked at me straight on. Then she pulled me inside, barkin' orders. For once I was glad of it. She grabbed the buffalo robes, threw them into my arms and told me to take them outside where Carl had the buckboard waitin'.

It took Skinner no time to eat, and I was standin' by the wagon when he come up aside me. "Sorry we hafta meet this way, Sarah," he said. He took the robes out of my arms and threw them into the back of the wagon as Nathan brought his horse to him. As soon as he took hold of the reins, he mounted and started to ride off.

"Be safe to ya all," was the words he threw over his shoulder.

I turned to go back into the soddy and met Carl comin' out carryin' a sack of taters and turnips. Hannah was right behind him with her arms full too. As I helped Hannah put ever'thing in the wagon, I caught a look betwixt Nathan and Carl that I didn't understand.

"Hannah's grabbin' her Bible. Then we'll go," Carl said.

As Hannah went back in the soddy one last time, Nathan helped me into the back of the buckboard. I'd not said anything since Skinner had come ridin' in—there'd not been time.

I finally took a deep breath as Carl climbed onto the wagon seat. Hannah come out with her Bible held against her bosom, and Nathan helped her into the back of the wagon with me. But instead of Nathan gettin' on the seat with Carl, he stood there, watchin' us leave as Carl slapped the reins on Bill and Barney's back.

"God be with you Nathan," Hannah yelled to him. It was then that I knowed Nathan wasn't comin' with us.

Nathan...

Sarah's eyes were wide with questions when she saw I wasn't going to the Walden place with them. I didn't have time to explain my reasons for not going and I didn't know if she would understand if I did.

I thought of the Walden children when Skinner told of the family who'd just been murdered. I hated the savages for those memories. I knew Carl didn't feel the same way I did. We'd argued about it one day.

"We've settled on the land they thought they was free to roam on. They seen their food supply killed off, like those two buffalo hunters who killed just for the hide— then left the meat to rot in the sun." He stopped his work, took off his hat and wiped his brow with his shirt sleeve.

"Their ways is different than ours," he continued, "but that don't make them wrong."

"But to massacre women and children?"

"White man's done the same to them."

I knew he had a point to his argument, but the vision of little Walter and Lizzie Walden being massacred, haunted me.

102

Hannah...

Carl drove Bill and Barney hard to the Walden place. It was late in the day when we first got there. No one had lived in the soddy since Skinner moved out. It looked like a mighty poor place to take refuge. But we could see for miles from there, and it would give us a head start if we had to make a run for the fort. We kept our supplies in the wagon and only took what we needed for the night into the soddy.

My Carl took watch that night whilst me and Sarah snuggled up on top of the buffalo robes, but we didn't get much sleep either. There was a bright moon shinin' outside, and Sarah said she seen shadows movin' all through the night.

"Ever' time a coyote yipped," she said, "I peeked outside to make sure Carl was still settin' out there watchin' for us."

I walked over to where my Carl was early the next mornin'. We set together for a bit and took in God's mornin' show of color in the eastern sky afore either of us spoke. I could see the tired in Carl.

"It's time you get some rest, whilst I watch," I said.

"First I need to check somethin' out," he said as he unfolded hiself and stretched. He handed me the rifle and said he'd be back soon. I watched him walk a ways and then turned my attention to the valley where I seen a small trail of smoke. I wondered if it was where the Indians camped. I seen no smoke at Nathan's place and I said a prayer for his safety.

It wasn't long afore Carl come walkin' back with a smile on his tired face.

"I found the spring Adam Walden told me 'bout," he said. "I wonder if it's the reason our creek don't ever go all the way dry. There's probably more in these hills."

"How'd you know where to look?" I asked.

He smiled, "I just watched God's creatures."

Sarah come out to where we was then, and Carl went back to the soddy to get hiself some sleep.

It was later that day when we heard the troops. They come ridin' from the south, headed to where Skinner said the Indians held the woman and her child. I felt a great relief that they was there to protect us, but I knowed they always made Carl remember days he wanted to forget. The three of us stood at the top of the hill as they passed by. We watched them ride 'til they was finally too far away to see anything but their dust, and we knowed they'd gone past our claim.

"We'll leave for home, first thing in the mornin'," Carl said. "I'll keep a watch out again tonight."

Carl had Bill and Barney harnessed and ready to go afore the sun was up the next day. They needed little encouragement when they knowed they was goin' home, so the ride was rough. Me and Sarah softened our ride a bit with each of us settin' on a buffalo robe. I was thinkin' of all the chores waitin' for me at home and I hoped the troops ridin' by didn't scare the feathers off my chickens.

Sarah had been so quiet the last couple days I wondered if she was regrettin' comin' to this land. I near asked her, when she asked me a question instead.

"It was because of Rebecca that he wouldn't leave, wasn't it?" I didn't answer, and she looked away from me and added, "Guess I'd done the same for my Jacob." Without lookin' my way, she asked, "Can you tell me a little 'bout her?"

It wasn't so easy to tell her how I felt 'bout Rebecca, but I thought she needed to know some if she was to marry Nathan.

"She wasn't raised like me and you," I explained. "I think her family must've been purty well to do."

A little frown passed over Sarah's forehead. I went on, "Her mama packed some fancy little tea cups in her trunk, and she loved to serve me tea—out here, on the prairie. She said her mama and herself had tea ever' afternoon. She knowed how to make a fancy cup of tea, but it took her a while to learn how to cook up a mess of beans."

"You liked her, didn't you?"

"She tried real hard to learn new things, but…"

Shots was ringin' out in the distance. Carl pulled up the team. We all listened, and I said another little prayer to myself. The shots stopped. We waited a long time 'til Barney snorted and a meadowlark sang off to our side. Carl looked at me and said, "I think we'd best get home as soon as we can." I nodded and he slapped the reins on the horses. Me and Sarah had to grab hold of the sideboards as we bounced our way home.

Carl...

We was back from the Walden place for a couple of days afore Skinner rode onto our place again. He told me troops was settin' up temporary camps in the area for the protection of the settlers.

"I think ya should be safe now," he said.

But when I asked 'bout the welfare of the woman and child that was captured, he looked up to the sky like he'd find a reason for the answer he give me. Then he looked away.

"We didn't find 'em in time to save the little one. The woman...well...she's alive." Then he told me again, "I think there's enough troops 'round that ya should be safe now."

Sarah come out of the soddy just then.

Skinner yelled out to her, "How-do Hannah."

Sarah grinned, and Hannah stepped into the doorway of the soddy. "How-do yourself, Skinner," Hannah laughed.

Skinner shook his head, chucklin' as he said, "Those two sure look alike."

Hannah and Sarah both wore ornery grins. It reminded me to give Skinner a message.

"Nathan wanted to talk to you too. Are you gonna stop by his place?" I asked.

I seen Sarah wait for Skinner to answer.

"I kin."

Sarah smiled at me and went back inside.

103

Nathan...

When I asked Skinner if he knew the nearest place I could find a preacher, his eyebrows narrowed a bit before his eyes looked off toward Becca's gravesite.

"Becca was in every dream I ever had for my future," I said. "Now I have to start thinking differently."

He stood quiet for a bit before he asked, "Hannah's sister?"

I nodded. "I've asked Sarah to be my wife."

Skinner took off his hat, and scratched his head, like maybe he could pull an answer out for me. He put his hat back on and said, "I've never been much for preachers myself, but I suppose you're in the need fer one. I knowed of a circuit preacher that come 'round east of here, 'fore all the Indian raids started. I heard he don't come 'round no more." He stopped talking long enough to spit out a stream of tobacco juice, before he added, "There's a chaplain back at Fort Harker. Maybe he'd be able to do you the honors."

The two of us shared a bit of silence until he spat out another stream of tobacco juice. "I'd best be gettin' on," he said.

"I'm obliged for your stopping by. It's good news to know the cavalry is camped near too."

His face wore disappointment before he looked away. "They'll be here if you need 'em. It's a shame they have to be here at all." He was shaking his head. "I thought things might end different, but I seen lots of good folks massacred—on both sides." He started to climb on his horse, changed his mind, and turned to look me in the eye. With a sadness in his voice, he said, "I gotta get back. I'll talk to that chaplain fer ya." He smiled, and added, "A man should have a partner in his life."

As he rode away, he reminded me of my father, before the war. I came to the conclusion that there are many sides to all men—myself included. I'd been hoeing potatoes when Skinner rode up, and I tried to finish the task when he left, but I had something else I had to do first.

I walked to Becca's grave, bent down and pulled a weed that mingled in the midst of the wildflowers she loved so much. The memory of her touch was with me. I ached to feel it again. But the memory of her insanity was mixed in. I could hardly catch my breath whenever I had the memory of her beautiful eyes turning into a dark nothingness at the end. She was gone, because of my dreams. I knew I'd never find peace with that admission, but if I was to ever find happiness again, I needed to go on.

"Forgive me, Becca," I begged. "I've asked Hannah's sister to marry me."

I wondered if my guilt would ever lessen. I stood there for a long time, knowing I had to learn to live again, without thinking of what my life with Becca would have been. I thought I might have another chance with Sarah.

Sarah...

After Nathan and Skinner talked, Nathan come to me and said, "We'll leave for Fort Harker tomorrow."

We was alone, down by the creek. I looked at him hard and finally said, "No."

He didn't understand. His brow creased and his next words was slow, "Did you change your mind?"

"No."

"What, then?"

I suppose this was a test to make sure I was doin' the right thing by marryin' him. "What did I tell you when I agreed to marry you?" I asked.

He didn't answer me right away, so I helped him a little with his memory and said, "You asked me if I liked the prairie."

"And you said you did," he smiled at me, "Sarah, I can't get rid of all the snakes on the prairie." Then I seen that he remembered. "Oh…and, you said any man you married had to treat you as an equal."

"Seems to me that I should have somethin' to say 'bout the day we decide to marry. If I'm to be an equal partner."

At first I thought he might take offense to my words, and I couldn't tell his feelin's 'til he smiled and spoke with a soft tone, "I've a lot to learn from you, Sarah."

We talked then, and made plans for our future together. We got to know each other a little bit better that day and made the mutual decision to leave for Fort Harker the second week in July.

104

Carl...

It was a Sunday in the second week of June when Nathan and Sarah told me and Hannah of their plans to wed in a month. They come up from the creek and was talkin' and laughin' together like they'd been friends all their lives.

First Nathan asked me if I'd watch after his place for a couple of days, and then Sarah asked my Hannah if she'd go with them to Fort Harker to be her witness. The women started makin' plans like the trip was for the next day.

Corky was layin' in the shade of the soddy when I seen his ears perk up. I shot a prairie chicken he chased up early in the mornin' and it must've tuckered him out, 'cause he didn't bark. He looked over at me, then turned his head to the top of the pasture hill to let me know we had company comin'. I seen a rider on a mule.

"Must be Herman Tinkerman," I said.

Ever'one looked in that direction.

Hannah was not of a kind mind when it come to that man. "Showin' up right at dinner time too," she said. She stood, then headed into the soddy, and by the time Herman got to our place, she and Sarah had dinner waitin' for all of us.

As we ate, Tinker told us the cavalry had one of their camps next to his claim. He added, "Guess I'm 'bout as safe as I kin be now, but it took my stock a while to settle down, with all the troops comin' and goin'."

Much as I could see the necessity of the troops, I hated the memories they brought to my mind, so I changed the talk to our lack of rain.

"You need to get that well dug," Tinker said. "I could help you get a start on it today."

My Hannah was quick to disagree. "Herman Tinkerman, we'll not work on our Sabbath."

Tinker sighed and turned a pitiful face to Hannah. "I didn't mean to offend," he said. "And my friends call me Tinker."

Me, Nathan, and Sarah watched the two. Funny how the wind howlin' seemed louder just then. We waited for Hannah to say somethin'. Tinker kept that pitiful look plastered on his face and waited with us.

She stood up, looked down at each one of us in turn. She shook her head and finally rested her eyes on Tinker. He was lookin' up at her, his wrinkled face beggin' for her to give him a kind word.

"We all want a well," she said. She finally added the wished-for word, "Tinker." She put her hands on her hips, looked him straight in the eye and said, "I can't bring myself to believe in your fancy witchcraft to find water though."

Tinker didn't bat an eye when his voice got soft and he said, "Hannah, when you find your water you will know it ain't witchcraft, but merely a gift." He grinned at her with a smile that was missin' two, bottom front teeth. "And thank you fer callin' me Tinker. It means we're friends now?"

The look on Hannah's face made me laugh out loud. When she turned to give me the same look, I caught Tinker's wink. It was good my Hannah didn't see it.

Hannah...

The day after Tinker was here, my Carl and Nathan started diggin' our well in the spot Tinker said we'd find water. For a week straight, they quit their field work early and dug a little each day, bein' real careful so not to let the sides cave in on them. Sarah seemed so sure they'd find water. I was sure they wouldn't.

It was into the next week, they started haulin' up buckets of mud. They quit early that night, and by next mornin' Carl went down into the well and was standin' in an inch of water. When he dug into it, the water started comin' in so fast he yelled for help, and it took three of us to dip out the water whilst Carl kept diggin'.

We didn't have time to rejoice just then cause we was all workin' so hard, and I felt a great relief when my Carl climbed up that ladder for the last time. He was soaked through and half mud, but he grabbed me in his arms and swung me 'round with the joy of it all.

When he let me back on the ground, I said, "I still don't believe Tinker had anything to do with this, but we was lucky with his gift."

Now that there was water in the well, Carl said we needed to get the sides shored up, or it would cave in. We all worked together one whole day gatherin' big rocks from atop the hill and haulin' them to the well. Then Nathan and Carl took turns back down in the well to lay up the sides. I fretted somethin' terrible ever' time one of them was down there.

"Say a prayer," I whispered to Sarah as Carl took one of his turns, and when he laid down the last big stone, I felt a great worry lift off me.

We dumped some small rocks from the creek bed into the bottom to let the mud settle for a couple of days. I could hardly wait to have my first drink from our well.

We celebrated by watchin' the sun light up the sky with yellow and oranges that night. My Carl put his arm 'round me and said, "Our gold lies in the western sky. We are truly blessed, Hannah."

I was so tired I near fell asleep right then. We had a well, and I was truly grateful.

Sarah...

Skinner come by the soddy the last week in June. Hannah was hoein' in her garden and I'd just hauled up a bucket of fresh water to take her a drink. It was a hot, sticky day. I held the dipper out to Skinner and he took a couple good gulps and asked,

"You and Nathan get hitched yet?"

"We're plannin' on goin' to Fort Harker next week," I answered.

"Would ya consider today?" he asked with a little cock-eyed grin on his face.

Hannah told me enough about Skinner's character that I knowed he was up to somethin'. I frowned at him, but didn't answer.

"I just come from the fort myself, with the chaplain ridin' by my side."

I raised my eyebrows, 'cause when I looked 'round I seen no preacher.

That brought on a roar of laughter from the man, and when he quieted down he explained, "He's just yonder, over the hills at the camp the cavalry set up. I took privilege and asked him if he'd do a weddin'."

"And, he said?"

"Said he thought it to be a grand idea." Skinner had a big grin on him.

"I need to find Nathan," I said.

Nathan...

Sarah was nervous when she told me what Skinner had said. I was relieved, because I knew it'd be simpler to get married right away instead of in the middle of our harvest. But I wanted to have some fun with her, so I said, "No."

When her face crumpled, I knew I shouldn't tease her on such an important matter. "Sarah, do you want to get married today?" I asked. "I was only joshing you, because you said *no* to me when I asked you only a couple of weeks ago."

First her mouth went into a flat line, then I saw the corners creeping up. She smiled and said, "I did give you a hard time."

"We're in agreement then?"

I nodded. It was to be my wedding day. My stomach gave a little jerk, and then we went to tell Hannah and Carl of our plans.

Hannah...

I never rode a bareback horse much, and my Carl laughed as he helped boost me on Barney.

"He'll not outrun an Indian pony, but you need to hang on tight and wrap your legs 'round him good. He'll shy if a rabbit jumps out in front of him, and you'll go tumblin'," Carl warned me.

Like we planned afore, Carl stayed home to tend the animals, whilst the three of us followed Skinner. I'd not ever come this far east. I was surprised by how many low hills there was. When we was atop the last hill we looked down to see Tinker's place at the bottom, and a little further on we seen a town of tents where the camp was.

We rode down the hill and straight to a creek where there was a lone cottonwood. Some troops was takin' advantage of its shade. Skinner talked to a couple of the fellers whilst we watered our horses, and one of the men got up and walked off. It wasn't no time, he come back to where we was. A very tall man all dressed in black was walking aside him.

"I hear tell you need my services for a wedding," the man said as he held out his hand to shake Nathan's. "I'm Chaplain Riddle. I have no certificate of marriage with me, but I can document a marriage if you brought your family Bible."

"I brung mine," I said. "I'm a sister to the bride."

"Excellent." The preacher come forward as I held out my Bible. "I see the resemblance," he teased. His eyes went back and forth from me to Sarah. Then he repeated his word, "Excellent. Let's get started."

As I witnessed the marriage of Sarah and Nathan under that cottonwood tree, I thought how my Carl would've liked us to have been joined together out in the open under a cottonwood. It didn't take long for the preacher to say they was man and wife. Then Skinner come up to him and whispered in his ear. The preacher nodded and made a motion to the soldiers that had stood 'round for the ceremony. Right away, they lined up in two rows and put their sabers together. Skinner wore a grin from ear to ear when he seen how it surprised Sarah and Nathan. They both had big smiles when they walked under the arch, and as soon as the parade was over, the troops all give a big "Huzzah!" It brung a color to Sarah's cheeks.

It was late in the day when we got back home. My eyes blurred when I showed Carl the new entry in our Bible.

June 29, 1869—Nathan Jacob Carter married Sarah Ruth (Lucas, Taylor) Carter

Carl took off his spectacles and laid them on the table. "I didn't know you had Jacob as part of your name too. I think my Jacob would approve." I could tell the words meant a lot to Nathan as the two friends looked at each other.

Sarah then fetched her Bible and handed it to Nathan. "This is our Bible now."

It had a record of her and Jacob's marriage and then of his death. "I think you should record Rebecca's life in it too," she said.

I knowed that Nathan never found Rebecca's Bible after she tore up the dugout. He swallowed hard and wrote with a steady hand, recording his old life with Rebecca and the beginnin' of his new life with Sarah.

106

Sarah…

The men started harvest the day after me and Nathan wed. Hannah helped me move my trunk and our mama's sewin' machine to my new home. Hannah told me I should have Mama's rockin' chair too, but I couldn't take it away from her. Hannah's smile looked so much like our mama's used to, when after a hard day's work, she would sit and rock slow and easy. She'd close her eyes as she rocked back and forth, lettin' the rhythm soothe her.

"I'll take the sewin' machine and you keep the rocker," I said.

"Sarah, why are you so attached to that machine? Have you ever used it?"

I closed my eyes, bit down on my lip, and shook my head. "No," I finally said. "And I never seen our mama use it either."

I set down on my trunk then and remembered how happy it made Mama. "Our daddy bought it for her, right afore he got so sick," I told Hannah. "He was so proud. He said it was to make her life easier." I got up then, opened my trunk, and dug deep into the bottom. I pulled up a piece of purty red and white calico fabric. "She bought this, and then when Daddy kept gettin' sicker, she laid it aside and talked 'bout tryin' to learn how to use the machine when he got better."

Hannah ran her rough hand over the smooth material. "Do you know *how* to use it?" she asked.

I shook my head again and tried to explain, "I didn't know…I thought…when I come out here, I didn't know

I'd be gettin' married. I thought maybe I could learn and then I could sew for other folks—to earn my keep."

Hannah looked at me and then looked around the barren room. "You've plenty of time to learn afore all the other folks get here," she said.

We both had a good hard laugh at that. I looked at the window thinkin' how much curtains would brighten the soddy. "I can learn some day, and make some curtains." I said.

It was a foolish thing, but I'd not been inside Nathan's soddy afore we was married. It was a surprise to see how sparse his belongin's was. "Hannah, I'll have to cook without a stove." I said.

"I'll help you learn." Hannah said, "Sarah, my stove…well…I got it after Rebecca died. It was hers. And afore that it belonged to the Walden family." She told me some 'bout the Walden family afore—how she got Edna's chickens and such. But she'd not told me 'bout the stove.

"After Rebecca passed on, Nathan took most of his meals with me and Carl and he thought I should have the stove." She frowned a little and ended her story by sayin', "If Nathan wants it back, I know how to cook on a campfire."

I looked down at the cookin' pit Nathan had made in the soddy. Even if Nathan did want it back, I couldn't take away my sister's stove. "Then teach me," I said.

107

Hannah...

Those long hot days of summer was easier when me and Sarah could spend them together. Whilst the men folk worked together at harvest, me and Sarah did a lot of our work together too. I taught her what I knowed 'bout cookin' on a campfire and she got real good at makin' some tasty meals. The four of us shared our supper with each other most ever' day, and once Nathan showed Sarah how to use a gun, she become real good at huntin' too. She brung fresh meat for our meals on many days.

It was the day we started talkin' of the well, that we had our disagreement. I felt blessed that we'd found water where Tinker told us to dig, but I didn't think Tinker wavin' a forked branch in the air had anything to do with where the water lay in the ground.

"But I felt it too," Sarah said. "It really does work, Hannah."

"I don't think it's right," I said. "Herman Tinkerman said you had a gift. I overheard our daddy tell you that once too."

Much as I thought the water witchin' was wrong, I was sorry for the words I'd just said. Sarah's face turned white and she asked me in a whisper, "What else did you hear when our daddy told me that?"

The day was hot, but Sarah gave a look that sent a chill over me.

"What else did you hear?" Sarah shouted this time.

"I...I didn't hear anything else, 'cause our mama caught me listenin' and she gave me a swat. She told me I shouldn't listen to private conversations and I shouldn't ever ask you 'bout it."

I never asked her 'til that day, and I wished I hadn't said nothin' then. I knowed Sarah could be quick to anger and I knowed she wouldn't hold it for long, but I don't think it was anger that made her walk away from me that day.

"Sarah, I'm sorry," I said.

She just kept walkin' away to her own place. I was left standin' in the garden wonderin' why a *gift* could cause her to get so upset.

Sarah...

When Hannah said she overheard my daddy tell me I had a gift, it took me back to a day when I was eight years old. I remembered the tight feelin' I had in my chest for days. I was so scared, but I didn't tell anyone. I thought I was gonna die, 'cause it hurt so bad ever' time I tried to take a deep breath.

I was settin' on the porch swing when my daddy come out of the house and looked down at me. His face told me he knowed somethin' was wrong.

"Did you and Hannah have a disagreement, Second One?"

I couldn't even smile at Daddy's twin joke. He eased hiself down aside me, and I let a tear fall. Daddy opened his arms and said, "Whoa, Second One, hold those horses back."

I remembered how good I always felt in my daddy's arms. I tried to smile.

"You want to tell your daddy what's wrong?" he asked.

"Daddy, I think I have the consumption."

He got a little frown on his forehead.

I told him how I'd been feelin' for days. I couldn't run and play 'cause it hurt to breathe heavy. "I feel like I got a hole right here," I told him as I pointed to my chest.

He got a strange look on his face and his voice was all wobbly. "Are you worried 'bout somethin'?" he asked.

"It feels like I done somethin' wrong. But I didn't Daddy, really, I didn't."

Daddy held me tight in his arms for a bit. Then he reached inside his pocket and pulled out the most beautiful, smooth rock I ever seen. It was the size of a pullet egg. Part of it looked like a bright green glass and part of it looked like a fine piece of polished wood. He put the rock in my hand and for the first time in weeks, I forgot how horrible I felt. The rock was cool and smooth.

"It's beautiful, Daddy," I whispered.

"That's my worry stone," my daddy explained. "I carry it with me and rub it whenever I'm worried 'bout somethin'. I could let you borrow it for a day or two and when you feel worried 'bout anything at all, all you have to do is rub that stone."

"I'm gonna go show Hannah," I said.

"No, Sarah, this has to be our secret."

"But Hannah won't tell anybody."

"Sarah, I think you have a gift," he said. "But others can't understand it, and it's a burden sometimes." He frowned. "Sarah, you can't tell Hannah. You can't even tell Mama," he said. "That's what a secret is, you can't tell anyone."

I didn't understand when I was eight, how a *gift* could be a burden. But I did as my daddy told me, and I told no one.

It wasn't long afore I found out what my daddy meant though. It come when my grandma died. It come many times after that.

Daddy seemed to know when I needed to borrow his beautiful stone. It was whenever I got the hollow feelin' in my chest. I'd rub the stone and feel better cause I knowed Daddy was feelin' it too, but it always meant a tragedy wasn't far behind the feelin'.

I had the feelin' once for a week and then it went away. I thought it meant I no longer had the *gift*, 'til the letter come 'bout my Jacob. I seen the date it said he died. It was 'bout the time I had the tight feelin' in my chest.

I knowed afore Daddy died too. And mama. I knowed somethin' bad was comin'. I couldn't find my Daddy's stone after him and Mama was gone. I looked all through the house afore I left Millersburg. I never found it.

When Hannah told me she heard Daddy that day so long ago, I first had a fear that she knowed I had the *gift*. But if she knowed it, she probably would've thought it evil. She didn't even like the water witchin'. It brought an anger on me from the memories of it all and I had to leave afore I said somethin' I couldn't take back.

When I got home, the anger was gone. I thought, why couldn't I have my own worry stone? I went to the creek. I walked aside the creek 'til I seen a place where the water was clear and runnin' over tiny rocks. I found the smoothest stone I could find. It didn't have all the colors

Daddy's stone had, but when I rubbed it, I was reminded of him. It was a good memory.

When I was walkin' back home, I was drawn to where the dugout was. I knowed Nathan didn't want me in there, but he was still at Carl and Hannah's place. He'd never know if I had a look-see. Besides, if we was equal partners, then the dugout was part mine too. I peeked inside, and when my eyes got used to the dark, I seen that part of the ceilin' had caved in. But then my eye caught somethin' layin' in the dirt on the floor. That's when I went inside.

A mouse scurried across the floor and near scared me half out of my wits. I kicked at what was layin' there and seen it was a book. When I reached down to pick it up, a tintype dropped out. Soon as I wiped away the dirt, I seen it was of Nathan and a beautiful young woman. I stared at it for a long time and knowed it had to be Rebecca.

My hands was shakin' so hard I dropped the book I was holdin'. I bent down to pick it up when I heard Nathan callin' my name. I couldn't think on what to do, so I quick put the photograph back in the book. That's when I seen the book was a diary. I covered it with some dirt. Then I stepped outside. Nathan was standin' there. He looked at me like I was doin' something wrong. He asked me what I was doin' in the dugout.

I don't know why I didn't tell him what I found. Somethin' inside me said I shouldn't. I never was good at lyin', so I said nothin'. I felt like I was lyin' though. I didn't like secrets either. Now I was plum guilty of both lyin' and keepin' a secret.

108

Nathan...

Ever since Carl suffered his spell in the heat, he had to be careful not to overwork himself during the hottest part of the day. We were resting ourselves in the shade of the stable, dreaming of future summers and discussing what tools and equipment we'd need when our fields would be larger. Hannah brought us some cool water.

"Where's Sarah?" I asked.

"She went home," Hannah said without looking at me. She took a quick look off towards my place, shook her head, and walked off. Something didn't seem quite right.

I looked at Carl, who shrugged. I wanted to take a short nap before I got back to work, but I decided maybe I'd better find out why Sarah had gone home.

I didn't find her at the soddy, so I went down by the creek. When I called her name, she stepped into the doorway of the dugout.

"What are you doing in there?" I questioned. I'd asked her not to go into the dugout. I thought I'd given her a good reason.

"I told you not to go in there. The roof isn't stable." I was irritated. I could see where part of the roof had already caved in. I didn't tell her my real objection was that I didn't want her to see what Becca had done to the place.

Instead of answering me, Sarah only gave me a quick glance when she stepped back outside. Then she looked away and started walking toward the soddy.

I caught up with her and grabbed her arm. "Sarah, what's wrong?" I asked.

Without looking at me she answered, "Nothin'…I thought it'd be a good storage place for our vegetables." She looked down at her arm where I had a hold on her. I let go. Without looking at me again, she walked away.

It was all so strange.. I didn't try to stop her, but I wondered for the rest of the day, why had she left Hannah's and why had she been in the dugout? I went back to help Carl.

Carl…

We'd scythed wheat earlier in the day. When Nathan come back from his place we started gleanin' and sheavin' the grain. I near couldn't keep up with him.

"Was Sarah feelin' okay?" I asked.

He stopped and took off his hat to catch a breeze. As he wiped the sweat off his forehead, he said, "Carl, I found her in the dugout." He looked up to the sky and let out a big sigh. "Now why would she go in there after I told her not to?"

When I stopped laughin', I explained to him the best way I knowed how. "Nathan, I've knowed Sarah as long as I've knowed Hannah, and I've got two sisters of my own back home. You tell any one of them not to do somethin', well, out of that bunch, she'll probably do it, just to find out why you told her not to."

I couldn't tell by his look what he thought of that, so I added, "We both got us some independent women-folk. And mighty fine women they are."

He shook his head, bent down, and gathered up another armful of grain. I could tell he was thinkin' on

my words 'cause he slowed down so I could keep up
again.

109

Sarah...

The days was long and hard. Just the heat alone wore a body out. But we was blessed with a wind most days that dried the grains for a good harvest. The men was working at our place now, so I was doin' most of the cookin'. I was lookin' forward to the day I'd have a cook stove. I knowed it had to wait awhile, so I did a right proper job of learnin' how to cook in the fire pit.

Ever' time I had to fetch water from the creek though, I wanted to go back into the dugout and read Rebecca's diary. Nathan said nothin' more 'bout the day he found me there, and I felt shame for not tellin' what I found when I held the secret inside myself.

Me and Hannah was still doin' our chores together too, but the fun wore off a little after our talk 'bout the water witchin'. I was sure we'd find water where Tinker had witched for Nathan. I had a plan for me and Nathan to have a well afore winter set in, even if I had to dig it by myself. I got up courage to ask him 'bout the witchin' part, on our day of rest.

Back home, if we wasn't able to attend church on Sunday, my daddy always read a Psalm from our Bible. I asked Nathan if he would do the same. He got a faraway look on his face afore he come back to my question, and without ever sayin' he would, he picked up my Bible and read for us. When he finished, we both set with our own thoughts for a minute. Then I asked him how he felt 'bout the witchin' part of findin' water.

"Hannah thinks it wrong," I said. "She didn't like Tinker tellin' me I had the *gift*."

Half frownin' and half smilin', his words was slow and careful. "Is that what's been between you and Hannah lately?" he asked.

I looked away from him and didn't answer.

"Sarah, I'd heard about water witching back in Eaton, when the farmers used to come into the store," he continued. "Some believed in it, others didn't. But it seemed to work for Carl. I say when we get ready to dig, we try it in the spot Tinker found."

"I want to start," I said.

His frown growed deeper and I heard his sigh, "As soon as I can, Sarah."

I smiled. I planned to start even sooner.

Nathan...

I didn't want to compare Sarah to my memories of Becca, but it happened every day. I'd loved Becca ever since I was a young man. I fell in love with a beautiful girl who I mistakenly thought loved horehound candy. Every day I missed her lovely eyes. I missed her touch, her laughter, and her song. And after she was gone, I nearly drove myself to an early grave remembering the way she died.

Then Sarah arrived on the prairie. I'd seen a practical need for both of us to marry. And after we said our vows, and lived together for only a short time, I found I could love again, but in a different way than I'd loved Becca. I felt like God gave me another chance with Sarah, and I prayed I'd do right by her.

One of the things I'd quickly discovered about Sarah, was that she was strong willed and independent. I knew there was something between her and Hannah, but she didn't talk to me about it. She didn't seem angry, yet the day I went to Carl's to cut prairie hay, she wanted to stay back to do all the chores herself.

"I'll be gone most of the day," I told her.

"I've plenty to do here. Tell Hannah I'll come see her tomorrow," she said.

110

Sarah…

I hurried through my chores that mornin', and as soon as I seen the men up on the hillside cuttin' prairie hay, I headed for the dugout. I didn't understand myself, why I couldn't tell Nathan 'bout what I found. Keepin' it a secret didn't seem right, but ever' time I'd tried to tell him, the words got stuck in my throat.

I looked up at the ceilin' when I went inside the dugout, bein' careful so no more roof fell in whilst I was in there. It looked solid enough, but I seen beady little eyes lookin' down at me. He'd been chewin' on somethin' and he stopped and watched me watch him. My heart near sank to my belly. How foolish I'd been to leave the diary here, a place that was runnin' over with rats and mice.

"Scat!" I yelled out so loud, I jumped at my own voice. The varmint disappeared, but that's when I seen there was somethin' else up there, aside where that mouse had been. It was wedged against the ridgepole of the roof, and when I stood on my tip-toes I seen it was a little hidey hole. I wanted to reach in, but knowed that'd not be the smartest thing to do.

I'd come for the diary. So I sifted through the dirt and grass, and when I found it, I seen a piece of broken pole that must've fell when part of the roof caved in. I picked it up and used it to poke in the hideaway. A book dropped down by my feet. I couldn't believe what I found. It had to be Nathan and Rebecca's lost Bible.

I knocked the dirt off the books and took them outside to the sunlight. I opened up the Bible first, and seen the delicate script that read…

April 1, 1868—Nathan Jacob Carter married Rebecca Louise Martin.

But it wasn't a purty thing. The fancy writin' that recorded their marriage was crossed through with ugly marks. It was an ungodly thing to do to a Bible.

I don't know how long I stood there lookin' at what I seen in the Good Book   I wanted to put it back where I found it. I wanted to put the diary back too. I wished I'd listened to Nathan and never gone in the dugout. How could I show him what I found, when it was all smeared and tore up? No mouse had done that. Those marks was made by somebody who was…what?

I looked over to the hillside and seen the men still workin' hard in the hot sun. I knowed I had to show Nathan what I found someday, but…I wanted to get to know Rebecca. I could do that if I read the diary first. I went back to the soddy with a heart mixed full of different feelin's.

I looked around the soddy to find a hidin' place to keep my secret. My trunk was what I decided on. I took the tintype out of the diary and studied it for a long time. Nathan looked so young and handsome. Rebecca was so beautiful. Together they looked happy.

I opened the diary, meanin' to put the tintype back. I seen the delicate writing. But I looked at the pages that was last written on and the purty script was gone. There was rough hard lines written, like the words didn't want to be put there.

"Okay, Sarah," I said out loud to myself. "What are you gonna do now?"

My head was startin' to hurt. I seen enough for one day. I dug into my trunk and got out the red and white calico that was to be my curtains. I put the photograph back in Rebecca's diary, and wrapped every'thing I found in the material. I hid it all, down deep in the trunk. Then I went outside, got the shovel, and started to dig a well.

111

Hannah...

I knowed my sister was up to somethin'. All the whilst the men was harvestin' we worked together, but things wasn't quite right. It was after I said I heard my daddy and her talkin'. I couldn't figure out why it upset her so. Did my daddy know she could point a stick and find water? Was that the *gift* she had when she was little?

Sarah didn't come to my place the day the men started cuttin' prairie hay. It wasn't like her to stay upset for such a long time, so I thought maybe I needed to smooth her feathers a little. I took a loaf of bread along when I went to see her, 'cause it was hard to bake bread decent in a pit.

It was a hot day. Corky was with the men, so I was bein' careful to avoid any snakes that might be in my path. Maybe it's 'cause I had snakes in my thoughts, but when I first seen Sarah, I thought the worst. She was a ways from the soddy and I seen her jump up and then down in a peculiar way. I feared she must've met up with another rattler. I ran to get to her. I was all out of breath when I got close enough to see she was puttin' one foot on the shoulder of a shovel, then jumpin' up and comin' down with the other foot on the other shoulder. She looked up when she heard me runnin' up.

"Hannah, what's wrong? Is it one of the men?" she said. Her face turned to the hillside where they was workin'.

"What are you doin'?" I was puffin' for air. "I thought you was choppin' on a snake."

Her look of concern changed to a look of pure stubbornness. "I'm diggin' a well."

"But I seen you jump…" I stopped what I was gonna say, and waited for an explanation.

"The grounds baked rock solid here. I couldn't get the shovel in any other way, so I jump on it."

"That's a good way to break a shovel handle," I said. "Or a leg."

"I'm fine."

The hen scratchin' she'd done on the hard prairie sod was pitiful. At least I didn't have to worry 'bout the sides of a well cavin' in on her cause at the rate she was goin' she'd be an old woman afore she got that far. I started to say so, but thought better of it when I remembered the last time we talked 'bout a well.

"I brung you a loaf of bread," I said.

"What I need is a nice cold drink of fresh well water," she looked at where she'd been diggin'. "But I'm grateful for a sister that brings me bread." She smiled.

"You're gonna try to prove me wrong…'bout the well."

Her look was pure stubbornness again.

I shook my head.

"I think I had enough for today, let's get out of the sun for a while," she said.

We talked then and laughed, and things felt right betwixt us again. But right afore I left to go back home, she looked over to Rebecca's grave and asked, plum out of nowhere, "Hannah, how did Rebecca die?"

It always brung me pain to think back to that night. I'd never told Sarah that Rebecca went mad, and I seen no point in tellin' her then. My mama always said it wasn't right to speak ill of the dead, so I tried to find a different way to tell her what happened to Rebecca.

"She was sick. Nathan was gonna take her to Ellsworth to see a doctor, but she died afore they went. Nathan was holdin' her in his arms when me and Carl seen her last. I...none of us knowed how sick she was, 'til it was too late to help her."

Sarah frowned and nodded. She was still lookin' at the grave.

"I got to go," I said.

She nodded again, whilst she kept starin' at where Rebecca was buried.

I met Nathan when I was goin' home, and I thought it should be his place to answer any more questions Sarah might have 'bout Rebecca.

"We got a lot of prairie hay put up today," he said. "Did you and Sarah have a good visit?"

"We did, but you got a surprise waitin' for you when you get home," I said. Then I smiled and went on, wonderin' what Nathan would think of Sarah's tryin' to dig a well all by herself.

112

Nathan...

I surely was surprised to see that Sarah had tried to start digging a well. I was plum tuckered out from cutting prairie hay all day and I misunderstood her intentions. I lost my temper.

"Woman, I told you I'd get to it as soon as I can. I can only do so much in a day's time." I said.

She'd had a smile of satisfaction on her face when she showed me what she'd done, but as soon as I said my words, I saw a fire come out of her eyes.

"I didn't ask you to do it," she shot back. "I did it." She put her hands on her hips and gave me my first lesson in how to deal with an angry Sarah—shut my own mouth and listen to what she had to say. "And I will continue doin' it. I didn't shirk on my own chores. I just got it started. I know you can't do it right now. I didn't ask you to. I won't nag you. I will do things when you can't. You're busy. I understand that. The horses will need to eat this winter. I'm not stupid. I just wanted to get a head start."

She stopped to catch her breath. I was immediately sorry and a whole lot confused. I started to open my mouth, but she wasn't finished with me just yet.

"Let's get one thing straight betwixt us. I can do some things myself and I don't need you to tell me I can't. If I have to dig the whole well myself, I will find a way to do it. It may take me a lot longer than you men-folk, but I can do it." When she stopped for another deep breath, I took the opportunity to hold up my hands in surrender.

"Sarah, I'm sorry."

Her face softened as soon as I said those three little words. Her eyes had spoken as loud as she had, and when they dimmed to a quieter glow, I smiled and took a deep breath of my own.

"You won't have to dig the well all by yourself. We'll do it together, and I'm sure Carl and Hannah will help too, just like we helped them. I'm proud of you."

I didn't tell her just then how durned scared I was going down into the hole when I'd helped Carl. We had nothing to shore up the sides when we dug. We were just lucky with his well that the deeper we dug, the more clay we took out. I hoped we'd be that lucky with our own. I had no intention of letting Sarah go down inside a well when it got over four feet deep. However, I didn't tell her that right then.

Carl...

Nathan asked me if my Hannah told him what Sarah was up to. I just nodded and chuckled to myself. I remembered how Jacob said the same thing of Sarah afore he asked her to marry him. He always talked 'bout how he liked her spirit. "It's quick as a flash and she wants things done yesterday," he'd say. I laughed out loud when Nathan said near the same thing to describe her.

"I can't let her dig down too far, Carl. Do you think she'll listen to reason?" he asked.

"Hannah told me she barely scratched the buffalo grass off the top of the dirt," I said.

"I know it's not a good time, but I think I need to put the well on my list of priorities."

"You'll not do it alone," I promised.

Workin' half days on our other chores, and half days diggin' for water, it took us near two weeks afore we finished Nathan and Sarah's well. My Hannah was not one to complain, but the well was a sore spot between her and Sarah.

"My sister never did have much patience for things," she said.

I held back my words and just smiled, 'cause I knowed better than to get betwixt the two. The day the water come in Hannah shook her head and told me how surprised she was that we found water in that spot, but I seen that Sarah had a real satisfied look on her face. Then it wasn't but two weeks later that the water in the creek started slowin'. We all said extra prayers for rain and thanked the good Lord for blessin' us with findin' water on our claims.

113

Sarah…

I watched ever' mornin' as Nathan walked to Rebecca's grave, and I wondered if he'd do the same if it was me layin' in the ground. He never stayed long, but ever since I seen that picture of Nathan and Rebecca, I had to fight a feelin' I didn't like 'bout myself. I knowed it wasn't right that I didn't show him what I found, but I needed to see for myself, what Rebecca was like. Her diary was a way to do that.

When we was busy with summer's harvest and diggin' the well, our days was so long and full that I never had a patch of alone time. Then one day after Nathan went to help Carl cut corn, I got my chance. My belly churned with guilt as I dug the diary out of my trunk and my hands was so sweaty they stuck to the pages when I opened it. I first looked at the last two times she wrote in it, and a cold shiver run down my back. The writin' was smeared. It had hard marks in it, like I seen in the Bible. There was no date on those pages, but she wrote that it was the month of August. On that last page she wrote …*If I am able to find a way to escape from this life, I shall never come back. I can trust no one.*

When Nathan recorded Rebecca's life in our Bible he put down that she died August 10, 1868. My hands was shakin' when I read that. Once again I wished I'd not found what I did. I closed the book, not wantin' to read more. Then I looked to make sure Hannah wasn't payin' me a surprise visit, and when I seen I was still alone, I knowed my chores had to wait a bit longer. I set myself down and opened the diary again. This time I started at the beginnin'.

I read for quite a bit, but it didn't take me long afore I seen how different me and Rebecca was raised. I wanted to set and read the diary plum through, but I had chores I had to do. So I took one more look at her image afore I wrapped ever'thing back up and put it in the bottom of my trunk.

Whilst I tried to hurry to catch up with my work, I found myself stoppin' and thinkin' of all the simple things I'd done since I was a little girl. That would've been when Rebecca was learnin' how to play the piano. We had no music in our house, 'cept when me and Sarah used to try to sing together. Our daddy often stopped whatever he was doin' and sang along. Our mama would smile and shake her head and then tell us all, "Not one of you can carry a tune in a bucket, but you all do a good job of keepin' the mice away." It stopped our singin' and made us girls giggle. We always sung even louder after she said it

The memory made me break into song. I'd not sung for years and my voice cracked. I sounded like one of Hannah's hens cacklin' and I started to laugh at myself. That's when I looked up and seen Nathan starin' at me.

"It's not that bad. Is it?" I asked.

He looked bone tired from shockin' corn all day, but his face cracked into a big smile.

"It's good to hear you laugh, Sarah," he said. Then he frowned a little. "But I thought you were hurt. What were you yelling about before that?"

"I was keepin' the mice away," I explained.

Nathan...

Sarah's laughter was an elixir for my spirits. I could be bone tired, but I couldn't help but smile and feel good when I heard it. I was once again laboring to build something I loved, instead of working to erase one night's memory Except for her paralyzing fear of snakes, I was of the mind that Sarah loved the prairie as much as I did, and she seemed to settle into our life together with ease. After our long hard days, we'd lie in each other's arms at night and share our dreams with each other.

114

Carl…

The heat of the summer was mostly gone and the days was gettin' shorter. Skinner brought us letters from my family a couple times durin' the summer, and it was time to let them know how we was doin'. It was up to me to do all our writin'. Hannah could no longer see good enough, even with her spectacles on, though she was still blessed with seein' good if there was enough light. It was a Sunday in the forenoon that she come runnin' in the soddy whilst I was writin' a letter.

"There's smoke, and lots of it," she said all out of breath.

I run outside and looked to the hills east of us. The land was thirsty for rain, and those tall grasses on the hills was like a tinderbox. We was lucky that the wind was gentle and in our favor, but I knowed that could change any time.

"I got to go," I told Hannah.

Her eyes was wide. "I'll wet down some gunny sacks," she said.

I looked to Nathan's place. He was headed our way, ridin' Jake. Sarah followed a ways behind. She was ridin' Polly and leadin' Molly and Patches.

"If it comes this way, wet down your quilts and cover yourself, and stay inside the soddy," I told Hannah. "The animals have the best chance in the middle of the field we just worked up, but take no chances holdin' them, 'cause I doubt they'd stay there. If fire is headin' their way, their best chance is to let them go free."

I ran to get Barney and then went back to the well where Hannah had the gunny sacks all wetted down. I slid off the horse and helped her put the sacks on Barney's back, and then I held her in my arms and kissed her, hopin' it wouldn't be our last.

"I'll be back," I said.

"I'll be here," she answered.

I met up with Nathan and we rode off to the hills. The smell of the burnin' grasses made the horses shake with fear and it was no small thing to get them to go to where the fire was. When we got near to where the ground was already blackened and smolderin' they refused to go another step. Their eyes was wild. We tied their reins up on their backs, and I hit Barney on the rear end with my hat. They both high-tailed-it for home.

We no sooner let the horses go than I could feel the winds changin' and the fire turned back to where it come from. That sent it straight to where me and Nathan was, and for a bit, I had to fight a real fear. But it was God's way of helpin' us out, for there was only a few patches of grass left to fuel it.

We couldn't see them, but we heard others shoutin' to each other. On the other side of where we was, they was beatin' down the few places that was still burnin'. We took our sacks and did the same, lest the winds picked up any more. Soon we was workin' alongside neighbors we'd never met afore. They come from far off to help with the fire too.

When we knowed we'd won the battle, we introduced ourselves, but we didn't know what anybody looked like. I recognized Tinker's voice in the group. He was black from head to toe, covered in soot, and he said he only knowed it was us because of our voices too.

Hannah...

When Barney and Jake come back without the men, Sarah's face went white. Then she took a deep breath, reached in her pocket, and said, "They're fine." The color come back to her.

"How do you know?" I asked.

She stared into my eyes and said again, "They're fine."

I prayed she was right. How she was so sure, I don't know. She started talkin 'bout our plans to trade in Ellsworth.

It was late in the day when my Carl and Sarah's Nathan come walkin' back. Corky ran to meet them, but he stopped when they got closer. He stood barkin' like they was strangers. They was so covered with black ash, all I could see was their eyes. Even when Carl talked to him, the dog put down his head and walked a ways behind them.

Me and Sarah ran to meet them too. They smelled mighty awful, but they was safe. We laughed with relief and ran into their dirty, open arms.

115

Sarah...

Me and Nathan and Hannah finally got to go to Ellsworth to do some tradin'. Our first stop was to post letters and to see what mail there was for us. Carl got letters from his family and Nathan's brother and mama sent him a nice long letter. He opened that letter the minute it was in his hand.

"I have a nephew," he announced to all who was in hearin' distance. "They named him Emil, after my brother. Will said he's the spitting image of me."

His smile was wide, but he had to swallow hard afore he could read on. When he was done, he turned to me and said, "You'll get to meet my family someday. We'll find a way."

My disappointment come from not findin' even one cookin' stove for sale in the town. So whilst me and Sarah did our tradin' for winter's goods, Nathan spoke to the mercantile owner and put out the money to order a stove.

"Now that the railroad runs through real regular, towns a growin' fast," Mr. Owens said. "Can't keep 'em in the store. 'Fraid you'll have to come back for it."

'Cause of Nathan growin' up in a store, he and Mr. Owens got along fine. I wanted a cookin' stove in the worst of ways and I was fretful of the cost, but on our way home, Nathan told me he got a fair price. When I asked what that was, he didn't answer. Hannah looked at me and waited. Then she grinned, cause my sister knowed how hard it was for me to not say more.

Nathan...

Mother's part of the letter said Father had mellowed some with the arrival of my nephew. They named the boy, Emil, after my brother who never came home from the war. Surely that pleased my father.

Maybe it was the letter from home that made me see some of him in myself, for when Sarah asked about the price I'd given for the stove, I just assumed she was like my mother, and couldn't understand numbers or money. But unlike my mother, Sarah wanted to make decisions together.

It was a trait I admired in her, that ability to be counted as an equal in our life. Sarah taught me a new way of thinking. As soon as we left Carl and Hannah's place, she looked at me with resolve and asked me again.

"And why is it that you won't tell me the price you paid for a stove that I will be doin' most of the cookin' on?"

It wasn't just a question anymore. It was a tone that let me know I'd better tread carefully. So what did I do? I jumped right into Sarah's anger.

"Do you really understand numbers and prices?" I asked.

Her eyes shot sparks. "If I was a man, would you ask me such a question?"

She didn't give me a chance to answer.

"Of course, I do. My daddy made us girls study numbers ever' day. It's true we didn't have school, but my mama and my daddy both taught us girls good. Who do you think took care of my daddy's business when he was ailin' and my mama got sick too? Who do you think sold the house? Yes, I knowed I didn't get all I should've. I should've got this straight with you when we got married and you wouldn't even talk 'bout what money I could bring in. It isn't much, 'cause I give Hannah half of it, but it's not mine now, it's ours."

She stopped and caught her breath, and started right back in. "And they taught us to read and write too. I can't do fancy script, but it's steady and neat, and…and, what if you get hurt? What am I supposed to do then, be at the mercy of another man?"

She quieted then and turned away from me. We'd arrived home and I'd stopped the wagon, but neither of us got down. Polly and Jake needed tending, but Sarah needed mending. I thought of my own mother not so many years ago, when I wanted her to stand up to my father.

"You're right, Sarah," I said as gently as I could. Jake snorted. We sat for just a bit longer without saying anything before we got down and each attended our own chores.

That night before we went to sleep, I told Sarah how much I'd paid for the stove. The next morning we put our money together, as partners would do. I was surprised with the amount she contributed, and she seemed surprised by what I still had. I didn't tell her some was left over from what Becca's father had given me. After all, he'd not wanted his own daughter to know.

My independent wife was always surprising me. As challenging as it was, I was thankful I had a strong partner.

116

Sarah...

At first I had a great relief when me and Nathan put our money together as one. I seen Nathan study me for a long time afore he did it though. Then he smiled and it was like we shared a good secret. But when I reached in my trunk to fetch my share of the money I had hidden there, the Bible and diary reminded me that I wasn't sharin' ever'thing. I willed my hand to pick them up too, and show what I found. I even touched the diary, gettin' ready to show Nathan, but it felt like a red hot coal on my fingers.

Next day I had a look-see in the trunk to make sure nothin' had disappeared, or worst yet, caught on fire. It was still there and I was still starin' at it when Nathan walked in.

"Got any more secrets in that trunk of yours?" he asked.

I jumped. I slammed the lid down too quick. My fingers was in the way. I yelped with the pain and opened the lid just enough to pull my fingers out. Now it was my face that burned. "You scared me." I managed to say.

Nathan come over and helped me off my knees and kissed my throbbin' fingers. My favorite story my mama told me as a little girl, was of a prince who kissed the hand of a princess. Nathan's kiss made me feel so elegant that I forgot the hurt, and Nathan's eyes made me feel like a princess.

Later that day my purple fingers didn't look very royal as I bent to pick up buffalo chips. How I wished I could've gathered wood instead. I missed havin' trees on the prairie, almost as much as I missed havin' visitors. I had a pile of chips heaped high for the winter, but not near the pile Hannah had, so with the cooler days of fall, I gathered as many chips and sunflower stalks as I could.

I was hackin' away at a stubborn stalk when I heard a rattle. I didn't move nothin' but my eyeballs, and when I seen him, I near fainted. He'd been sunnin' hiself in the grass, not close enough to strike, but too close for me. I wanted to run, though I knowed that'd be foolish. 'Cept for my insides shakin', I stood dead still. I didn't even blink and I must've stopped breathin' too, 'cause when he finally slithered away, I was gaspin' for air. It's when I realized I'd been standin' there, frozen, with a corn knife raised above my head. I wondered if I could have even used it, if he would've come my way.

I was shakin' so hard I had to vomit, and after my innards was empty, I shook even more. I'd done the same thing yesterday, though there'd not been a rattler around. And it wasn't 'til later in the day, as I was takin' another peek in the diary that I realized why my belly wasn't feelin' so good.

When I finally got back to the soddy, Nathan was still helpin' Carl, so I got the diary out to read where I'd left off afore. I set outside where I could see if he was comin' home, so I'd not have to worry 'bout him sneekin' up on me. Ever so once in a while I checked 'round me, makin' sure there was nothin' slitherin' up behind me either.

I read 'bout Rebecca havin' a secret and bein' ill almost ever' day. It was clear that she was in a family way. Hannah never told me that.

I stopped readin' and looked up. I seen my Nathan comin' home. So I went back in the soddy and hid the diary again. And that's when it come to me, that I wasn't havin' belly aches 'cause of my guilt 'bout the diary. I counted. I was in a family way too.

117

Carl...

Nathan and Sarah was back from Ellsworth again. This time they carried no letters for us, but Sarah was a happy woman with a new stove in the wagon. As I helped Nathan wrestle with puttin' it in their soddy, Hannah and Sarah talked 'bout how fast the buffalo chips would turn to ash.

"You'll need a bigger pile of fuel to keep you from freezin' this winter," I heard my Hannah say.

"Maybe Corky can go with me next time to scout out for snakes. I don't want to meet up with another rattler," Sarah said. "I 'bout died from fright the last time." She turned to Nathan and said, "Maybe we ought to get us a dog of our own."

We was puttin' up the stovepipe. Nathan stopped ever'thing. His face showed the same pain he wore the day he put Rusty down. He turned and walked out of the soddy. I was left holdin' the stovepipe.

Sarah's eyes followed Nathan. She turned to Hannah and whispered, "Oh, Rebecca had a dog, didn't she."

There was a bit of quiet afore Hannah asked, "Did Nathan tell you about Rusty?"

"No, uh, you, uh..." Sarah said.

"I don't remember tellin' you 'bout him."

Sarah's eyes was dartin' back and forth from me to Hannah, but she didn't say more. Instead she turned and walked out of the soddy too.

Hannah frowned.

I put the stovepipe down and we walked outside together. Nathan and Sarah had walked off a ways and was talkin' in a quiet voice.

"There's some things Sarah should know," I told Hannah.

"I'll not speak poorly of Rebecca though," she said whilst noddin' her head.

Her sayin' that confused me a bit, but I didn't always understand Hannah's reasons for what she did. When it come to her and her sister, I didn't even try.

Nathan put his arm 'round Sarah and looked our way. Then they come walkin' back together, and he said, "Let's get that stovepipe through the roof so we can let Sarah cook us something on her new stove."

Nathan...

Sarah followed me outside.

"Nathan, did I say somethin' wrong?" I was glad she was standing behind me when she asked, for it took me a while to figure out what to say to her.

I turned around. "No, you didn't say anything wrong." Then I tried to explain, "I never told you about Rusty, Becca's dog. He tangled with a skunk and he got rabies. I had to put him down. Becca hated me for that, and it was right after that...that Becca...Becca became ill."

"I'm sorry," Sarah said.

"You had no way of knowing."

She nodded. I saw a question in her eyes, but she said nothing. For that, I was grateful.

I managed a smile and said, "Let's go hook up that stovepipe now."

Hannah…

Me and Sarah didn't talk 'bout Rebecca much. Truth was, I seen Rebecca changin' a while afore she went mad. There was things 'bout her that I didn't understand, and I didn't want Sarah puttin' even more questions in my thinkin'.

After Sarah asked me the first time, how Rebecca died, I looked back on it and I really didn't know. I knowed she wasn't right in the head, but the night she died, she'd been strong enough to give me a big goose egg, and my Carl said him and Nathan wrestled an ax away from her. When I wrapped up her body so we could bury her, I seen how tiny she was. Could she have died from her madness? It was all such bad memories. Maybe it was even rabies, 'cause I never seen what they could do to a person. I didn't want to remember it.

118

Sarah...

When I told Nathan we was gonna have a little one of our own, he got the same joy on his face that he had when he found out he was an uncle. There was no question that it brought him pleasure. He picked me up and twirled me in his arms. When he let me down on my own two feet, he asked, "Are you sure?"

I laughed and nodded. My worry that Nathan would grieve for the loss of his first-born with Rebecca was gone. It was later that day when I told Hannah our news, I took into consideration Rebecca had never told anyone that she was carryin' a child.

As soon as Hannah seen me, she asked, "What are you up to, sister?"

My happiness was hard to hide. It was when I shared my news that I seen a pain come over her, and she turned away from me. I didn't understand at first. As I tried to think why my sister wouldn't rejoice at my news, the worry come back. Maybe Rebecca never told Nathan, but she must've confided in Hannah. Before I thought long enough on it I said, "Is it because of Rebecca's baby?"

She turned 'round real slow. "What?" she asked. She frowned and said, "Rebecca didn't have a baby."

My face felt like it was on fire. I swallowed hard, "Oh, I..." I started to explain.

"Where did you get that idea?"

"From you," I lied, and tried to think what I should say next. "Aren't you happy for me?" I asked.

Hannah looked down with the saddest face I ever seen on her. "It's me," she whispered. "Sarah, I'm barren."

She hid her face in both her hands and her shoulders started shakin'. I held her in my arms then and we both cried, like we'd not done since we was little girls.

We talked of how our mama would not approve of so many tears. Then I told her how many tears Mama had shed that last year of her life, and we cried some more.

Our chores suffered, and we had to scurry when the men come in to eat their noon meal. Nathan and Carl was laughin' and jokin' with each other. Carl come over to me and said, "Sarah...I," he stopped. He was lookin' in my eyes. He looked at Hannah, then he looked at Nathan. Nathan gave a little shrug. I seen Hannah's eyes was all puffy and red. I suppose mine looked the same. Nathan and Carl got real quiet then, and none of us said much whilst we all ate.

Hannah...

When Carl asked me if ever'thing was good betwixt me and Sarah, I nodded. He told me how happy Nathan was when he told him of Sarah's condition. I took a big deep breath and told him how happy I was for her. Then I told him how sorry I was that I'd not given him a child. I wasn't able to even look at him when I said it, 'cause I didn't want self-pity to come over me again. But my Carl always had a way of makin' things right. He reached over with a gentle hand under my chin and raised my face to look his way.

"God's blessed me with you, my Hannah," he said. "We have to trust that He knows what's right for us." He wrapped his arms 'round me then and held me for a long time.

I knowed he was right. I was happy that I would soon be an aunt, and I was ashamed that I wasn't more grateful for that. But I longed to hold a baby of my own in my arms.

119

Sarah...

The longer I kept my secret from Nathan the more I fretted. He'd almost forbidden me to go in the dugout, so how could I tell him where I'd found Rebecca's things. I worried myself sick that I'd not be able to keep it from him much longer, 'cause I knowed it was wrong. But then, I got the chance to read the rest of the diary one day, when Nathan said he was hungry for some fresh game. He grabbed his gun, and as soon as he went out the door, I went to my trunk, dug out the diary and read what I'd not been able to finish afore.

I didn't have much left to read. I already knowed what the last page said and when I read those words again, I got the same feelin' I had the first time I read them. *If I am able to find a way to escape from this life, I shall never come back. I can trust no one.* There was more, but it was only scribbles and deep ugly marks.

I don't know how long I set there starin' at the book, but I jumped when Nathan's gun broke the silence of the quiet day. Thinkin' on what I just read, I finally understood why Hannah never talked 'bout Rebecca. It was clear Rebecca wasn't in a good way. Her thinkin' she'd had tea with her mama and Martha showed me that. She said she could trust no one. Did that mean Hannah too? Did Hannah know that?

So instead of tellin' Nathan what I done, I hid the diary deep in the bottom of the trunk again. Those words was makin' an echo inside my head—*If I am able to find a way to escape from this life, I shall never come back.* I was sick at the thought of how those words might make Nathan feel, and I knowed that I could never tell him what I found.

When he come home he had a big old turkey and an even bigger smile, but he was shiverin' with cold.

"The weather's changing," he said. "There's a drizzle coming down, and it's getting colder."

I was happy to talk 'bout the weather, so I didn't have to think 'bout what Rebecca might've done to herself. The words *find a way to escape* kept with me, 'til I realized I needed to pay heed to Nathan. When he'd gone out in the drizzle I thought he just got chilled. Then I seen it was more than that.

The drizzle changed to rain and he decided he'd stay in for a while.

"Not much sense in trying to work outside today," he said.

He got busy greasin' Jake and Polly's harness whilst I got busy cookin' the turkey. But then Nathan started coughin' like I heard my daddy do when he was dyin'. For a while, I forgot 'bout ever'thing else. Then I noticed Nathan couldn't stop his shiverin' as he was tryin' to work.

I walked over to him and put my hand on his face. It scared me.

"You're burnin' with fever."

"I'll be fine," he said. Then he started coughin' again.

"You'll be fine tomorrow," I said. "Today you need to take care of yourself."

He argued with me at first, but then I got him to lay down. I could tell by lookin' in his eyes, that he needed my mama's cure afore he got sicker. He slept between his coughin' spells. I got busy.

Nathan...

I must have slept most of the day. When I woke up the rain had stopped. Sarah came in from doing the evening's chores and I tried to sit up, but everything started spinning around me, and I was overtaken by a wicked cough. I laid back down.

"Good, you're awake," Sarah said. She went over to the stove, added more chips to the embers, and then washed her hands.

"Don't know if I'll ever get used to cookin' with chips," she said. But it wasn't the chips that was smelling foul—it was the concoction she had been cooking. She held a spoonful of the syrupy liquid to my lips.

"Here, you need to take this."

I opened my mouth to protest. She took the opportunity to pour the contents in. I swallowed.

"What in tarnation is that?" I croaked. "It tastes awful, and it smells even worse."

"My mama used to give this to me whenever I had a bad cold comin' on. It's onion syrup, and it's good for a cold."

"But I killed you a turkey for supper."

"And I'm gonna eat some of it. But I'm not sick. You are."

Just when I was going to object to the cruelty of her remedy I started to sneeze. I must have sneezed ten times. Sarah wore a satisfied smile.

"That's what Hannah used to do when our mama gave her onion syrup. I didn't take to it the same way, but it still worked." She held another spoonful in front of me, and I shook my head, but she didn't move. I took it quick. I swallowed quick. Then I had another sneezing fit that tuckered me out. I laid back down and closed my eyes while my stomach protested, but when I awoke the next morning I felt good enough to get up and do my own chores.

120

Hannah...

When the colder weather come, my Carl and Nathan started workin' at the quarry again. The same as the year afore, Nathan still did most of the huntin' for fresh meat and we took our noon meal together. But this time my Sarah was with us, and Nathan didn't carry the fresh hurt of losin' Rebecca.

Whilst the men was workin' in the quarry, me and Sarah decided to take a break from huntin' buffalo chips. They was gettin' harder to find close to our claim, now that the buffalo herds had moved further west. We was always lookin' for ways to add to our fuel supply, so one day we worked together twistin' hay into cats.

My sister had changed a bit over the last year. I suppose I had too. But we had a closeness from bein' born together. I could tell Sarah was frettin' over somethin', but it didn't come out 'til we was in the soddy, workin' on the hay twists. I grabbed a bunch of hay when I seen Sarah lookin' at my hands.

"You're bleedin'," she said. Lookin' at her own hands, she seen they had tiny cuts from the prairie hay too.

"My hands are so dried out, I wasn't sure I had any blood left in them," I said.

"Our daddy's hands got so soft when he was sick. He said a man's hands should never get soft."

Memories of Rebecca come to me then. "Remember how Mama said you could tell a real lady, by how soft her hands was? Rebecca's hands was really soft," I said.

"You don't talk 'bout her much. Was she a real lady? Havin' tea and all?"

"Not all the memories are good," I said.

Sarah looked away from me. She was settin' and starin' at the door, like she was expectin' someone to walk in. Somethin' was botherin' her.

"Sarah?"

She turned my way, lookin' pale.

"Sarah? Are you feelin' poorly?"

She took a deep breath and blurted out a question, "Hannah, did Rebecca end her own life?"

"What?" I asked, "Why'd you think that?"

She looked away again and said nothin'.

I didn't have any idea why she was askin' me. Maybe it was just somethin' she needed to know 'cause when my sister got somethin' in her head, it wouldn't leave 'til she could see it clear, so I tried to be careful with my words.

"No." I finally said. "But, Rebecca was raised to be a lady, not a farm wife."

"Nathan told me she didn't like the prairie."

"The day Nathan had to put down Rusty, it was more than she could take."

"But you said she didn't take her own life?"

"She went mad," I said. I realized I'd not ever said that, even to Carl. I went on, "I even wondered for a while if she'd got the rabies from Rusty, but I don't think so."

Sarah's eyebrows creased. She asked, "But how did she die?"

"Nathan was gonna try to find her a doctor. I was the only one she'd listen to, so he asked me if she could stay with me the night afore. Carl and Nathan slept outside and Rebecca slept in here with me. I don't know what happened. Carl woke up and seen her goin' after Nathan with the axe. They wrestled with her and Carl come in here and found me on the floor with a big old goose egg on my head. When me and Carl went back outside she was gone. Nathan was holdin' her in his arms."

I seen a shudder pass through my sister. She got up and went over and opened the door. She stood there for a long time, just starin' out east to where the men was workin'. I started twistin' hay again, and when I looked over to where she was standin' she was lookin' down at her belly and rubbin' it real gentle. After a bit she set herself back down and helped me twist more cats. I could tell somethin' was still troublin' her, but we didn't talk 'bout Rebecca the rest of that day.

Nathan...

We had fashioned enough limestone block, that we started hauling one or two back with us whenever we came from the quarry. When we compared our abilities with the stone we'd cut the first year, it was easy to see that we were learning as we went.

"By the time we get our house built, we might figure out what we're doin'," Carl joked as we unloaded the buckboard.

Sarah and Hannah came outside as we were stacking a couple of blocks in the pattern of how we would lay them out for a building.

"It'll be a few years, but what do you think of that for a house someday?" I asked.

Sarah's eyes lit up. Her smile and questions told me she thought it would make a fine home.

"How are we gonna make mortar for it? How many windows will it have? Will we have to have a dirt floor?"

Carl interrupted her questions with a question of his own. "When are you women gonna feed us hungry men?"

It was a lively conversation around the supper table that night as Carl and I tried to answer the questions both women had. It was getting late in the day when Sarah and I left for home. We had to face a sharp wind from the north, but in our excitement it was still a pleasant walk.

"It will take us time, Sarah," I said. "The land won't be ours for three and a half more years."

"It gives us plenty of time to decide where we should put the house," she said.

How good it was to hear the word 'us' in her words. How good it was to have a dream we both shared.

121

Sarah…

Nathan still had a bit of a cough when winter got closer, but he didn't take kindly to the idea of another dose of onion syrup.

"It'd end that cough for good," I said.

"Or end me," he argued, as he scratched his chin where his beard had growed in.

It seemed like all the critters knowed that winter was comin'. The animal's coats turned thick and heavy. And near ever' day I heard geese honkin' as they flew over our place. I liked to watch as they took turns leadin' each other south, to wherever they was goin'.

The bugs, spiders, and mice was all tryin' to move inside with us too, burrowin' into the walls of our soddy. I fought with them all the time. Maybe that's why I liked the outside so much.

One day I was busy makin' breakfast, when out of the corner of my eye, I seen somethin' drop out of the ceilin'. When I seen it was a snake, layin' there on the floor, hardly movin' at all, I near fainted. He was betwixt me and the door. I felt trapped. I didn't even know I was screamin'. Nathan come runnin' in from doin' his chores. He reached down and picked up the evil creature by its tail.

"It's only a little bull snake. He won't hurt you, Sarah," he said as he stood there holdin' him up for me to see.

"Nathan!" I screamed. "Get him out of my house!"

I knowed my fear wasn't rational, but I couldn't stop shakin'. When Nathan took the snake outside, I went outside too. I took deep breaths and watched him as he started to lay the snake in the grass. I yelled at him again, "If he finds hiself a way to get back inside the soddy, you'll have to sleep outside with him next time."

Nathan was shakin' his head as he walked all the way to the creek carryin' that snake by the tail.

When I went back inside the soddy I could feel snakes watchin' me as I did my work. I jumped when Nathan come back inside.

"We've got company," he said.

Skinner was standin' aside him, holdin' a buffalo robe in his big arms. "Thought you needed a weddin' present," he said. He had a big fat grin on his face.

I forgot all 'bout the bull snake, and wrapped myself in that warm robe. Now we had a robe to lay ourselves on and Nathan's robe to cover ourselves. We was ready for the cold of winter—if the snakes stayed away.

Whilst Skinner ate breakfast with us, Nathan told him 'bout our mornin's excitement. He laughed so loud I thought more snakes might drop down from the roof, but I could tell somethin' wasn't right with him either. We visited for a while, afore he left to go see Hannah and Carl. We told him we'd see him at their place later that day.

There was a quietness hangin' on all of them when we got to Hannah and Carl's. Skinner said he was headin' for the fort to bed down for the winter, but he didn't act like it was where he wanted to be.

Carl...

Like the year afore, when the winter started to settle in, Skinner come callin'—the difference bein' that my Hannah wasn't near as lonely for company after her sister come out on the prairie. She'd grown fond of Skinner though. His stories had always been a little raw, but they'd mellowed of late with a sorrow when he talked of the Indians. He had a great understandin' of their ways, and it was plain he didn't think they'd been treated fair.

"Don't really think there's much need fer me to hang 'round these parts anymore," Skinner said. "Think maybe I'll be headin' out West in the spring."

Hannah was stirrin' a pot of stew whilst we talked. She looked over at us when Skinner was explainin' how he'd done his part in gettin' treaties signed.

"It's been near a year since Black Kettle was massacred," he said. "He was a good man, and look where it got him."

I seen Hannah start to say somethin', then think better of it.

"Well, the Indians have been beaten back, and I don't think you'll have any more difficulties with them. I hate what's happened to them though."

This time Hannah spoke her mind. "How can you say that, after what they did this last spring? They signed treaties, didn't they?"

Skinner nodded his head real slow. "It's true," he said. He raked his hands through his wooly hair. "At the time, I thought the treaty was a good thing." He bowed his head, lookin' at his boots.

"I ain't seen either side keep their end of those treaties." He let that settle on Hannah for a bit afore he went on. "The Indians got their own way of life that the white man will never understand."

Hannah listened to him like I seen her listen to her own daddy when she was a little girl. I was thinkin' that Skinner was explainin' his feelin's to hiself, as much as he was to her.

He kept on talkin'. "Ever'thing they knowed was taken from 'em. They was put on land they didn't choose, with rules that make no to sense to 'em. They was told not to leave their reservations, yet the government doesn't give 'em provisions they was promised. Their people are hungry, yet they're no longer allowed to use the huntin' grounds they've always relied on."

Hannah frowned and looked confused.

"What are they to do, Hannah?" he asked.

She turned away from him, and gave attention to the stew she was stirrin'. She had no answer for him. It got real quiet in the soddy for a bit 'til Corky's bark told us Nathan and Sarah had come.

122

Hannah...

There was somethin' betwixt me and Sarah. 'Cept for the secret of her *gift* that our daddy said she had, we'd never kept secrets from each other. Yet I felt it now. Maybe it was the blessin' she carried inside her.

I don't think she knowed she did it, but sometimes Sarah stopped whatever she was doin'. She'd get a far-away look on her face, and reach down and rub her belly real gentle. I watched and had a joy for her, but a heaviness in my own heart, 'cause I'd never get to feel whatever it was she was feelin'.

It brought a bittersweet memory to me too—of our own mama doin' the same thing when me and Sarah was 'bout seven years of age. One day the doctor come to our house. I heard a baby cry that day and shortly after that, me and Sarah was sent to the neighbor's house. We didn't understand why we had to stay there for days, but when we come home I didn't see our mama rubbin' her belly anymore. She seemed to be sad for a long time.

When I got old enough to read and my eyes was still good, I seen the name Mathew Lucas in my mama's Bible one day. There was two dates aside his name. They was both the same. So I asked my mama 'bout it. She gave me the strangest look.

"You had a brother," she said. Then her face turned hard. "He died." She turned and walked away from me. I told Sarah 'bout it, and our daddy heard. He told us girls we should never again talk to our mama 'bout havin' a brother.

I wondered if Sarah had those memories too.

Sarah...

The weather was mild yet, so the men worked at the quarry and I spent most days at Hannah's. Nathan had traps set all along the creek. He always went out early to Rebecca's grave and then checked his traps afore he did anything else. He said he couldn't stand to see an animal suffer any longer than need be. If he was lucky with catchin' us a meal, then me and Hannah shared in the chore of cookin' it.

Me and my sister always liked to keep busy, so it was the quiet times that was the hardest. We was settin' at her place, patchin' overalls, when she told me how long the days got the winter afore I come. It brought on a melancholy spirit for both of us.

"I'm grateful that you was there with our daddy and our mama," she said. "But now I'm grateful that you're here."

I nodded and smiled. I laid my mendin' down and got up to stretch my legs. When I opened the door to look to where the men was workin', I seen my sister watchin' me like she wanted to say more. Then I realized I was standin' there with my hand on my belly, wonderin' if I was carryin' a boy or a girl.

Whenever I thought of the baby growin' inside me, my thinkin' went to the diary. Rebecca had a baby growin' in her too. She kept it a secret, even though she was scared. I felt her loneliness and it mixed with the happiness I had. I wanted to tell Hannah what I read— what I found. I thought it would hurt her to know that Rebecca didn't trust her though. I couldn't do that to her.

I prayed ever' day, askin' God what I should do with the things I found, and I seen no answer. So I kept the secret and wondered why He let me see it in the first place.

Whilst we all set down to eat rabbit stew for supper that night, we heard the wind come roarin' in from the north. We hurried with our meal and then me and Nathan headed for home. I pulled my shawl up over my face, as there was ice fallin' out of the sky, and it felt like needles pokin' into my skin. It made me see why Nathan wanted a beard for the winter.

By the time we reached our place my hands was so stiff with the cold I did a poor job of milkin' Molly. Nathan tended the horses and as soon as we was done, we went in the soddy and snuggled betwixt our buffalo robes.

"It's gonna be hard to drag myself out of here in the morning to stoke the stove," Nathan said.

I knowed how fast chips and cats burned and I said a prayer afore I fell asleep, that I'd have enough fuel to get us through the winter.

123

Nathan...

When the weather turned bitter, it was surely a pleasure to have Carl and Hannah come to our place for a change. It was too cold to work at the quarry up on a hillside with no protection from the biting wind. It gave Carl and me a chance to plan the best way of using the limestone for building material.

We were discussing how to make a mortar with slaked lime, when I heard the women talking about using the sewing machine.

"Let's get that material you showed me, and make curtains," Hannah said. She was standing beside Sarah's trunk. When she reached down to open it, I couldn't believe how fast Sarah moved.

"Let me get it," Sarah snapped. A look passed between the two that I didn't understand, but it was plain that Sarah didn't want Hannah in that trunk. It made me curious as to what she had in there.

While Carl was talking about slaking lime and making a kiln in the creek bank, I half listened to him, and half listened to the two sisters as they pondered how to use their mother's sewing machine. Together they moved it closer to the window where there was more light, treating it like it was a fine piece of china. Sarah had never said much about it to me, although I knew it was something very special to her. I was surely surprised when I realized she'd never used it.

They were both hovered over the machine, debating the threading of the needle.

"There is no way I can see to do it with this poor light inside," Hannah said.

"I can do this," Sarah said, "let me try to remember how it's supposed to go."

Carl saw me observing the two. He stopped talking and listened too. Hannah caught his look.

"Sarah doesn't know what she's doin', and we have no manual," she explained.

"I read it once, when our daddy brought the machine home. When our mama got the material to sew, our daddy was taken ill," Sarah said. I heard a frustration in her voice. "I lost it somewhere…I…I suppose when I closed up the house."

"Well…" I started to add my consideration to the conversation. Carl' eyebrows arched, as if in warning. I heeded his caution and said no more.

"Let's take a walk to the creek and see where we might fashion some kind of kiln," he said.

Carl and I weren't gone long, for the freezing temperatures and wild winds soon chased us back to the soddy. But we were gone long enough that when we returned Sarah had indeed figured out the complexities of her mother's sewing machine. The sisters were marveling at the stitching it accomplished.

"Now, you are ready to sew for all the fine folks around here," Hannah said. I surely didn't understand what brought on all the laughter then, but both women thought the remark very entertaining.

Carl chuckled. It was always that way with him, when he heard Hannah laugh. He didn't question it. He just enjoyed the sound.

Sarah...

Hannah surprised me when she had the idea to make curtains. We'd talked 'bout it once afore, and said we'd use our mama's sewin' machine. When I got into the trunk to get the material, I forgot 'bout the manual. It was in my trunk too, and I'd read it many times, but I couldn't take a chance on findin' it that day 'cause it was down in the very bottom, under the diary.

I told another lie. How I suffered with guilt, for I knowed it was a sin to lie. I wanted in the worst way to confide my secret to my sister, yet I didn't. I held it all inside of me.

124

Carl...

We was all lookin' forward to Christmas. Nathan shot a wild turkey the day afore Christmas, and my Hannah asked if she could be the one to make it into our dinner for all of us. She had a special surprise for Sarah too. She'd been workin' on it ever since she found out Sarah was in a family way.

"I'll get this done afore Christmas," she said more than once. Yet to make it a surprise, she could only work on it when Sarah wasn't 'round, and when she did work on it, her eyes had to strain with the effort. Still, it seemed to bring her such joy.

"Now tell me, Carl, are my stitches even?" she would ask. They all looked good to me, but when I told her so, she said, "I ain't never made fine stitches anyways, so you got to tell me if they're straight."

It was Christmas mornin' when the sun was shinin' bright, I seen her put on her spectacles and step outside to inspect it. She held it close to her face to see. She come back inside wearin' a smile and put the little quilt under the buffalo robe to hide it from Sarah's eyes.

"Guess I'd best get back to Christmas dinner," she said.

The weather was mild that day though my bones felt like there might be a storm brewin'. I went outside in the forenoon to see if Nathan and Sarah was comin'. I seen them first leavin' their place, when Corky let me know we had another visitor too. Skinner rode in from the south. We'd be sharin' our Christmas dinner.

When we put his horse in the stable with Bill and Barney, he pulled his saddle bags off and carried them with him as we made our way to the soddy.

"Letters?" I asked.

"Letters, and a couple things to show my appreciation for you makin' me feel like I'm family." He smiled. Somethin' in the way he said it, made it sound like a good-bye.

Hannah...

Skinner's visit for our Christmas dinner was a gift to all of us. As soon as Sarah and Nathan come, Skinner winked at Carl and said he'd brung us letters from home. The letters was from Carl's family. Both me and Sarah felt like we was a part of them. When Carl read his letter to all of us, they all had good wishes and blessin's for Sarah and Nathan too. I seen that meant a lot to Sarah.

Nathan got letters from his mama and his brother too, and both talked 'bout how big baby Emil was gettin'. When Nathan shared that with us, he looked over to Sarah, like he couldn't wait for his own child to be born.

As soon as Nathan finished his letter, I gave Sarah the baby quilt. I knowed it meant a lot to her, and I think it pleased Nathan as much as it did Sarah.

"I have somethin' for you too," Sarah said. She went to the basket Nathan brung in earlier and set out a molasses cake on the table. I started to thank her for it when she reached in again and brung out the curtains she'd finally finished on our mama's sewin' machine. She unfolded them and held them out to me. "I think these will look mighty purty on your window," she said.

I thought them to be the most beautiful curtains I ever seen. I wanted to put them over the window right then and there, but I turned my attention back to gettin' our dinner on the table.

It wasn't 'til we all had our bellies full that Skinner said he had somethin' more he thought we might like. He reached behind where he was settin' and pulled a parcel out of his saddlebag. Whilst he untied the string to the small bundle, he explained, "I got no family of my own, and you women-folk have always made me feel at home. This is for you both. The merchant in the dry goods at Ellsworth, said this was popular with the ladies." He folded the paper back to reveal the purtiest pink and gray cotton fabric I seen in a long while.

I don't know what my face looked like, but Sarah was wearin' a mighty big smile on hers. "Oh, I can make more curtains," she said.

The men all agreed they didn't understand why we wanted curtains. "Why, when there's so little light in a soddy anyways, would you want to put somethin' up that would block more light?" asked Carl.

Me and Sarah laughed at that.

"No use explainin'," I said.

Skinner picked up the material and handed it to Sarah. Under it lay two pouches of tobacco. "This is for those that don't understand the magic of the curtains," Skinner said, as he handed one pouch of tobacco to Carl and the other to Nathan.

The men went outside to enjoy their smokes. After Skinner left later in the day, Carl and Nathan told me and Sarah what Skinner told them when they'd been outside.

Skinner couldn't bring hiself to tell me and Sarah that he might not see us again for some time. His plan was to catch the first wagon train headin' West in the early spring.

125

Sarah...

Instead of makin' curtains out of the fabric Skinner brung us, I thought how our mama had made us matchin' dresses when we was little girls.

"There's not enough for dresses," I said, "but we could make aprons. There's enough for us to each have a nice apron."

"And we could wear them when we go to town," Hannah said.

"And on Sundays," I suggested.

Hannah clapped her hands together. "Then we would get to wear them more than once or twice a year," she said.

So me and Hannah made fine, even stitches on our mama's sewin' machine. We had fun makin' those aprons, and the time it took us to do it, helped to pass the long winter days whilst we waited for a sign of spring.

It was after we made the aprons together that I dug into the trunk one day when Nathan was outside for a while. I read the sewin' machine manual over real good and was just 'bout ready to put it back when I heard Nathan comin' in. I turned 'round and held the book behind me and then set myself down on top of it. He come in stompin' snow off his boots, sayin' how cold it was outside. I set there like a rabbit that was too scared to move, tryin' to think of some reason to send him back out into the cold.

"Sarah, are you feeling poorly?" he asked. It must've looked stange to him, with me just settin' and doin' nothin'.

"Afore you put any more snow inside on the floor, would you get us more water?" I asked.

He looked over at the water pail that was not near empty yet. "But, it's half full," he said.

I couldn't look him in the eye, and I couldn't think of anything else to say. He stood there lookin' puzzled for a bit, shook his head, and put his coat back on. He grabbed the pail, emptied it into my cookin' pot, and went back into the cold to get the water I didn't need.

I breathed a sigh of relief and whilst I hid the manual again, I made up my mind right then, that next chance I got, I'd get rid of all the secrets I hid in my trunk. I'd burn them to a cinder and I'd never have to tell anyone anything.

I reached in my pocket and rubbed my worry stone. My chest felt like it did afore a tragedy, but I knowed it was from the lies I told. I also had a fear that if I burned a Bible, I'd surely go to hell. I was no good at keepin' secrets. I rubbed the stone harder, and just then my baby let me know he was growin' inside me.

126

Hannah...

Even Carl was anxious for a trip into town when the weather started showin' signs of spring. When we was doin' mornin' chores and we heard geese honkin' he watched them head north, and said. "They're tellin' me it's near time to be doin' the spring plantin'. Lookin' skyward, he smiled and added, "Best we go to Ellsworth now, afore we get so busy that you and Sarah have to go alone."

But when we all talked it over, it was decided me and Carl would make the trip ourselves.

"Don't think I could take all that jostlin' in the wagon right now," Sarah said. She stood rubbin' her hand betwixt her hip and her back.

Next mornin', me and Carl did our chores in the dark so we could head out as soon as the sun lit up the east with a bushel basket full of reds and yellows. Carl gave Bill and Barney a "giddy-up," and we rode silent for a while, breathin' in the fresh scent of spring and lookin' to the east at the beauty of the sunrise.

When a meadowlark's clear notes broke the silence, Carl said, "God's got a mighty big paintbrush this mornin'."

I smiled and held on tight as we hit a bump in the trail. It always give me a good feelin' when I seen how my Carl was such a part of the land, though I still yearned for his family and wished they'd not be so far away. I mostly held it inside me, but I had a deep need for news from back home, so I asked, "Can we post our letters and check our mail first thing?"

There was two letters from Carl's family and one letter from Nathan's kin. Carl stuck all three of them in his overall pocket and we hurried to do all our tradin'. After we had all our supplies loaded we found us a nice place to camp right outside of town. It was near dark by the time Carl set down to read the letters.

Each of his sisters wrote a letter. Cora's letter was full of happy news, but Elizabeth's letter, dated two days later, told of an accident that left their daddy's leg twisted and broken in two places. It was the same leg he broke when his sons was all off to war. It was hard to think of their daddy hobblin' on crutches again. It left us both with a sadness as we slept in the buckboard under the stars that night.

What a difference it was the next mornin' when we woke up to find ourselves covered in a heavy fog. Ever'thing was damp and dreary. Even Bill and Barney seemed burdened by the fog. I said a prayer to myself that the sun might come out and lighten our spirits.

'Bout when we was half way home God answered my prayer, but he lifted the fog with a sharp wind from the north that we had to face all the way home. When we seen our place it was a relief, until we seen Nathan, hurryin' to meet us. He yelled out to us as soon as we was close enough to hear.

"Hannah, it's Sarah. She needs your help."

127

Sarah...

Right after Hannah and Carl left to go to Ellsworth is when a heaviness come over me and I had the old familiar fear of knowin' a tragedy was comin'. Ever since my daddy first told me what my *gift* was, it was always a mystery as to who would suffer the calamity that I knowed would happen. I carried my worry stone with me and thought of my daddy each time I rubbed it. It helped the ache in my heart.

Then I remembered back to that conversation with my daddy, when I was but a young girl. I told him it felt like I done somethin' wrong. I grabbed onto the hope that maybe the heaviness was not an omen this time, but it was my guilt at hidin' what I found. 'Cause I'd not listened to Nathan, I had a burden put on me. I didn't want him to know I'd gone behind his back. I found somethin' that was rightly his, and I couldn't tell him. How would it make him feel to know of Rebecca's wantin' to escape? Havin' the diary and the Bible made me downtrodden with shame.

That mornin' when I woke up feelin' so bad, I near confessed all to Nathan. I waited 'til he went out to do chores. Then I dug the diary out of my trunk and threw it in the stove to burn whilst I made breakfast. Nathan would never see the words that would hurt him so.

I couldn't bring myself to put the Bible in the fire though, and so my plan was to go back to the dugout and put the tin type and the Bible back where I first found them. Then I would stay out of that place, like Nathan told me to.

As we ate our breakfast, I knowed the diary was ashes. I thought I'd feel some of the burden lift off me, but my breathin' come even harder. Nathan noticed it too.

"I'll take care of Hannah's chickens for you this morning," Nathan said, gettin' up from breakfast and headin' for the door. "You don't look well, Sarah. Take it a little easy today."

I nodded. But as soon as he left, I headed for the trunk and dug for the Bible. It was my chance to get to the dugout and get rid of the rest of the secret, afore Nathan would get back home. I put the photograph inside the Bible, closed the lid to the trunk, and stood up straight.

A pain hit me so hard it knocked me down to my knees. I bent over like a dog on all fours, 'til it let up enough for me to try to stand again. Though it was a cool day, I was covered in sweat with the tryin'. I managed to get the trunk open again, and get the Bible back inside, but as soon as I closed the lid another pain come.

The agony put me on my knees again and I had to crawl over to my bed where I found some relief in layin' down. I tried to calm myself by rubbin' my worry stone inside my pocket. Then real panic hit me. I'd convinced myself that my anxieties was only my guilt for the secret I kept. I never thought my baby might be the tragedy this time.

Nathan found me in bed when he got back from carin' for Hannah's critters. The pains had lessened some, but he told me I'd better stay put for a while. I fell asleep for a bit then, but midafternoon the misery was back. Nathan stayed close by my side 'til Corky started barkin'. We looked at each other with new hope.

"Maybe they're back," he said. He went outside and come back in, tryin' to smile when he said, "It won't take me long, I'll go fetch Hannah for you."

Carl…

A man feels helpless when nature doesn't go the way he intends it to. I seen that weak look in Nathan's eyes when he fetched Hannah to help Sarah. And when Hannah got to Sarah's side, he near buckled under with relief.

We was right outside the soddy where we could hear Sarah's cries of, "It's too soon, Hannah." She said the same words over and over. She made the hard sounds a woman makes durin' labor. Then she said again, "It's too soon, Hannah."

Hannah's voice come back clear and strong, "You're doin' fine. You have to push him out, Sarah."

We heard more sounds then. They was sounds that men don't know how to handle, but it was the quiet betwixt the moans Sarah made that was the hardest to listen to. It was durin' a quiet spell that Nathan looked at me and asked, "Should I see if I can help?"

I shook my head and told him, "No, she'll be fine and Hannah will let us know."

So we waited, and listened, 'til near daybreak.

Nathan…

It's strange what a man thinks of when he's under stress. I remembered back to my schooldays as a young lad, when one of my classmates was yelling "sic-em" to his dog. I watched in horror as his dog tore into a cat that was caught in the corner of a fence. Others had watched too, and when the blood spurted from the cat they cheered while I backed away from them and puked in some bushes. Later that day I found the poor creature dead, and my thought was that he didn't have to suffer any longer.

Carl's reassuring words were the only thing keeping me of a sane mind. When Sarah's cries reached me, I would have welcomed the pain for myself if it was possible. And when Sarah didn't cry out, all I could think of was when I held Becca in my arms and she suffered no longer. I was so ashamed of myself. I wanted to run and puke in some bushes.

It was dawn when Carl stood up slow and said, "I'll go take care of your chores."

Just then, Sarah screamed. It was different than all her other cries in the night.

Hannah...

When the baby finally come, I couldn't get him to take his first breath of life. I tried ever'thing I seen or heard others do, but to no avail.

When Sarah seen the baby had no life in him, she set up and screamed, "No! No! No!"

I yelled for Nathan to come in. I handed the baby to him and turned back to Sarah. She'd laid herself back down. She was starin' at the ceilin'. I tried to talk to her, but she wouldn't even look at me. It was like part of her was gone somewhere else and it scared me that I might lose my sister too. I wanted to cry with her, but she had no tears. I wanted to comfort her. But all I could do was tend to her needs as best as I knowed how.

128

Nathan…

I'd never seen a baby so tiny before. I begged God to let him live. I don't think God was listening to me. I would've gladly died if my baby would've lived. It had to be a mistake. I couldn't think of anything I'd ever wanted so much as to hear my first born cry. The soddy was so quiet, except for Hannah speaking. Her voice was soothing at first, but then it changed. There was a panic in her words.

"You got to help yourself Sarah," she said. "Sarah! Listen to me. You got to help yourself."

Sarah had always seemed so strong to me that until I listened to what Hannah was saying, I never thought she might die too. When she wouldn't answer Hannah, I knew I needed to find a way to reach her. If I lost her too, I don't think I could have lived with that.

I was holding my boy in my arms when I saw the little quilt Hannah had made for him. I laid his still body on it and wrapped it around him. Then I took him over to Sarah and knelt with him by her bedside.

"Sarah," I said.

She wouldn't look at me. She was facing the wall. I didn't even know if she'd heard me.

"Sarah, please hold him," I pleaded. I reached over her and laid him in her arms. It was a long time before she acknowledged him there, but I waited. When she gently pulled the quilt away from his face so that she could see him better, she spoke.

"His name is John," she whispered. She gently stroked his face with the tips of her fingers as though she was etching his features in her memory. Finally, she pulled the quilt over his face and without looking at me, said, "Take him. Put him aside Rebecca."

As I lifted him away from her, she shut the rest of us out of her world.

Sarah was too weak to join Carl, Hannah, and me when we buried John Joseph Carter later that day. I knew Sarah had named him John after my father, so I chose the name Joseph after her father. Hannah said a prayer for him and a prayer for Sarah, and then she went back to be with her sister again. Carl walked away too, and once again I was left alone, to mourn for a son I'd never get to know.

Hannah...

I thought I was doin' the right thing for my sister, when I went to fetch her Bible so that Nathan could record the baby's day of birth and death. The Bible was layin' right on top of Sarah's other things she kept in her trunk. I picked it up and somethin' fell out. I bent over and when I seen what it was, I didn't know what to think. Rebecca had showed me that tin type many times when we first found our claims, and I knowed that Nathan looked for it when she died. Then I looked at the Bible I was holdin' and knowed it was Rebecca's too. I opened it up to the page of testimony, and even though I didin't have my spectacles, I seen it was all marked up with an ugly crisscross.

Sarah was finally restin'. I thought the danger of losin' her was past, but I seen her heart was broken. I watched her stir in her sleep and wondered where she found Rebecca's Bible and photograph. Maybe Nathan finally found them. But why was the Bible so marked up.

Had Rebecca done that—or even Sarah? I heard the men walkin' back to the soddy so I quick put the picture back in the Bible and put them both in the trunk. There was too much sadness in the day already. I was sure my sister would tell me 'bout what I found when her loss was not so fresh.

129

Carl...

When we first found out Nathan and Sarah was to start a family, it grieved Hannah that we'd never have a child of our own. But instead of feelin' sorry for herself, Hannah had nothin' but joy for her sister.

I remember tellin' my Hannah, "We'll love their little one, like it's our own."

When the baby died, we mourned the loss like it was ours too.

For Hannah it was more than one loss. Weeks passed, and she still fretted over Sarah's well-being.

"Sarah's up and movin' to do her chores, but I never seen her so sorrowful," Hannah said. "She hasn't even been out to where we laid him yet."

It was somethin' in the way Hannah didn't say the baby's name that bothered me. "Did you offer to go with her?" I asked.

"I did ever'thing but drag her out there myself."

"Maybe there's a way. I got an idea, but let me talk to Nathan first," I said. I gave Hannah a kiss and got on with my chores for the day.

Sarah...

Hannah later told me 'bout the things I done the weeks after John was born, but I remember none of them. She said she seen my body heal, but I scared her the way my eyes wouldn't look at her or anyone else. I couldn't bring myself to see his grave. I knowed Nathan laid him aside Rebecca. He said I asked him to.

It was many days afore my body let me get 'round good. Then my sister said she come to my place and helped me plant my garden. She said she had to tell me ever'thing to do, like I was a child. I don't remember that. I remember I wanted to scream at her to go home and leave me alone. I didn't.

She said she told me I needed to say good-bye to my baby too, but she couldn't get me to go to his grave. She said she stopped askin'. Then one day Carl and her come over in the buckboard. When they drove it over to where the graves was, Nathan went out to meet them. Hannah come on over to the soddy and said they had somethin' to show me, but she still couldn't get me to go to my son's grave. I don't know why. I don't think I let myself feel much of anything for a while.

When Nathan come back to the soddy, Hannah said he said nothin' to me, but he picked me up like a sack of taters and threw me over his shoulder.

I remember the rest. I started kickin' and screamin' and told him to put me down. I pounded my fists on his back whilst he carried me to that little knoll where Carl and Hannah was waitin'. He finally put me down on the ground. I kept my eyes closed.

"Sarah," he said. "I lost one wife to madness, I'll not lose you too." His words was pleadin' with me, but I didn't care. I kept my eyes closed tight. I couldn't face it that the baby I carried inside me for so long was layin' in the ground.

"Damnation! Sarah, open your eyes and look at our son's grave."

Nathan had hold of my shoulders and was shakin' me when he shouted those harsh words. He'd never talked to me like that afore. How dare him cuss at me! I opened my eyes, ready to scream at him, but when I seen how pained his face was, I finally looked over to my baby's grave.

At the head of where he laid, was a limestone marker with the name John Joseph Carter carved into it. There was only one date on it.

No words come to me. I stared at the headstone made for my baby—John. Our son had been real. Nathan mourned him too.

I finally looked at my husband. How selfish I'd been to let him carry this burden by hiself. He knelt down aside me and held me. Betwixt the two of us, we let the tears come. I didn't even hear Carl and Hannah leave us.

130

Hannah...

I didn't have the pleasure I usually got from spring, for it was into summer afore Sarah come back to us. I seen a sadness in her that I didn't think would ever go away. We worked together most of the time, and talked 'bout things that we done when we was girls. It seemed to help lift her spirits. Then one day I asked her 'bout findin' Rebecca's Bible. Her eyes turned scared with the same look she had when we was girls, and she'd done somethin' wrong.

"What was you doin', goin' through my things?" she whispered. Her face went white.

"I only wanted to find your Bible so Nathan could record your baby's birth."

We was hoein' in my garden. I seen Sarah start to wobble afore she set down in the middle of the tater patch. I squatted aside her.

"Sarah, what's wrong?"

"Oh, Hannah, please tell me you didn't tell Nathan."

"I didn't tell Nathan. I didn't even tell Carl," I said. Rememberin' what the Bible looked like, I wondered again if it was Sarah's doin'. "I seen the Bible was all marked up." I said.

"I know, that's why Nathan can't see it."

"Did you do it?"

"Oh, no...no...that's the way I found it."

"Let's get you to the shade, and we'll talk." I helped her up and we walked over to the well. I let the bucket dip down and hauled us up a cool drink. Sarah took a couple big gulps afore she started cryin'. "Oh, Hannah, I think God took my baby from me, 'cause I been keepin' this secret. I can't let Nathan know though."

We walked over to the shade of the soddy. There was somethin' more she wasn't tellin' me, and it was hard not to ask her questions. I could feel how tormented my sister was. She told me how she found the Bible and the tintype in the dugout. She said Nathan never wanted her in there, but she went anyway.

She took a deep breath and looked out to the field where the men was hoein' corn. Then she started talkin' real slow, like I wouldn't understand, and I didn't at first. There was such a sadness in her voice.

"She hated Nathan, and…and…she was pregnant too." Sarah turned and looked at me. "You didn't know, did you?"

"No." I shook my head. "Nathan didn't tell us."

"Nathan didn't know," she said. She sighed again, like she had a big weight on her shoulders. "Hannah, I found her diary. It was in the dugout too."

I was tryin' to make sense of ever'thing she was sayin', but I was afraid she was gonna tell me things I didn't want to hear. She said Rebecca felt betrayed and wanted to escape. She told me Rebecca didn't want any of us to know 'bout her expectin' a baby.

"Hannah, I feel like I knowed her too. And I know it's wrong that I didn't show Nathan the diary, but Hannah, I know how much he loved her. It would hurt him so."

"Won't it hurt him more if he finds it, and he finds out you lied to him?"

She looked away from me. "He won't find it. And he won't see the Bible either."

"How can you be sure of that?"

"I burned the diary," she said.

"Sarah, no."

It sounded so wrong when she told me that. I told her so. I told her how Rebecca was my friend too, and asked her why she didn't let me see the diary. She didn't answer me. She was lookin to where Carl and Nathan was workin'.

"But I can't bring myself to burn a Bible, she said. "I just can't."

I don't think she even heard what I'd been sayin'.

131

Nathan…

One morning in late June I was at the graves, bent over pulling a weed from around John's headstone. I didn't realize Sarah had joined me until I saw the edges of her skirt out of the corner of my eye. The vista was aglow with daybreak's colors. The silence was broken with a meadowlark's song.

"This is my favorite time of the day," Sarah whispered. Her voice was resigned. I thought she was finally at a place of acceptance.

I stood up and put my arm around her shoulders. Though the day promised to be miserably hot without any wind, it surely was a beautiful morning. I didn't want to break the sounds of the prairie's awakening with my voice, so I said nothing for a bit. Then Sarah told me what was on her mind.

"The limestone…the stone you carved for John," she said. "It made him real, like he had a place in this world, even if he never took a breath."

I bit my lip so hard, I tasted blood.

Each in our own thoughts, we stood for a bit longer. A crow cawed in the distance, and Molly answered with a "moo" to let us know it was milking time. We smiled at each other.

"Sounds like she wants to get on with her day," I said.

Then Sarah surprised me by saying, "Rebecca, should have a headstone too."

I swallowed the lump in my throat and nodded. As we walked back to the soddy to start our day, I told her that I'd started to fashion one for Becca, after I'd finished John's.

Carl...

After we'd finished our work on a blisterin' day in August, Nathan asked if I'd help place Rebecca's headstone at her grave. I wondered why he picked that particular day, 'til I seen the carvin' he did on the stone. It said August 10, 1868. It was exactly two years since she was gone.

We just got the job done when Corky gave a woof and jumped up. Tinker was ridin' in from the south. He was whistlin' some tune I couldn't quite make out, and when he rode closer and seen what we was doin' he stopped with the song. As he pulled his mule up aside us, he looked like his thoughts went somewhere else, and he took off his hat and bowed his head.

"Those stones look mighty good. Wish I'd had one to mark my wife's final restin' place."

Nathan nodded his head once, but said nothin'. We was done with settin' the stone, so I gathered up our shovels, and me and Tinker walked back to the soddy. When Hannah and Sarah poked their heads out the door, Tinker teased them.

"Think I can beg for some supper?" he used his most pitiful voice.

Sarah smiled at him whilst Hannah tried to act like she was givin' it much consideration. Then I seen the corners of her mouth start to turn up just a bit.

"Course, I could pay ya with what I picked up whilst I was in Ellsworth," he laughed. He reached in his pocket and pulled out a letter. "It's addressed to Carl though."

He handed me the letter. I didn't have my spectacles with me, and the letters blurred, but I could make out it wasn't from family. Sarah was standin' aside Hannah.

"Sarah, can you see who it's from?" I asked.

She took the letter, frowned a little, and said, "Mrs. Xavier Birdy." She looked up at me to see if I knowed who that was. "Don't know if I'm sayin' that right though."

We was all so interested in who the letter was from that none of us paid any heed to Nathan, who had come back to the soddy too.

"Who did you say that letter was from?" he asked. He had a half-grin on his face, like maybe he knew. Sarah handed the envelope over to him.

"Mrs. Xavier Birdy," he read. His grin grew into a smile, then a chuckle, then he laughed out loud. "It's Skinner," he said. "Xavier is really Skinner."

Not one of us was convinced, 'til I told him to open the letter and read it to us. As he tore open the letter he told us how he overheard Samuel talkin' to Skinner one night on the wagon train. He said Samuel called Skinner by that name, and Skinner told Samuel that he'd show him where he got the name Skinner from if he ever told anyone his real name.

"I figured I'd better not tell on him either," Nathan said.

"Nah," Tinker said. "You're teasin' us all."

"Are you sure it says Mrs.?" I asked.

Nathan assured us it did.

"Let's hear it then," I said.

Nathan read the letter he was holdin'. It was written by Skinner's new wife, and explained how Skinner caught a wagon train earlier in the spring. When he got as far as Colorado, he met up with Lila, who run a boardin' house. She said she knowed a good man when she seen one, and she didn't let him get away. She wrote the letter at his request, to let us all know he'd finally settled down and married.

None of us could imagine it to be true, but we all was wearing big smiles at the thought of it.

132

Sarah…

Me and Hannah never talked 'bout the diary anymore, though we worked together near ever' day all that summer. Now that I wasn't holdin' that secret from her, it was more like it was when we was little and sometimes we didn't have to say anything to know what the other was thinkin'. It was like that one day in the late summer when we was out together gatherin' any fuel we could find for the comin' winter.

We was quite a ways away from our homesteads when we seen a big patch of goldenrod bloomin' against the grasses that was turnin' brown. Without needin' to say anything, we both walked to it and each of us picked a big bunch.

"I bet it'll dry real purty," Hannah said, "and…"
I started to agree with her, when I sensed she was brewin' some idea.

"Do you still have Rebecca's Bible?" she asked.

We'd not talked 'bout the Bible since that day I confessed my secret to her. I didn't answer' her, but I reached inside my pocket and rubbed my worry stone. Instead of just bein' there when I knowed a tragedy was gonna happen, I found it calmin' at other times too. It gave me time to think afore I spoke when my temper was quick. It also helped me whenever I fretted on what to do with the Bible. I nodded my head real slow. It was one of those times Hannah was tryin' to tell me somethin' without sayin' all she meant.

"Rebecca would've loved goldenrod," she said. "She left us afore it flowered out that season."

When she seen I didn't understand, she added, "I wonder if we can get some it to grow back at our places?"

I seen where her words was goin'. I had the answer I'd been lookin' for, and somehow it seemed right. Rebecca's Bible should be with Rebecca.

Hannah...

Me and Sarah never told the men what we was doin' when we took the wheelbarrow and spade, and went back to that place for goldenrod. The men was workin' at our place that day so when we got back to Sarah and Nathan's, we first planted some of the goldenrod around Sarah's soddy. I left some clumps with Sarah, and I took what was left with me.

My Carl and Nathan already ate their noon meal of cornbread afore I got home. They was restin' a bit afore they went back to the corn field.

"Wondered where you two ladies was all mornin'," Carl said.

"We thought maybe we could transplant some color round our places," I answered. Then I set down and ate some cornbread myself.

When they left, I heard Carl say somethin' 'bout curtains and wildflowers. I seen Nathan was lookin' to his place, and when I looked I seen that Sarah was already busy out by the graves.

I finished my cornbread and got busy plantin 'round my soddy, afore the clumps of roots I brought home got all dried out.

133

Carl...

Once again nature was tellin' us the season was changin'. Hannah come outside when she heard the geese honkin'. We both liked to watch them followin' their leader on their journey to wherever they was headed.

"You suppose they're all tryin' to tell him where to go?" Hannah asked.

I chuckled at that. Then I thought how Hannah had followed me to this land where I needed to be. My Hannah understood how nature always lent its hand in helpin' me to heal. It wasn't easy. Sometimes it was the toil and sweat that helped the most. And when we first come out onto the prairie, I wanted us to be alone. But God knowed me and my Hannah needed friends, and it's my thinkin' that God had somethin' to do with Nathan landin' in his place too.

I knowed it wasn't easy on any of us. Nathan had his share of grief. I didn't understand it all. That's when I remember back to what my daddy always said whenever there was hardships in my family. He said, "Maybe it's for the best".

That's not somethin' people always want to hear when things don't go their way, but I suppose it was my daddy's way of sayin' God does things for a reason.

Hannah...

When I seen the pleasure my Carl got from watching birds tellin' us that winter was comin', my bones ached, but my heart warmed. I guess I'd followed him just like the geese was followin' their leader. We lived in a house made of dirt, but he'd build us a fine house of stone some day. I believed in the dream he seen, though sometimes it seemed mighty far away.

It was Sunday, and Sarah and Nathan was comin' to our place for dinner. I looked up to see Sarah walkin' our way by herself, and wondered why Nathan wasn't walkin' aside her. Sarah seen me and waved, but she seemed in no hurry.

Much as I loved my Carl, life was not near so lonely for me since my sister come to live out here. I said a silent prayer and thanked God for that.

Sarah...

Nathan still felt a need to go to Rebecca and John's grave ever' mornin'. I walked out to where he was and stood aside him. I mourned the loss of my little John, but I had a new hope. I was in a family way again. I'd not yet told anyone. It was a secret I would keep to myself for a bit longer. It was a good secret that gave me happiness and no shame.

"I didn't think you'd have any luck when you planted that goldenrod, but it looks like it's taking root here," Nathan said.

I smiled. "Not like up by the soddy. I don't think Hannah's took root by her soddy either."

"Funny how its growing here, and not there," Nathan said.

"Seems right, somehow."

I reached inside my pocket and rubbed my worry stone. Then I reached in the pocket on the other side of my dress and pulled out the little tintype of Nathan and

Rebecca. "I have somethin' for you," I said. I held it out for Nathan.

His mouth dropped open as he reached for it. "Where?" he asked. "Where did you…I looked and looked…"

I couldn't say the lie out loud, so I said nothin'. Nathan's brows come together in a frown afore he forgot I was even there. He was studyin' the picture. It was a moment for him to go back in time, and I knowed I did the right thing by finally givin' it to him.

I held a good secret in me now. I wouldn't have to keep it to myself for long. I turned and walked to Hannah's place whilst Nathan had some time alone. I breathed easier than I had for a long time.

Nathan…

I don't know how long I stood there, staring at the tintype. I'd forgotten how beautiful Becca had been. We looked so happy, and so young. My last memories of her always went back to the night I'd seen her go completely insane. I questioned my own sanity at bringing her to a place where she wasn't meant to be.

And the night she died, I still didn't know for sure what happened. She was coming at me with an axe. The moonlight let me see the wild in her eyes—the same pain Rusty had before I put him down. She was suffering.

Carl and Hannah were there that night, looking at me as I held her. I've nearly driven myself mad, wondering if it was my own hand that killed her. I suppose I'll never know until I die. I'll never know until God accepts me, or condemns me to hell.

The ferrotype—where had it been? I turned to ask Sarah and saw that she had gone on. I watched her walking away from me, and wondered where she'd found it. I decided it didn't matter. This was the memory I'd been longing for. It was how I needed to remember Becca.

"Thank you, Sarah," I whispered into the cool morning breeze.